"Newcomer Jill Elizabeth Nelson has crafted a fast-paced, captivating tale peopled by characters you not only care about, but would love to have in your circle of friends. (Especially on those days when crazed international assassins and art thieve!) *Reluctant Burglar* is a wond

—KAREN BALL

be   e and *The Breaking Point*

"*Reluctant Burglar* is a hands-down, thumbs-up winner. Jill Elizabeth Nelson packs her story with all the suspense and mystery a reader could want. The added bonus: two strong characters reluctant to fall in love."

—DONITA K. PAUL
award-winning author of romance and fantasy

"Jill Nelson's *Reluctant Burglar* offers a unique blend of whodunit mystery and high stakes thriller, with a touch of humor and romance."

—SHARON DUNN
award-winning author of the Ruby Taylor Mysteries

"Take one beautiful reluctant burglar and add: one eye-sizzling FBI agent, an international terrorist, riveting suspense, delicious romance, trials of faith. Then buckle your seat belt for a wild, heart-pulsating read. Jill Elizabeth Nelson's debut novel will leave you breathless!"

—LINDA WICHMAN
award-winning author of *Legend of the Emerald Rose*

"Jill Elizabeth Nelson wrote a gripping debut novel."

—ARMCHAIR INTERVIEWS

RELUCTANT BURGLAR

A NOVEL

JILL ELIZABETH
NELSON

Multnomah® Publishers *Sisters, Oregon*

RELUCTANT BURGLAR
published by Multnomah Publishers, Inc.
© 2006 by Jill Elizabeth Nelson

International Standard Book Number: 1-59052-686-4

Cover photography by Steve Gardner, www.shootpw.com
Interior design and typeset by Katherine Lloyd, The DESK, Sisters, OR
Unless otherwise indicated, Scripture quotations are from:
The Holy Bible, New International Version
© 1973, 1984 by International Bible Society,
used by permission of Zondervan Publishing House

Multnomah is a trademark of Multnomah Publishers, Inc.,
and is registered in the U.S. Patent and Trademark Office.
The colophon is a trademark of Multnomah Publishers, Inc.
Printed in the United States of America

For information:
MULTNOMAH PUBLISHERS, INC.
601 N. LARCH STREET • SISTERS, OREGON 97759

Library of Congress Cataloging-in-Publication Data

Nelson, Jill Elizabeth.
Reluctant burglar / Jill Elizabeth Nelson.
    p. cm. -- (To catch a thief ; #1)
ISBN 1-59052-686-4
1. Fathers--Death--Fiction. 2. Security systems--Fiction. 3. Art museums--
Security measures--Fiction. 4. Art thieves--Fiction. I. Title. II. Series: Nelson,
Jill Elizabeth. To catch a thief ; #1.
PS3614.E44585R45 2006
813'.6--dc22
                                                                    2006010874

06 07 08 09 10—10 9 8 7 6 5 4 3 2 1 0

To my dad,
Robert Field,
who always thought I could make it as a writer.
He is no longer on earth to see this day,
but I trust he knows in heaven.

Acknowledgments

*H*ow does one begin to thank the Lord for the fulfillment of a dearly held dream…or for any of the other countless blessings we so often don't even recognize? I have no doubt that He knows how happy He's made me to have the privilege to publish this novel and the others to come. My loving heavenly Father has sent many people my way to help in my growth as a writer and specifically to polish this book to the best of my current ability. I'd like to thank them all from the bottom of my heart.

Bev Huston, you believed in me and supported me when I was a wide-eyed infant in the world of publishing. Thank you! Humble gratitude to the crit buds who worked with me on *Burglar*—Donita K. Paul, Linda Wichman, Sharon Hinck, Molly Bull, and Virginia "Ginny" Smith. A special thank you to Brandilyn Collins, who encouraged a fledgling writer in a way that kept my feet to the fire lo these many years, until that first contract offer came. It's not an easy road, nor is it quick. To my agent, Andrea Boeshaar of Hartline Literary Agency, who persisted with me. And to the lovely people at Multnomah and my editor-extraordinaire, Karen Ball. Finally, to my family who continually encouraged and supported me in my writing career, even during the times when it looked like it was going nowhere. We've come a long way together!

Author's Note

The Boston Public Museum of Arts and Antiquities is an entirely fictional invention, not based on any existing institution. The National Antiquities Society is also fictional, though art preservation and protection societies do exist.

While I am aware that security companies do not normally make a business practice of staging thefts, it is a possible scenario and makes for fun fiction.

*Trust in the LORD with all your heart
and do not lean on your own understanding.
In all your ways acknowledge Him,
and He will make your paths straight.*

PROVERBS 3:5–6

One

D esiree Jacobs schooled her breathing as she handed her
ID to the museum guard.

Relax...just relax. This guy has no idea what you're up to.

The man scowled at the card, then at her, then back at the
photo of a blond, blue-eyed, thirtyish female—a reasonable
facsimile of the live version. With a curt nod to the receptionist seated behind a high mahogany desk, he handed the
card back to Desiree. Then he stalked off on the rounds she'd
interrupted when she showed up insisting on access to the
restricted area.

Desi turned a smile on the perky receptionist. The woman
grinned back and offered a broad wink—a much nicer welcome than old Sour-Britches.

The receptionist lifted her telephone handset and
punched in a few numbers. "Olivia Layton from the National
Antiquities Society is here to see you, Dr. Plate." She hung up
and looked at Desi. "You can go right in." The woman pressed
a button under her desk, and a thick door to Desi's left swung
open with a slight buzz.

Desi felt the impassive eye of the security camera follow
her as she turned on the heel of her designer pumps and

marched into the private inner sanctum of the Boston Public Museum of Arts and Antiquities. Dingy beige walls begged a fresh coat of paint, but who would notice the improvement in this dim hallway?

Shadows loomed. The place reeked of ancient secrets. Desi's skin prickled.

Just call me Indiana Jane…

She stifled a laugh. The "ancient secrets" she smelled were cleaning solutions used to preserve the priceless art the museum displayed, as well as a few extraordinary items not so open to scrutiny.

The palm of her right hand, curved around the handle of her leather briefcase, felt dry, cool. The soft fabric of her pantsuit shushed against her skin. Assurance blanketed her down to her little pinkie toe. Prayer and planning were the linchpins of any successful operation, her father always said.

A great deal rode on the outcome of her first solo run. Dad might finally have to admit that he could entrust the high pressure end of the business to someone else. He needed to take care of himself now that the doctor said—

A door at the end of the corridor sprang open, and a round man stepped out. "Ms. Layton." He ran a pudgy hand across the bald dome of his head. "I'm Dr. Sanderson Plate, chief curator. We'll meet in here." He shook her hand and ushered her into a stuffy cubicle.

Dog-eared magazines and stacks of treatises littered the desk and floor, even the guest chair. Vintage museum office. Government-funded facilities didn't often have money or space for decent offices. Boston Public was no exception.

Plate scooped a stack of periodicals off the chair and motioned for Desi to be seated. He took his place behind the desk and folded his hands across his paunch. A smile widened his cheeks but stopped below his nose.

Does he know more than he should? Desi's chest tightened.

She set her briefcase on the floor beside her. Leaning back in her chair, she crossed her legs. Whatever the outcome, she'd play the caper through with style.

A Jacobs can do no less.

"What did my office tell you about the purpose of my visit?"

Plate returned a sober gaze. "You question the authenticity of our most recent acquisition. Evidently, the Society esteems your opinion more than that of our conservators." Resentment trickled through his voice. "I agreed to your examination of the piece to silence any doubts. I am confident your suspicion will prove unfounded." He lifted his chin.

Desi lowered her gaze to the desk, where three of his fingers performed a muted tap dance. "May I see the painting?"

"As soon as you sign this affidavit assuming responsibility for any damage caused by your testing." He shoved a piece of paper and a pen across his desk toward her.

Desiree grinned on the inside. *Gotcha!*

Plate apparently hoped that the threat of liability might deter her examination, allowing the original authentication to stand unchallenged. The curator would try that bit of fancy footwork on her only if he believed her credentials from the National Antiquities Society. Museum personnel hated having their judgment questioned, especially by a third-party watchdog organization like the NAS.

Desi took the pen and signed *Olivia Layton*. "May we get

started now? I don't wish to take up any more of your time than necessary."

The curator rose and led her out of his office. They went up another corridor; then he unlocked a door that let them into a small room containing glass cases with items in storage. Desi admired a collection of Native American black-on-white pottery while Plate scanned his key card through the lock of a large metal door. When the door unlatched, they entered a halogen-lit, climate-controlled room. Cupboards and shelves laden with supplies framed the perimeter. A large worktable sat in the center.

On the end of the table nearest them lay the Renoir—a charming pastoral scene recently discovered in a forgotten bomb shelter in Germany, where it had been collecting dust since World War II. The painting lay unframed and ready for her analysis...er, rather, Olivia Layton's analysis.

Desiree drank in the beauty of the work. Like her father, she could wander for hours in art galleries and museums, but neither of them had a speck of artistic talent. Too left-brained. No doubt the reason they chose instead to do what they did.

Plate fussed with the angle of the gooseneckd table lamp. "If you don't mind my saying so, you seem young for such a level of expertise."

"I hear that comment often." *Stop mooning and get with the program, girl.*

Desi opened her briefcase. Donning her headgear, she slid the magnifying loupe in front of her eye and leaned over the picture to examine brushstrokes and cracks in the paint.

Plate hovered like a hummingbird. He fidgeted and paced, never more than a few steps away. Desi curbed an urge to kick him, though she couldn't blame him for a display of nerves. Based on Boston Public's expert opinion, one of the museum's most generous donors had paid major bucks for the picture. If the NAS cast the smallest doubt...well, Plate's smooth dome might be handed to him in a basket.

She took a small scalpel from her case and harvested an almost microscopic fleck of paint, then sealed the fleck in a tiny container of epoxy. She lifted her ultraviolet wand to scan the painting's surface for tampering. So far the Renoir looked genuine—not that she'd had any doubts.

Precious seconds ticked past. *Where is Max?*

A shrill alarm sounded. Sanderson Plate jumped. A shiver ran through Desiree. *Good old Max.*

The curator touched her arm. "I need to see what caused the security breach. Once I leave, you will be locked in here until I return or unless the fire alarm sounds and releases the door automatically. Is that acceptable to you?"

"By all means." *Oh, please, do go.* "You can never be too careful."

Plate's round face colored. "Just following policy. If you can't trust a representative of the National Antiquities Society, whom can you trust?"

The man bustled out. Desiree watched the door shut behind him. A leap of her heart echoed the lock's click.

Desi smiled. *Whom, indeed?*

She turned back to the painting and set about her true business.

Curator Plate returned to the locked room ten minutes later, shaking his head. "Another false alarm." He took a narrow-eyed look at the painting on the table. "You're finished?"

Desi nodded. "For now."

"Very good. Allow me to escort you to the door."

A few minutes later, Desiree walked into the sunshine of the April afternoon. She paused at the top of the stairs leading down to the street. A breeze ruffled her shoulder-length hair. *Ah, the sweet scent of success.* Just an ocean tang overlaid by vehicle exhaust and the smells of busy humanity, but it was her Boston. Just like the brownstone buildings and Victorian architecture on this edge of historic downtown.

The people, however, belonged to the twenty-first century. Wheeler-dealers with cell phones, iPods, and BlackBerries. Speed walkers and Rollerbladers. No one so much as glanced in her direction. *Perfect!* She moved toward the sidewalk doing mental backflips and cartwheels.

Midway down, she halted. Her whole body went stiff.

Up the street, a man in a dark gray suit stood, his back to her, beside a car bearing the logo of the city police. He was talking to an officer through the open window.

There was no mistaking the square set of those shoulders and the curly black hair that refused to lie flat. Special Agent Tony Lucano from the Organized Crime Division of the Boston FBI Field Office. The man handling the legwork on an art theft ring operating in his backyard.

Would he know me if he turned his head? Her pulse rate climbed.

She looked away, slipped her sunglasses on, and finished her descent. A white commercial van waited half a block in the opposite direction of Agent Lucano. Her legs wanted to run toward the vehicle, but she held herself to a brisk walk, blending in with sidewalk traffic.

If Lucano caught her, he wouldn't care that she was within feet of her documentation. He'd enjoy hauling her in for questioning. The man delighted in harassing her. Well, maybe not her so much, but her father for sure.

Desi's stomach rolled. Great. She'd concluded Phase I of the operation without breaking a sweat but was reduced to acid indigestion by the sight of one bright but grossly mistaken man. Her father would never—

No! She wouldn't go there.

Desi reached the van and yanked open the passenger door.

"Hey!" The plump, red-haired woman in the driver's seat lowered a disposable cup from her lips. "You almost made me spill my cappuccino. Where's the fire? Did you get caught or something?"

Desi slid into the seat. "The operation went smooth as glass. But I can tell you right now that they need a surveillance camera in that workroom of theirs." She set her briefcase on the floor by the center console. "Great timing on the alarm, by the way. Hope you got a few ideas for security measures while everyone scurried around."

Max snorted. Apparently that little assignment didn't rate a mention. "What gives, girl? You don't often get that look on your face. Like a cross between a mule and a bronco. Last time was when that hot Italian agent came around and…ohhhh…" She narrowed her cat-green eyes, then laughed. "Tall, dark, and intense musta been hangin' around again. And he missed you? What a hoot!"

A knot loosened inside Desi. "I'm soooo glad ten years of East Coast haven't messed with your West Texas sense of humor. I needed your perspective." She looked at her watch. "I'd better change for Phase II. The museum director expects me in less than half an hour."

She climbed into the cargo compartment of the van, the back half of which held racks of electronics. The front half served as a changing room, complete with a dresser and small mirror, an array of cosmetics, and several wig stands.

While Max filled Desi in on observations she'd made about security in the museum, Desi removed the blond wig. She brushed her sable brown hair and then fluffed it into waves that ended in a tapered cut just below her ears. Next she took out the blue contact lenses and put them in their case. She fluttered her lids to moisten her hazel eyes. Cold cream and tissue scrubbed away the heavy makeup the fictitious Olivia Layton favored. Desi reapplied foundation, blush, and eye makeup with a light hand. Then she changed into a navy pin-striped skirt suit.

Max blinked at her when she resumed her seat in front. "I never get used to the way you do that. Take off this, put on that, and here you are—no trace of the woman who just robbed a museum."

Desi laughed and patted her briefcase. "Better get this back where it belongs. Do you have the contract?"

"One get-out-of-jail-free pass comin' up." Max fished in the glove compartment and pulled out a manila envelope.

Desi took the packet. A lump formed under her breast-bone.

This next part of the operation was as delicate as the first. She had to finesse the return of the painting in a way that smoothed raised hackles and enticed museum management to follow HJ Securities' recommendations. Her dad, Hiram Jacobs, was legendary in the business as diplomacy personified.

How can I measure up? The lump grew. *I'm his daughter, that's how. I've been trained by the best. I can't fail. I can't!*

Max bumped her arm. "What brought the frown back?"

She shook her head. "This isn't my favorite part of the operation, you know." She stepped out of the van.

"Oops! Almost forgot." Desi plucked her real ID card out of the pouch on the side of the seat and put it in her blazer pocket. "Best go back in as myself. Do you think that grumpy guard will notice he's admitted me before?"

Max clucked her tongue and grinned. "That's the least of your problems, girlfriend. What are you gonna say if Agent Pacino stops you on the way back in?"

"That's Lucano, Max."

"Yeah, but doesn't he just remind you so much of Al in *Serpico*?"

"Mr. Clean-Cut *Gentleman's Quarterly* and a seventies hippie cop? Hardly."

"Oh, forget the hair and beard from the movie." Max waved a hand. "That's window dressing. It's in the eyes, Des. They could x-ray lead."

Desi hooted. "The X-ray eyes must have malfunctioned this afternoon. I got clean away, right under his nose."

She left Max chuckling and headed back toward the museum. The next few minutes meant the world to her future. Her dad's health was on the line. She *had* to land this client—prove to her dad that he could back off and let her take a greater share of the responsibility. When he came home tomorrow from his business trip in Europe, she'd have all the ammunition she needed to make him listen to reason about the company he served like a slave.

He's got to take good advice this time. Please, God, I don't want to lose him.

Thick carpet cushioned Desi's walk across the mile-wide office toward Director Jacqueline Taylor's desk. Model slim and attractive in a Julie Andrews way, the director stood and gave Desi's hand a squeeze.

"Make yourself comfortable." Taylor motioned toward the only unoccupied guest chair. Two men rose from the other seats. "This is Edgar Graham, our security manager, and Dr. Plate you've met. Gentlemen, this is Desiree Jacobs of HJ Securities Company." She settled into her leather executive chair and picked up a sheaf of papers. "Please allow me a moment. I'm reviewing the contract once more."

Desi exchanged handshakes with the men and sat down. She crossed her ankles and held the briefcase on her lap.

Plate leaned toward her. "If we had met, surely I would remember."

Desi smiled. "We were introduced under rather odd circumstances. I would be surprised if you knew me as you see me now."

"A mystery." Graham's deep-set eyes bored into her from beneath bushy brows. He was a sharp-nosed man with thinning hair.

"All will be explained in due time." Taylor's firm tone squelched conversation.

Desi's hopes sank. *She doesn't sound too interested.*

With nothing else to do, Desi took stock of her surroundings. Polished teakwood furniture. Wet bar recessed into the wall. Marble pedestal displaying a massive brass vase of silk flowers. And the carpet…a girl could lose her shoes. *Someone's got great taste on the expensive side.* All show to snag potential donors and impress board members.

Ms. Taylor commanded the room from a leather executive chair. Her steel gray hair, trimmed close around her head, and the maturity lines in her face said upper forties or early fifties. Either she made regular use of a tanning bed or her Nordic features hid Mediterranean blood. The woman twirled a pen between slender fingers.

Now *there* was a good sign.

Taylor laid the pen and the contract down and focused on the two men. "I asked you here for this." She nodded toward Desi.

Filling her lungs, Desi rose. *Be confident. Breathe deep and even. Smile, but let them see that you understand their feelings. No one likes to be duped, even for their own good.* She slid the Renoir from the false side of her briefcase and laid the picture on the desk.

Graham bounded to his feet, glaring; Plate sank back like a deflated balloon. He stared up at Desi.

His mouth flopped open. "Olivia Layton?"

Desi nodded. "You have a sharp eye. I've fooled my best friend a time or two."

"But the painting was on the table when you left."

"A copy made in the nineteenth century worth a few hundred dollars on the open market."

The security chief let out a strangled noise. "Ms. Taylor, you knew about this?"

The administrator sat forward. "You were informed several weeks ago that the board had authorized hiring a security consultant. I challenged HJ Securities to prove that our museum needs them. We signed a provisional agreement, pending the outcome of today's contrived heist. I was aware of every detail in advance." She inclined her head toward Desi. "I was surprised that you proposed such a simple plan…and that it worked." A smile softened the severity of her words.

Desi bottled an urge to crow. *Too soon.* The ink wasn't dry on the signature line yet. She glanced at the security manager. His face still resembled rare beef. Time to define the issues, then apply balm to the wounds. Warmth flowed through Desi. She could do this.

"Master criminals dropping from skylights and slipping through laser detectors are the exceptions in the art theft world. Low-tech heists, such as what happened today, are far more common. The patrons streaming through your doors, as well as people who appear to be on legitimate business, are potential threats. But that's not the worst. Employees are the most frequent culprits and the most difficult threat to guard against."

Taylor pursed her lips and stared at the ceiling. Plate paled as he ran a hand across his smooth head. Graham scowled.

"Yes, I know that suspecting your coworkers is a bitter pill to swallow. HJ Securities helps museums and private collectors develop methods to protect against all types of theft, as well as establish fire and disaster plans. We're not here to cost anyone their jobs, but to enhance their ability to do them."

She motioned toward Curator Plate. "For instance, when you got the call from the National Antiquities Society requesting to send someone over to test authenticity, you should have instructed your receptionist to call the NAS to confirm the appointment. Such an inquiry would have uncovered one of two things: that no Olivia Layton works for the NAS or that the real Olivia Layton has no knowledge of an appointment. Voilà! One imposter exposed. You could then have caught me in the act, and I'd be cooling my heels in a jail cell right now."

Desi suppressed a shudder at the thought.

The curator grinned. "That's so easy."

"Oh, yes. Simple procedures can save your museum from irreplaceable losses."

Furrows smoothed from between Graham's thick brows. "You mentioned disaster plans. Does that mean you can help me update that pesky plan that never seems to get off my desk?"

"Of course." Desi nodded. "In fact, I have a sample manual in my case. I'll give it to you before I leave today. You can study the material, and our firm's experts will work with you to fit the specifics to Boston Public's needs."

"One moment, everyone." Director Taylor waved her pen. "I haven't signed yet."

"Sign it," Plate said.

Graham bobbed his head. "Please."

Tension dissolved in shared laughter.

Desi restrained a grin. *Oh, Dad, I can't wait to tell you about my day.*

Taylor cleared her throat and shifted in her chair. "I just have one final question. Well, not a question. More of a comment, since I don't believe the rumors about a man who's been on the cutting edge of the security business for the past thirty years, but—"

A chill flowed through Desi's veins, but she kept her tone level. "I assume you're referring to the nonsense that got started when a federal agent began making careless and unfounded inquiries? I assure you, Ms. Taylor, our firm has filed a protest with the man's superiors. This is a prime example of overzealous investigation harming a legitimate business."

The director nodded. "Good. Then let's execute that contract. Everyone at Boston Public will feel much safer when we have a tight rein on security."

Yeah, and I'd better get a tight rein on my temper, or I may just feed a certain federal agent his badge.

The signed contract safe in her briefcase, Desi took a cab to the office. Max had gone ahead with the van so she could start systems analyses at her computer while Desi wrapped up business with the museum director.

The international headquarters of HJ Securities operated out of a modern single-story wood and glass building that took up a corner lot in a prosperous district. Quiet and a hint of floral potpourri welcomed her in the reception area. She chatted with the administrative assistant, who was seated behind a marble-topped counter, to gather an update on the day's activity. Then she headed back toward her office.

Desi passed Max's open door, and the redhead looked up from her work. Raised eyebrows begged the question. Desi did a little two-step. Max shot her a thumbs-up. They shared a grin; then Max returned to her computer screen.

Settled behind her desk, Desi began putting together a schedule for interviews with key museum employees. An hour later, she rubbed a hand across her face and sat back. *Concentrate, woman.* She eyed her dismal progress on the computer screen.

Too bad tar and feathers went out with the colonial days. Lucano was shredding an innocent man's reputation and had yet to uncover a single piece of real evidence.

Desi shot from her chair and paced to the window overlooking a strip of manicured lawn. *Stop fuming. Just stop.* Agonizing got her nowhere. She knew chapter and verse on a Christian's obligation to forgive.

Might be easier if I didn't see the hypocrite every Sunday.

A few months ago, Lucano had possessed the gall to join the church she and her father attended. Even pretended to be a believer. Hah! The only thing that man believed were his trumped up suspicions.

"How about hittin' Chi-Chi's with Dean and me for supper tonight?"

Desi jumped. She turned to find Max leaning against the door frame.

"You deserve to celebrate." Her friend laughed. "Boston Public hasn't hired a security consultant in its entire 150 years of existence. Thanks to you, they've joined the twenty-first century after skippin' most of the twentieth."

Desi forced a smile. A spicy Mexican meal usually tempted her, and Max's husband never treated her like the odd person out when they made it a threesome. But she wouldn't make very good company.

"Thanks for the offer, but I need to get home. In fact, I'm leaving right now. Dad will be calling with his flight schedule for tomorrow, and I want to make sure his precious jade collection is dusted and his plants are watered."

"Well, soon then?"

"You got it."

Forty-five minutes later, Desiree crossed a small wooden porch and walked into a two-story clapboard home in the Boston district of Charlestown. She'd grown up in this house as the only child of a widower. Dusk had fallen, so she flipped on the lights in the enclosed foyer, then turned to the panel on the wall and punched in the code to neutralize the alarm system. The house lay quiet except for the ticking of a clock on the vestibule table.

A door to her right led into the downstairs living area, but she unlocked a door on her left and climbed the stairs to her second-floor apartment. She loved being able to stay in familiar surroundings, yet have her own space.

Dad was canny that way. When she turned twenty-one and returned from college without Mr. Right in her hip pocket, he had remodeled the upstairs for her use. He never visited without knocking first and expected the same courtesy of her. They led independent lives, despite the fact that they were wedded to the same business.

Desi grinned. Like father, like daughter. If only he'd lighten up on her social life—or lack thereof. Before he left on his sweep through England, France, and Italy, he'd given her another "You need to get out, have more fun, find a nice guy" lecture. Like he should talk!

She plunked her briefcase onto the coffee table and

headed for her bedroom to change into jeans and a sweatshirt.

Hiram Jacobs had made no effort to remarry after his wife was killed in a car accident soon after Desi's birth. If he didn't need a woman, then why did he think his daughter needed a man to make her complete? If marriage was God's plan for her, then He'd have to drop Golden Boy in her path, because she wasn't interested in looking. She'd seen too many desperation matches in her singles group at church. No, that was not for her. She was happy with her life the way it was, thank you very much.

Humming, Desi prepared a supper of soup, and peaches with cottage cheese, all washed down with hot green tea. She rinsed the dishes and put them in the dishwasher, wiped her hands, and headed for the stairs. She stopped in the middle of the living room. Headlights glared through the twin dormer windows. A car was turning into their driveway.

Now, who...?

Dad? Early? How like him to try to surprise her with his homecoming. He often came and went at odd hours, especially these past few months. If she didn't know better, she'd suspect he was hiding something. Maybe even a girlfriend. She smiled at the nutso thought. Well, he wasn't going to put one over on her this time. She would be right there to welcome him.

Desi hustled down the stairs, stepping into the foyer just as the doorbell rang. Her shoulders slumped. Dad wouldn't ring the bell. She glanced through the diamond of beveled glass in the door. Her hand froze on the knob.

Tony Lucano stood there, grim-eyed and frowning. What else was new?

Desi opened the door. "My father isn't here."

"I know."

Despite her firm resolution to dislike everything about this man, the mellow timbre of his voice wrapped around her. She steeled herself against it, studying him with a critical eye. His knee-length coat hung unbuttoned over his suit; his black hair was even more disheveled than usual.

All of which only made him more attractive.

Desi gritted her teeth. Fine. The man was nice looking. She'd concede on that point. But that didn't mean she liked him. And it certainly didn't mean she trusted him.

Lucano gestured with his hand. "May I come in?"

Desi hesitated.

"It's important."

His urgency stopped the refusal on her tongue. She stepped back, crossing her arms over her chest. Anything to provide a barrier against his intrusion on her space.

The agent took a single stride over the threshold. His presence filled the foyer as he closed the door. Desi looked up into the face she knew so well—one seemingly chiseled from granite. Hard. Cold. Except…

Lucano's eyes were warm. She'd never seen them any way but hard and assessing. Her breath hitched.

This softer look scared her.

He stuck his hands into his coat pockets, glanced at the floor, then back up at her. "I'm sorry to bring bad news, but I thought it should come from me since I took the call."

"Daddy?" The word squeaked between her lips.

Lucano nodded.

"Let me guess. You arrested him, right?" Her fingernails bit into her palms.

The agent shook his head. "I'm afraid that's no longer possible. It happened in Rome. He's been—"

"Oh, it's his health then! The doctor warned him his heart could be a problem." She gripped her hands together, refusing to let fear overwhelm her. "We'll get him the best medical care. Dad'll be all right. He's tough—"

The agent's hands clamped around her arms. She gazed up into dark eyes.

"Miss Jacobs, your father was murdered in his hotel room in Italy. I'm sorry, but he's dead."

Subzero vacuum squeezed the breath from her lungs. *Liar! Liar!* She struggled to scream, but the sound stuck in her throat. She could only shake her head.

"Miss Jacobs—"

Desi's fist struck out, hitting the broad chest in front of her. Again. Again. She lunged at her enemy—

Then she was crushed in arms too strong to fight. Shards of light exploded behind her eyes, and her knees buckled as she surrendered to something she'd never known before.

Despair.

Two

Tony gripped the slight figure in his arms.

How had this happened? She was hitting him, coming after him. He grabbed her. She fell forward…

Blast! He should have tried harder to find a female agent to come with him, but the bull pen had been a zoo tonight. Oh well, time enough to kick himself later.

He scanned the foyer. No place to help her sit down.

Sobs wrenched Desiree's body, sending shock waves up his arms. Her fingers dug into his suit jacket and clung for dear life. He frowned as an exotic fragrance drifted around him, teasing his senses. Was it from her hair?

He'd always seen Ms. Jacobs calm, cool, and collected. Too collected. The ice in her eyes when she looked at him would freeze the fiery furnace of Shadrach, Meshach, and Abednego. He could handle that. But this…

Now what did he do?

He tried a few pats on her back. Lame. No words of sympathy popped into his head. What could a guy say to the daughter of a thief whose buddies whacked him? Maybe he should just let go of her and back away. But what if she collapsed?

Tony held on.

Okay. Maybe he should just imagine she was his mother or the sister he didn't have. How would he act with them? The patting loosened up and came more easily. *That's it. You're getting it.* "Um, I'm real sorry this happened. I—"

Desiree Jacobs went rigid, and a strangled cry puffed against his shirt. She shoved away from him, eyes wide, cheeks bright. She staggered back until she hit the hall table with her hip. The table scraped a few inches across the hardwood floor. A vase of silk flowers teetered, then settled.

"Don't." Her voice was husky. "Don't be nice to me now."

Huge eyes smudged with mascara glared at him. There was the look he'd come to know so well—like she'd found a bug in her soup. He should be glad. He was back on familiar footing. So why did he feel like he'd lost something?

Don't be an idiot, Lucano. He'd just held her up so she didn't fall. That's all. Nothing had changed.

She moistened her lips. "Tell me." Her jaw flexed. "I need to know what happened. Did he suffer?"

He shook his head. "No. It was quick. He wouldn't have felt the bullets."

A shiver flowed down her body. She closed her eyes, then flipped them open again. "Where is his...where did they take him? I'll have to make arrangements..." She scrubbed her forehead with the heel of her hand, as if trying to wipe the last few minutes from her memory.

Tony buried his hands in his coat pockets. "Do you have anyone you could call to help you?" He hoped she could think of someone. From his investigation into their backgrounds, Hiram and Desiree Jacobs were very alone in the world. Few relatives remained, all of them distant. He figured that was one reason Ms. Jacobs and her father were so close—and to believe she was in on the theft ring? No way the father could have kept his crooked activities a secret from his daughter.

Ms. Jacobs bit her lip, then nodded. "They're not home right now, but I know where they are. Chi-Chi's…"

Tony pulled a card from his pocket and held it out to her. "Here's the number for the police station in Rome. Talk to Detective Raoul Gaetano. He'll know when the body can be released to you and will help make transportation arrangements."

As she accepted the card, a sob escaped her. She turned her back on him, spine stiff. "I'd like you to go now." The words came out a throaty whisper.

Tony checked the impulse to lay a hand on her shoulder. He didn't need it to get bitten off. Instead, he gripped the door handle. "I'll need to interview you tomorrow. I'll answer as many of your questions as I can and ask a few of my own. Should I come here for that?"

She shook her head. "The office. I'll be there. Come in the morning. I want to know—" she cleared her throat— "everything."

Tony nodded, though she couldn't see him, and let himself out into the cool spring night. The turf was spongy beneath his feet. He crossed the yard toward his Bureau car. His partner waited in the passenger seat of the nondescript sedan. Not the kind of guy you took with you when sharing delicate news.

Steve Crane's heart was one big callus. Nobody wanted to work with him.

What did his squad supervisor, Rachel Balzac, have against him that she'd paired them up when Crane transferred into their squad six months ago? It was like she'd singled him out, stuck him with Stevo, then handed them rinky-dink cases that only took the two of them, not the usual teamwork. This art theft case was the biggest thing they'd handled, and it was going nowhere fast.

Until now.

Tony reached the Bucar. He glanced back at the house. Stars sparkled in the mellow sky, framing the pitched roof. The upper middle-class neighborhood lay quiet, except for the purr of the sedan's engine. Not even a dog barked. An atmosphere too peaceful for the bomb that had just been dropped on one of the residents.

The fallout would hit come morning. Tony climbed into the driver's seat, one hand massaging his chest. For a little thing, she packed a decent punch.

Crane grunted. "That went well, I take it."

"Like a root canal without Novocain." Tony put the car in gear and backed out of the driveway. "She says she's going to call friends to come be with her."

Crane snapped the wad of gum in his jaw. "People going into the house are fine. It's stolen items coming out while we're not watching that makes me nervous."

Tony glanced at his partner. The man's blunt features were softened by the gloom, but Tony could imagine the steely glint in Crane's pale blue eyes.

"Relax, Stevo. Stakeouts in residential neighborhoods may be the pits to arrange, the way people notice strangers and unfamiliar vehicles, but we cut a break today. The owners of the vacant house next door agreed to rent. The Jacobs home will be under surveillance all night long."

"*Yes!*" The gum popping picked up tempo. "When the judge comes through with those search warrants in the morning, things ought to get real entertaining. I'm going to enjoy every minute. This is our golden opportunity, while she's shook up."

Tony swallowed a sharp reply. Crane's attitude sickened him, but so did so-called believers who lived double lives. Tony had arrested too many "fine, upstanding churchgoers" to harbor any illusions that Christians were exempt from giving in to temptation. How did they excuse their actions—to themselves, to God? Didn't they consider the cost? Ms. Jacobs had to be doing exactly that right now. She'd lost her father and, if she was in on the theft ring, would soon lose her freedom.

"Drop me off at Sporty's." Crane's voice came out with brittle cheer. "I need a couple of beers to help me sleep."

"Sure, like you need a good case of the flu."

"Don't ride me, pard. I'm no wino. I don't invite you to the bar; you don't nag me about attending church. That's our agreement." Crane laid his head back against the seat and chomped his gum, a not-so-subtle reminder that Stevo had also agreed not to smoke in the Bucar.

Tony drove in silence.

Should he file his concerns about Crane's drinking with the ASAC? He had little solid evidence of drunkenness on the job to give the Assistant Special Agent in Charge. A few late days, a surly attitude, bloodshot eyes, and bad breath didn't add up to much.

Crane had a top-notch arrest record—he delivered results.

Which no doubt was why the Bureau continued to put up with him despite his reputation as an irritant and potential embarrassment. Besides, Tony didn't know if he could forgive himself if Crane was put on a forced leave of absence for the remaining months until his retirement. To a guy like his partner, that would be like shooting him in the stomach and not letting him die.

But could he take the chance? What if Crane's drinking affected his work? When an agent couldn't think straight, someone could get hurt—most often himself or his partner. *And that'd be me.*

Tight-jawed, Tony pulled over to the curb near a flashing red marquee that advertised a popular bar.

Crane climbed out. "See you in the morning." He slammed the door and walked away.

Tony sat still, taking in slow, deep breaths. If his partner showed up for work hungover again, he'd have no choice.

He'd have to write that report.

Desi took the key to her father's half of the house out of her jeans pocket. She opened the door and turned on the light. A hint of Dad's woodsy cologne hung in the air. A book of acrostic puzzles lay on the end table. Too normal!

Why did her heart beat, her lungs breathe? Why did the clock tick on? Time that had no right to march forward without her father.

Desi's eyes stung.

She gazed at the familiar furnishings. Oriental carpets scattered on a polished oak floor. Genuine textured plaster walls painted soft gray. Rich blue drapes at the picture window. Cozy fireplace. Leather sofa and easy chair, the latter well worn. How often had she found Daddy there with his feet up, enjoying his puzzles or a weekend baseball game?

She turned away and slumped against the doorjamb.

"Dad, you can't be gone. Not like this."

Murdered! Not possible! But that's what Tony had said.

Tony?

Desi frowned. She'd never thought of the agent by his first name before. Heat rushed through her. What had she been thinking to collapse against him? She *hadn't* been thinking, that's what. And his arms were strong. She'd felt safe, comforted. For all of two seconds. She'd bet her last nickel that his ridiculous allegations of theft had contributed to her father's death. She should have slugged him again.

Desi drew herself up. She wanted answers, and she wanted them now. She'd been too furious with Lucano—and too embarrassed by her own weakness—to tolerate his presence long enough to ask more questions. It might be the wee hours of the morning in Rome, but police stations were always open, right? Desi looked at the number on the card clutched in her hand, then strode for the phone in the kitchen.

Ten minutes later, she banged the receiver into its cradle. Deciphering the night attendant's butchered English had been hard enough without running into a brick wall.

"No, Detective Gaetano not here… Yes, I tell him you call… No, cannot give officer's home number."

She pressed the sides of her head and rubbed her scalp. What should she do next? Call Max. Her friend would offer true comfort, not some Judas hug.

Desi dialed Chi-Chi's, but the Webbs had left. She tried their home number. On the fourth ring, the answering machine picked up. Max's cheerful voice started her spiel. Desi hung up. Let Max and her husband have an evening of peace before the nightmare began in the morning for the staff at HJ Securities—all the family left to Desi now.

She got up, shut off the kitchen light, and wandered back into the living room. She fingered her father's precious Chinese jade figures displayed on the fireplace mantel. Five in all. Large, heavy, needing two hands to lift. Dad had been so proud of his collection, adding to it a piece at a time over the past several months.

A sob bubbled from her chest. She whirled and headed for the exit, snapping off the light switch as she went by. At the door, her feet refused to budge another inch. She had intended to flee to her own apartment but couldn't go. Couldn't leave the place that held so much of her father.

All right. She'd stay a little longer.

With a ragged sigh, she turned back. Moon shadows dappled the room from a sliver of light that crept between the drapes.

A suede throw pillow on the sofa caught her eye. She picked it up and clutched the softness to her chest. Her father's scent caught in her nostrils. Tears spilled down Desi's cheeks as she sank onto smooth leather and let the river flow.

God, how could You let this happen?

An odd noise jerked Desi awake. She lay on the sofa, curled on her side in an awkward ball around her father's pillow. Deep darkness shrouded the room.

Desi took shallow breaths, ears perked to hear a repetition of the thump that had pulled her out of uneasy slumber. From the kitchen area the floor creaked. Once. Again. Like stealthy footfalls.

Someone was in the house! A cold burn prickled across her skin. Why hadn't the alarm gone off? Then she remembered. She hadn't set it like she always did when she went to bed. Terrific! A burglar had picked the one night she slipped up to break in.

Silence. More silence.

Desi relaxed the fingers that had clawed into the pillow. Her keyed up emotions had made her imagine things. She sucked in a deep breath and let it out. The small sound had an echo. Not imaginary. Real.

And close.

A beam of light flickered over the room. Whoever held the flashlight stood behind her, near the kitchen doorway. The back of the sofa shielded her from the intruder's view. But for how long?

Dear Jesus, help me!

The beam of light and the sound of agitated breathing moved closer.

Boulders weighted Desi's arms and legs. Blood rushed like the surf in her ears. She couldn't lie here and wait to be discovered. She should do something. But what? Start a pillow fight?

"Where did you put them, Hiram?" The whispered voice was masculine, accented. "I warned you not to hide things from me, but you did not listen."

Desi's scalp tingled. This was no random burglary. What if this was her father's killer?

White-hot lava erupted in her brain. Desi shrieked and sprang from the sofa. She hurled the pillow in the direction of the voice.

A masculine yelp answered her, and the flashlight clattered to the floor and rolled. Crazy patterns of light and shadow spiraled across the walls as a dark hulk lurched toward Desi.

Still screeching, she snatched up the table lamp and swung it like a bat. The blow caught the intruder on the shoulder. Glass tinkled. The man staggered away, sputtering in a foreign language.

Desi dropped the stump of the lamp and raced toward the fireplace. Arms stretched, she groped for the tools. There! The rack tipped. Fireplace tools thumped to the hearth rug, and Desi lunged for the poker.

A heavy body slammed into her from behind, driving her to the floor. She landed on her stomach, the intruder on top of her. The breath wheezed from her lungs, cutting off her cries. Pain stabbed through her chest and legs where she'd fallen on the metal implements.

Hot breath, stinking of wine and garlic, panted in her ear. "The daughter, yes?"

Desi wriggled beneath her captor, then gasped as iron jabbed into her flesh. She'd have a lovely set of bruises in the morning. If morning came for her.

"Be still!" The voice hissed in her ear. "I'd hate to hurt you. You could prove useful."

The weight lifted; then strong hands grasped her arms and hauled her to her feet. The intruder shoved her on the sofa, towering over her. The man leaned forward and traced something cold and metallic against her cheek. Desi smelled gun oil.

"Don't move. Or I *will* kill you."

Tremors began in her middle and radiated outward. "Wh-what do you want?" She wasn't sure her choked voice would carry to his ears.

His chuckle said he'd heard all right. "I will ask questions. You will answer. We will get along. Perhaps very well, eh?"

The suggestion in his tone turned her stomach. He stepped toward his fallen flashlight, and Desi tensed. Could she make it to the door while he was distracted? The man bent and reached, his hawkish profile haloed in the flash-light's aura.

"Freeze! FBI!"

Both Desi and her captor jumped at the voice erupting from the blackness of the kitchen. A splintering crunch sounded from the front door; then the foyer door burst open and hit the wall with the crackle of chipping plaster. Light spurted as a gun blasted to Desi's right. Her assailant. Shots answered from the kitchen and the foyer.

She dove for the floor just as a crash sounded near the picture window. Glass shattered. Fabric ripped, followed by a muffled thud. Feet pounded past Desi's prone body. Another crash. Bits of debris rained down on her back. Cool air rushed in.

Shouts and curses rang outside, not all in English. The sound of running feet faded into the distance. Then...

Blessed quiet—except for the rasp of heavy breathing. Her own? Not entirely.

The overhead light flicked on.

"Are you all right, miss?"

At the sound of the deep voice, Desi looked around her. Glass and wood slivers littered the floor. The heavy curtains from the picture window dangled by one twisted fixture. Most of the fabric lay in a mound on the floor. The window itself was a gaping hole into the night.

Desi rolled over and sat up. Her heart did a giant *ka-bump*.

Two men in Kevlar vests stood over her, cradling automatic weapons. With their night-vision goggles flipped onto their foreheads, they looked like four-eyed space aliens.

She stifled a burst of laughter. Now was not the time to turn into gibbering mush. Too late! Her sangfroid was wheezing on its deathbed, but no one else needed to know that.

She wasn't a Jacobs for nothing.

Three

Tony stood in the doorway between the kitchen and living room and watched Desiree. She sat hunched on a stool by the kitchen island, clutching a blanket around her shoulders. What could he say to make this situation easier?

Wrong question, Lucano.

An agent could get into big-time trouble for sympathizing with suspects. How well he knew! When people broke the law, bad things happened to them, plain and simple. Regret tumbled through him. Yeah, if only it were that simple. Sometimes the innocent got hurt along with the guilty. Which one was Ms. Jacobs?

Tony let out a long sigh.

Around him, the evidence collection progressed. An investigator on his knees checked the rear door for prints where the lock had been picked. Other agents moved around in the living room behind him. More scoured the lawn outside and fended off nosy neighbors in the pale dawn.

Tony stepped toward Desiree. She was staring at the counter as if nothing in her world would ever be right again. Maybe it wouldn't.

"Ms. Jacobs?" He touched her arm.

She jerked and shuddered. When he arrived about a half hour ago, she'd been shaking so badly he brought her the blanket. Outer warmth didn't seem to be helping much. She turned dull eyes on him.

"Is your friend coming to be with you?"

She nodded without a word.

"I need to take your statement now."

Her lips quivered. "The guy got away."

"Not for long. He won't get out of the country. You can help us track him down."

Desiree frowned. "How? I couldn't even identify him in a lineup. You seem to know more about him than I do. Who is he anyway?" A flush rose on her face.

Good. She needed the strength anger would give her.

"Leone Bocca." Tony sat on the stool next to her. "He'll smuggle anything for a profit. Art. Arms. Drugs. People. He's an anomaly in the antiquities theft world."

"How's that?"

"Most criminals trafficking in art and antiquities shy away from violence. Bocca will kill in a heartbeat."

Fear flashed through her eyes, replaced at once by a stony expression. "Tell me something I don't know."

"He didn't shoot your father."

Desiree gaped at him.

Too bad he couldn't tell her who *had* done it. This case had more twists than a Gordian knot, and tonight's events added one more loop.

"Bocca was in the States when Hiram Jacobs was murdered. We know that much. This particular theft ring is run by someone with more smarts and a lower profile than Bocca.

We thought it was your father, but now—"

"You don't." Desiree straightened her shoulders. "I've been trying to tell you so."

"If he wasn't part of the ring, why was he killed?"

Heat flared in her eyes. "Maybe because you made some baddie *think* he knew something he shouldn't."

Tony's jaw clenched. This woman really believed he didn't know his job, that he was pulling suspects like her father out of thin air. Either that or she was continuing her snow job on him.

"Follow the logic on that, Ms. Jacobs. It doesn't go anywhere. If he was uninvolved, Hiram was worth more to the theft ring as a live red herring than as a dead end."

She paled and looked away.

Tony clamped his mouth shut. He hadn't meant to be so blunt. Referring to the deceased as a "dead end" to the newly bereaved's face was hardly the soul of tact, but Desiree Jacobs pushed more buttons than he knew he had.

"Let's move on to what happened these past few hours." He took out his notebook and pen.

"All right." She pursed her lips. "What do you want to know?"

"Start from what you did after I left here."

She took a deep breath. Her statement came out with no stuttering or stammering and very little coaxing. Good witness for details. His pen raced.

"Stop!" His pen halted in midair. "Say that again."

She blinked at him. "What?"

"You threw a *pillow* at Leone Bocca?"

"It was all I had in my hands." The pink in her cheeks

brightened. "Listen, I wasn't thinking about anything but that this guy maybe killed my dad. I hit him with a lamp, too."

Insane. But gutsy. Tony hid his smile with a frown. "Start again with the pillow incident, and go on from there."

"I got 'em."

Desiree's head whipped around at the gruff voice from the kitchen doorway. "Bocca?"

Tony turned toward his partner. "The search warrants?"

Crane waved two sheets of paper in the air. "You bet. One for the house. One for the office. After tonight's little dustup, we rousted the judge out of his beauty sleep and got the go-ahead early."

Crane's clothes were rumpled, and Tony smelled cigarette smoke from half a room away, but at least the man's eyes were clear and his speech unslurred. Small miracles were always welcome.

Desiree threw off her blanket and stood. "You're *searching* my property?"

Whatever lines of communication the interview had begun to form between he and Ms. Jacobs evaporated like water on a hot skillet. He felt the sizzle.

"Desi—*girl!* Oh, hon!" A stocky woman with a mop of bright red hair barged past Crane and made a beeline for Ms. Jacobs. "I'm so sorry you couldn't find me earlier. I should have been here. I…" She folded the smaller woman in an embrace.

Desiree melted into the offered shoulder. The women rocked together.

Tony slid off the stool. He recognized Maxine Webb from his background check photos on everyone at HJ Securities.

His interview with the intriguing Ms. Jacobs would have to continue later.

He took his partner on a tour of the scene in the living room but kept his ears tuned to the murmur of feminine voices in the kitchen. Little reached his ears outside of his own conversation with his partner. They went back into the kitchen. The women glared at them.

Tony tapped Crane's arm. "I'll supervise the search here. You take a team and head over to the business."

"Wait!" Desiree stepped in front of them.

Her eyes blazed in a tear-stained face. "I'm not having you break down another door." She looked toward her friend. "Max, please go to the office with the agent. Don't let him take a *step* outside the parameters of his warrant." She fixed Tony with a hard look. "I'll defend our rights here."

Tony motioned toward his partner. "This is Agent Steve Crane. If you provide him with a key, as any innocent citizen would be happy to do, your door will be safe." He arched his eyebrows at Desiree.

Her face flamed, and those glaring eyes narrowed.

Maxine Webb stalked over to Crane and looked him up and down, as if sizing him for a casket. "C'mon, big boy. And watch your step, like the li'l lady said. You people have made an unholy mess in here. Don't even think about doing the same to our office." She swept toward the door.

Crane stomped off in her wake.

Desiree stuck her hands on her hips and looked around the room. "Where do we start?"

Tony pointed a finger at her. "This is outside protocol, but if you must, you can follow me around. You touch nothing, and you do not interfere with agents performing their duties. Including me. Got that?"

Her lips compressed, but she jerked a nod. "Whether you believe it or not, I want to catch these people twice as much as you do. Dad must have had something that Bocca creep wanted. I'd like to find it and get it out of my home, if you don't mind."

"Well, all right then." What was she up to now? Genuine cooperation, or would he get a few clues from her body language about where illegal items might be hidden as they searched? Either way, his little step outside the regs might pay off.

Two hours later, they were still combing the house. They'd been upstairs in Desiree's apartment, all through the main floor, and even poked around in the musty half cellar under the house. Desiree hadn't kicked up a fuss about anything until he appropriated her father's laptop computer for evaluation at the FBI office. After reading the fine print in the search warrant, she had to give in on that one, too. He'd be sure to tell the lab people to pay special attention to the laptop.

From the gray cast to her skin and dark circles under her eyes, Tony half expected her to drop. He didn't feel far from it himself, though that was more out of frustration than anything else. Whatever Bocca had been looking for didn't seem to be here. Desiree had been a great help in the search. Her behavior seemed open and genuine, but she hadn't been able to identify a single thing out of place or unusual. Certainly nothing an international art smuggler would want.

They returned to the trashed living room. Agents had taped clear plastic over the broken picture window, and the sun's rays shone through the cover, bathing the room in hazy light. Tony picked the lamp shade up off the floor and set it on the side table. "Are you sure your father didn't have any secret hiding places around the house?"

"I grew up here. I know every nook and cranny." Desiree flopped her arms.

"Just keep your eyes open then. I don't think Bocca will be back, but we've got surveillance on the house from next door."

Desiree frowned but didn't protest. She'd better not. FBI presence last night had saved her life. Not that she'd offered a word of thanks.

Tony glanced at his watch. 9:00 a.m., and the day had already been more eventful than most. "I need to leave now. You should get some rest."

"Are you going over to my office?"

"One of my first stops."

"I'll grab a shower and be right behind you." She started to turn away, then gasped, her gaze fixed on the mantelpiece.

Tony tensed. "What is it?"

Desiree hurried over and cradled the bull in both hands. She moaned. "It's been damaged. See?"

Tony looked over her shoulder. A deep gash ran the length of the animal's body where a stray bullet had creased the stone. Desiree turned the sculpture around and over. A strip of white under the base caught Tony's eye.

"Wait. What's that?"

She turned the sculpture bottom up. Her brow furrowed. "Just Dad's record-keeping system. He put a tag on the bottom of each acquisition, telling when and where he bought it and the provenance of the piece. 'Bang' stands for Bangkok, Thailand, which is the place of purchase. Then comes the date of purchase. The next two lines, 'Sung Dynasty, circa A.D. 1200, Hunan Province, China,' tell where the sculpture was made or found. That's its background—or provenance."

He eyed her. "I know what a provenance is. But what are those numbers in the fourth line?"

She frowned, peering at them, and the barest hesitation preceded her casual response. "I couldn't say for sure. Maybe a general ledger code. You know, for bookkeeping. Dad was meticulous that way."

Tony shifted in stance to catch her attention, but she didn't make eye contact. Instead, she set the bull back on the mantel, then gazed up at him, features composed. "How did Dad die?" Her voice throbbed.

Tony laid a hand on her arm, and she didn't flinch like she might have done a few hours ago. "He was found in bed in his hotel room, two bullets in his chest, one in his forehead. It was a professional job. From all indications, he was asleep and never woke up."

Air whooshed from her lungs. Muscles in her throat pulsed. After a few seconds, she nodded. "Thank you. I needed to know. And tell that SWAT team thanks for showing up when they did."

"Will do. Is there anything else you need?"

She gave him a strained smile. "No, I'll be fine."

Tony walked out to his car, a slow burn in his gut. Desiree Jacobs had lied to him about the numbers on the jade figure—and about being fine. Yet everything else she'd said to him today had struck him as the truth. Either she was the most calculating criminal he'd ever met, or she was a coura-geous innocent.

His heart leaped. He wanted her to be innocent. But that wouldn't make her safe. Far from it.

Lord, I hope You can get her to tell the truth before it's too late. I can't seem to make a dent in that independent front.

Ms. Jacobs had better decide to come clean with every detail pretty soon, or things were not going to turn out well for her. People like Bocca and his faceless boss weren't inclined to mercy.

Not even when their victim had hair as soft as a mink coat and a heart-shaped face that haunted a man's dreams.

As soon as she was alone, Desi lifted the bull down from the mantel. She stared at the label on the bottom. She hadn't lied to Tony...Agent Lucano. But she refused to let those kill-me-or-kiss-me brown eyes lure her into saying more than she should.

She really didn't know what the numbers meant but doubted they were a general ledger code for use in the com-pany's books. This was a private purchase. Desi fingered the label. The configuration of numerals seemed familiar, but the application escaped her. She frowned.

Dad never did anything without a reason. The numbers meant something...

Letting out a pent-up breath, she set the figure back on the mantel. She didn't have time to decipher her father's per-sonal notes right now. She needed to call Officer Gaetano in Rome. He'd better be in, or she'd give new definition to the term Ugly American. Nothing was more important than getting her dad's body home.

Mysteries, no matter how intriguing, were on hold until she buried her father.

Desi stood by the checkout counter and glanced around the video store at people browsing the shelves. *Last Thursday, Max and I were in here wrangling in the classics section like our lives depended on picking between James Dean and Jimmy Stewart.* Who would have guessed she'd feel nostalgic for a time less than a week ago?

"Hi, Ms. J."

Desi turned to see a pimply-faced teenager grinning at her from behind the counter.

"Sorry these are late, Decker." She handed him the stack of overdue DVDs and turned to go.

"Want to pick out some new ones?" Decker's voice followed her. "We just got a set of remastered Katharine Hepburn movies."

"Not today." She didn't look back as she took a step. "I really don't care." Her voice cracked, and she stopped to clear her throat, then swiveled to face him. She didn't owe this kid an explanation, but she'd done business here long enough that even the part-time help knew her taste in movies.

"My dad was k—my father died three days ago. I'm not doing so great at the moment."

Nothing like baring one's wounds to a casual acquaintance. Of course, with Dad gone, besides Max what other sort of contacts did she have? How had she become so isolated?

Barrenness settled in her heart like an endless desert.

Decker's grin faded. "Aw, Ms. J. That's tough. How about I let you take a few freebies. I can fix it right up on the computer."

A smile snuck up on Desi and touched her mouth. What an absurd condolence offer! But cute and from the heart. Dad always did say she had an odd sense of humor. "Thank you, Decker." She waved and headed for the door.

"Wait, Ms. J! I almost forgot. Something came for you yesterday."

Desi came back to the desk, and the young man held out a VHS video. A gift card was taped to the case with her full first name spelled out in large, dark letters.

"Where did that come from?"

Decker shrugged. "Some dude phoned in the request. Then he sent money order payment and this card to attach. Said it was a surprise and to give it to you next time you stopped in. Guess he wanted to remain anonymous. Unless he signed the card. But I sure didn't open it to find out."

Desi took the package and clutched the video to her chest as she walked to her car. The hot sun on the tarmac sent waves of heat up her body. Or maybe it was nerves. She slipped into the driver's seat and turned on the car and the air-conditioning.

Who would send her a mysterious gift? Her money was on the bad guys.

With fingers not quite steady, she flipped up the envelope to see what she held: a copy of Orson Welles's 1946 release *The Stranger*, still in its shrink-wrap. She'd seen it before. The movie was about a man who lives a quiet, respectable life as a

New England prep school teacher...until he's exposed as a Nazi war criminal and commits murder to keep his secret safe.

Dad, what did you know that got you killed? Who is protecting himself? And from what?

Desi shook her head. She was jumping to conclusions, reading into the choice of video a message that might not be there. The card was the important thing. She set the tape on the passenger seat and then paused. Some unseen menace knew she was a classic movie buff and where she rented them? Tiny ants crawled across her scalp.

She glanced around the parking lot, then up and down the street. There. A dark sedan with two men sitting inside. Her FBI tail. They must be wondering why she didn't drive away from the store. Let them.

Desi ripped open the envelope and drew out a square of stiff vellum card stock. The message looked like it had been run on an ordinary computer printer.

One can never be too sure of those closest to them. When you find what Hiram left behind, keep quiet. You will receive instructions. Disaster would follow a chat with the authorities.

The word *disaster* hit Desi between the eyes. Her fingers tightened on the envelope—and she realized there was something more inside. Her throat squeezed as she pulled out a folded newspaper clipping. The scrap of newsprint was yellowed with age. She unfolded it and found a photograph of a burned-out office building. The caption spoke of a tragic explosion and fire that claimed the lives of many employees.

The date and the name of the business had been cut out, leaving little square holes where that information should have been.

Horror and fury ripped Desi into equal parts. She flung the offending card and news clipping away from her. They fluttered to the floor on the passenger side.

No mistaking this message. The threat wasn't even subtle. *Play this my way, or your office may go up in flames.* Innocent people—her staff, herself—could die, just like in this tragedy recorded in an unknown newspaper. She slammed her fist against the armrest. The slimy killer had threatened her where she was the most vulnerable. He thought he could control her.

Not!

Desi jerked her car into gear and peeled out of the parking lot. She headed for downtown Boston and the FBI office building. Never mind the agents assigned as her tail. She didn't even care if they kept up with her. This demanded a certain man's attention.

Special Agent Tony Lucano was going to get an earful from her.

He could put the full power of his agency into finding out who sent her this vile note. She was not going to be held hostage at the whim of a murderer, even if she had to close down her offices to keep the staff safe.

Yes, that's what she'd do. A lot of them could work from their homes. She'd keep the business going that way and spit in the killer's face at the same time. It might not work as well in their foreign branch offices, but she'd think of something.

She plotted and planned through twenty minutes of hectic

Boston traffic. The FBI office loomed close. She cruised past and then circled Scollay Square. Again, she went by the building. Her rebellious foot never let up on the gas pedal.

What was she doing?

The answer was immediate.

The FBI had brought her nothing but grief and more grief, with little or nothing to show for it. As much as she wanted to spite the mysterious messenger, as much as she longed to see him brought to justice, sharing the note with Lucano would be a waste of time. Whoever had sent it was too smart to leave fingerprints. From what she could tell, there was nothing unique about the paper or the print or the envelope. The newspaper clipping was gutted of clues as to its origin. The bravado of rushing to the "authorities," as this jerk put it, might even reap more death. No, she needed to be smart.

If she hadn't blown it already.

Desi drove home at a sedate pace. A strange calm enfolded her. Somewhere along the route, she noticed that her FBI tail had stuck with her like the proverbial burr. They were good. After her erratic behavior, no doubt Agent Lucano would come around with searching questions. Fine. She'd give him a nugget of truth. Tell him she had wanted to know the latest on the investigation—which as far as she could see was going nowhere—but couldn't bring herself to drop by his office and face more disappointment. That ought to rattle his cage.

She smiled without humor.

Lucano had nothing to worry about with her. Same went for Mr. Murderer. She didn't know anything that could help either of them.

Her father's remains would arrive in Boston tomorrow.

She was due at the funeral home after lunch today to plan the service. She needed to keep her focus on what was within her scope of responsibility. Anything else she'd have to leave with God.

Desi bit her lower lip. Yeah, right! She wasn't very good at "letting go and letting God." Action was in her blood. It drove her nuts not to be able to right a wrong. Just give her the tiniest bit of opportunity, and she'd jump in and mess up some lowlife's devious plan with a few head games of her own.

A small voice in the back of her mind mocked her. *Big talk for a woman without a plan...or even a clue.*

Four

Scents closed in on Desiree—freshly turned earth, wet spring grass, roses from the casket bouquet, perfumed bodies packed under the funeral canopy. She inhaled but couldn't fill her lungs. The chair under her was as hard as the lump beneath her breastbone. She looked outside, seeking a glimmer of sunlight, but found only knots of mourners huddled under umbrellas in the sullen drizzle.

She ran a hand under the collar of her black suit. Max squeezed her other hand.

Pastor Grange stood a few feet away, Bible open. He read her father's favorite Scripture. "…giving thanks to the Father, who has qualified you to share in the inheritance of the saints in the kingdom of light. For he has rescued us from the dominion of darkness and brought us into the kingdom of the Son he loves, in whom we have redemption, the forgiveness of sins."

The pastor's gaze rested on Desi, and he gave her a gentle smile. "Hiram Jacobs knew the truth of these words from Colossians chapter 1. In my frequent conversations with him, his words were salted with grace and thanksgiving…"

Desi shifted her weight.

Dad's faith was always more solid than mine. Kinder, too.

Shouldn't such goodness come with some reward? Yes, he was in a peaceful place now, safe and surrounded by love. United with his wife, the mother Desi couldn't remember. Yet here his name was still being dragged in the mud. The newspaper accounts stopped short of outright accusation, but word got around in the art community. Several clients had given notice to terminate their contracts with HJ Securities. No grace for a man not yet buried.

God, where are You? She ached in the place where her sense of His presence used to be. Had He taken His business elsewhere, too?

An elbow nudged her ribs. Desi turned her head toward Max, who nodded toward the grave. Expectant silence had fallen. Time to stand up and take a rose from the casket before it was lowered into the ground. Desi went through the motions, and the service ended.

Standing under the canopy, she accepted a steady stream of condolences. Teary-eyed company employees hugged her. Sober-faced clients and business associates patted her hand. The same murmurs and replies over and over again.

And there's a bull's-eye on my back, too.

With FBI surveillance ongoing, unseen eyes watched her from a distance. At such a public event as the funeral, it'd be Lucano, no doubt, and probably his thug of a partner. They would be watching for Leone Bocca or someone connected with him, and Bocca could be watching her. Desi's spine prickled, and she stiffened.

Just let him try to approach me. He'll be so busted!

Her breath hitched. Perhaps her father's killer was here.

Gooseflesh traveled down her arms. Had she shaken hands with him today? Had he been laughing at her behind one of those funeral smiles? He'd been so clever and so bold with that communication through the video store. Nothing for anyone to trace. No way for the FBI to know she'd been contacted, unless she told them.

Desi swallowed. Had she done the right thing in keeping quiet? The blackened devastation of the picture in the newspaper clipping appeared in her mind. Her throat tightened.

"Desiree Jacobs?"

She started at the soft voice beside her.

"Monsieur Dujardin, you came!"

"Would I miss saying a proper farewell to one of my dearest friends?"

The slim, white-haired gentlemen leaning on a four-pronged cane raised pale brows, but his eyes smiled. He resembled a dapper Gene Kelly in a double-breasted suit and black wing tips. Had he been thirty years younger and had this been a happier day, Desi could picture him tap-dancing and singin' in the rain like the 1950's film star.

"Daddy would have wanted you here. He mentioned you often."

"And likewise he spoke of you to me. Your papa was very proud of you."

Desi blinked back tears and made her lips form a smile. "I've always enjoyed our conversations when you call the office. But the last time I saw you I was young enough to appreciate the teddy bear you gave me. Did I ever properly thank you, monsieur?"

He cupped her palm in his. "You must call me Paul. This is not business, and you are not a little girl any longer but a beautiful young woman."

He bowed over Desi's hand.

Old-world elegance. A woman's charm-o-meter would have to be broken not to love this.

Tears glistened in his dark eyes. On impulse, Desi hugged him. He patted her back, making little harrumphing noises.

They drew apart, and he looked at the ground. "It seems impossible that Hiram is gone. I shall miss him a great deal."

"Did you fly in from France just today?"

Paul shook his head. "When I heard the news of Hiram's passing, I was at my Washington DC estate helping my son with his campaign for reelection to the Senate."

"A U.S. election campaign? Oh, yes. Daddy said you have dual citizenship."

"My father was an impoverished aristocrat who married an American heiress, an exchange of title for money not so uncommon in those days." Paul laughed. "And now they are both gone, and I have outlived two wives. Who'd have thought I would also outlive a friend so much younger than myself?" His gaze sharpened. "Hiram was at my villa right before he left for Rome. If I had been able to stay and host him a little while longer, perhaps…" His nostrils pinched, and he blinked rapidly.

A touch on her arm distracted Desi. She looked around to find Sanderson Plate offering a smile and a handshake.

"On behalf of Boston Public Museum of Art and Antiquities, I would like to extend my sympathies."

"Thank you. So kind of you to be here."

Now leave so I can finish my conversation with Paul about Daddy.

Stay cordial, girl. You don't need another client to withdraw from a contract because you're more interested in what someone else has to say.

Plate nodded. "We won't hold you to your schedule with us tomorrow if you need more time to get your affairs in order."

Desi's stomach clenched, but she managed a smile. "That's very thoughtful, but the staff interviews will be conducted as planned. HJ Securities will continue to serve our clients with the usual standard of excellence."

"Good, good." Plate rubbed a hand across the top of his head.

"Let me introduce you to Paul Dujardin." She motioned toward the elderly gentleman. "Paul, this is Dr. Sanderson Plate, head curator at Boston Public. The two of you share a devotion to fine art, I believe."

"P-Paul Dujardin? The art critic?" The curator's pink cheeks lost color. "I didn't expect…I mean…an honor, monsieur."

"My pleasure to meet you." Paul held out a hand.

The curator gave it a quick grip and then hurried across the lawn without another word. His furled umbrella whipped back and forth in his hand, while his smooth dome and suited shoulders got wet in the increasing rain. He made for a car parked up the street, where a slender female figure climbed into the passenger seat. Desi narrowed her eyes. Must be Jacqueline Taylor in a hurry to get back to the office…or maybe she didn't want to talk to Paul either.

Desi exchanged looks with the Frenchman.

His shrug was as eloquent as his laugh. "I had no idea I was so fearsome."

"Did you do a scathing review of one of their displays?"

"If I did, I have forgotten. But who can comprehend the oddities of the human mind—mine or Monsieur Plate's?"

For the first time in days, Desi laughed.

When Desi arrived home after the funeral, her purse hung like a lead weight on her shoulder. She dragged her feet through the front door and reset the alarm. Since the break-in, she kept the door and window alarms activated at all times, not just when she was out.

Her heart sank at the sight of the climb to her apartment. *Mount Everest. Not going there right now.* She wandered into the downstairs living room.

The picture window's panes had been replaced and the curtains rehung. No glass splinters or wood chips remained on the floor. Except for the missing table lamp, everywhere she looked her father's things sat undisturbed, as if awaiting his return. She let out a gust of breath.

Loneliness and sorrow lumped in her stomach. Thank heaven she still had the business to give her a reason to get up every morning.

Dad, I promise you, I will keep HJ Securities afloat. And your good name will be cleared.

So far, the FBI had made no arrests, nor had the Italian police, who were on watch for Leone Bocca. The search at the HJ Securities office had uncovered nothing incriminating or even suspicious. Analysts were dissecting data from the firm's computers, but they weren't going to find anything. If her father had been part of anything criminal—which she didn't believe for a millisecond—he was too smart to leave evidence in the usual devious places that attracted investigators like bees to honey.

No, he was more likely to hide something in plain sight, where no one would look at it twice. Dad swore simplicity was the most effective subterfuge.

Desi stopped. Stared.

If her father had stumbled across something that got him in trouble with Leone Bocca and his mysterious boss, it was still here at the house! Probably in this very room where her father had spent the most time.

Waves of electric energy washed up and down her body. Heart pumping in overdrive, she slipped out of her high-heeled shoes and took off her suit jacket. Time for another search, Jacobs style. Either she would find something that would prove her father a man of integrity—a man who simply discovered something that got him killed—or she would find nothing at all. Either way, she could rub Tony Lucano's face in her father's innocence.

Beginning in one corner of the room, she ran a hand along the plaster walls. No unusual bumps or anything out of the ordinary. Definitely no secret passage. She grinned. The top of the door lintel yielded nothing but dust. No key to a safe-deposit box in the Cayman Islands, or wherever crooks hid their loot these days. She took a flashlight from a drawer in the kitchen, then got on her knees on the hearth and peered up the chimney.

Yuck! Oh, gross! Desi backed away, brushing at black

smudges on her white blouse. *I won't be wearing this again.*

She stood up, tossed the flashlight onto the easy chair, and planted her hands on her hips. She was still thinking too cloak-and-dagger. Tapping a finger against her lower lip, she scanned the room. *Plain sight. Plain sight.*

Her gaze halted on her father's prized jade collection. First, the mandarin duck. Then the ox. Then a Qing Dynasty white jade cabbage. Next came the Kwan Yin figure.

Could have bowled me over with a feather when he bought that one.

The goddess represented admirable qualities such as kindness and justice but was steeped in Buddhist philosophies of reincarnation and collective human godhood. When Desi had asked him about his purchase, her father gave her a one-armed hug and said, "I have no belief in this piece of stone shaped by human hands. The object can't hurt me or help me, but it's just what I need for my collection."

Just what he needed? Desi's skin prickled. *Daddy was buying with a purpose, not a collector's passion.*

Last in line on the mantelpiece, the damaged bull stood frozen in a humpbacked snort.

Desi swept the order of figures again. Duck. Ox. Cabbage. Kwan. Bull. In an acrostic, the first letters of each item would spell...*dockb*. Dockb? Desi frowned, concentrating. Then her eyes widened. No, not *dockb*...

Dock B.

In a harbor town like Boston, those words meant something. And Daddy had loved his acrostics.

Desi clenched and unclenched her fists. Maybe she was making things up in desperation.

Maybe not.

She strode to the mantel, flipped the duck over, and read the white tag on the bottom. If she hadn't been looking for it, she would have missed the abbreviation in the four lines of text about the background and purchase details. *EBOS*. East Boston Harbor.

Desi set the duck down and grabbed the ox. Nothing cryptic this time, but the place of purchase read Pier 1 Imports. *Hah! I know good and well Dad didn't get this at the import store. He bought it online from a previous owner.*

What did she have so far? Dock B at East Boston Harbor on Pier 1.

Desi picked up the cabbage and discovered *WRHS*. She nodded. Of course. Warehouse. The numeral five was included in the provenance information. Warehouse 5.

She set the cabbage down and leaned her forehead against the cool marble of the mantel's edge. Her breath came in harsh gasps. She so did not want to complete this puzzle, because once she did she'd have to do something with the knowledge.

But the truth wouldn't go away just because she hid from it. Making like an ostrich wouldn't exempt her from being the target of a killer like Leone Bocca. In fact, ignorance could be fatal if she had no idea what she was up against.

Desi swallowed. She made herself pick up the Kwan Yin. The label's acrostic had to be an abbreviation: *CONT*. But the purchase date didn't make sense: 1-1-93. Dad hadn't started his jade collection until six months ago. Cont. 1193?

Her heart fell. *Container 1193.*

She moved on to the final figure. No acrostic. Nothing

unusual. *What? Ooooh!* What a sludge-brain! She and her father worked with these types of codes all the time. The string of numbers in the fourth line was a keypunch sequence for a brand of electronic lock.

Tremors began deep inside. She stared unseeing at the numerals. Everything fit. So logical. So neat. So like her father.

Only someone who knew Hiram as well as she did would pick up on the clues. Who else was that close to him? No one. The message was for her alone. Dad had known this day might come, and he was speaking to her from beyond the grave.

Speaking…or confessing.

Daddy, no! What have you done?

A cry left her lips. The jade figurine slipped from her fingers, and the crash of splintering stone jerked Desi from her trance. She whirled and raced from the room, pounding up the stairs to her apartment. She slammed and locked the door, then leaned against the jamb, panting.

She couldn't believe… But what if—? Not possible!

Her father was an honest man. End of story. Whatever had happened, when the truth came out, the world would know that Hiram Jacobs had good reason for hiding something from evil people.

Desi's breathing slowed. She'd vowed to restore her father's good name. Now that she had a direction to investigate, she needed to sit down and plan. That's what Dad would have done.

She went to the kitchen and brewed a cup of herbal tea—good old brain juice. With the mug cupped in her hands, she curled up on the corner of her sofa.

Getting to the container undetected by the legal beagles

or the bad guys would be difficult. She was watched everywhere she went. Was the house bugged? Probably thicker than an infestation of cockroaches. Were her phone wires tapped here and at the business? She would have to assume so. Hemmed in by human and electronic surveillance, she had limited options.

Should she involve Max? A helper would be worth her weight in Rembrandts. Desi shook her head. No way would she involve her best friend in something that might get her hurt. Max was a wife and mother, for pity's sake.

The odds against solo success were the pits. But she had one thing going for her: Neither Lucano and company nor Bocca and boss understood the extent of the training she'd received under her father's instruction.

She smiled and took another sip of tea, savoring the minty tang.

Dad, if you were here, we could have fun with this.

Desi's spirits plummeted into the dust. Dad wasn't here.

She didn't trust Tony Lucano and his guilty-before-charged system of law enforcement. She feared Leone Bocca's violence and the terrorist threats of his faceless master. But both paled in comparison to what she dreaded most...

Finding out what was hidden in Container 1193 of Dock B, Warehouse 5, on Pier 1 of East Boston Harbor.

Tony barged through the second-floor bedroom door of the surveillance house next to the Jacobs home. "What have you got?"

The Asian-American technician looked up from her receiving unit at the lone table in the bare room. She pulled off her headset and shrugged. "I may have called you in for nothing."

"Tell me anyway."

"No, really, I—"

"Humor him." Crane's voice came from the doorway.

Tony turned to see his partner saunter into the room. The tip of a toothpick peeked from between his lips. Not much of an improvement over the gum-smacking.

Crane shot the young technician a toothy grin, jaw clamped around his pick. "He'll just keep bugging you until you give him the details. He's got a *thing* for this investigation."

Tony glared at his partner. Was Stevo implying that Tony had something personal at stake?

"Very well." The woman's expression didn't indicate that she considered Crane's comment out of line. "Desiree Jacobs arrived home from her father's funeral about an hour ago. For about five minutes, I picked up soft breathing from the downstairs living room area. Then I started hearing noises that sounded like a search. This went on for, say, thirty minutes. Then it got all quiet again, but the breathing got louder. Like she was agitated. Pretty soon, *bam!* Something hit the floor and broke. She cried out, and then I heard feet running across the room and up the stairs. That's when I called you. I thought maybe we had an intruder situation again."

"We don't?" The question came out harsher than he had intended.

"Nah. If I thought so, I'd have sent the boys over. Besides, an ant couldn't get in there without us spotting it or an alarm going off. For the last twenty minutes, I've picked up ordinary sounds. Someone rattling around in the upstairs kitchen. Relaxed breathing in Miss Jacobs's living room."

Thank heaven! Tony's muscles relaxed. Why should he feel relieved? They *wanted* to catch a burglar. Yeah, but he didn't want Desiree in danger. The stark fact stared him in the face.

Crane chuckled. "That Jacobs lady is a piece of work. Knew it the minute I laid eyes on her. She must have been looking for whatever loot her dad stashed, got upset when she didn't find it, and threw a tantrum." He slouched out of the room.

Tony's hands fisted. If they didn't catch Bocca pretty soon, he might just strangle his partner to let off some steam.

The fear that knotted in his belly—not for himself, but for the class act next door—shouldn't be there. She was a suspect! But for a woman like Desiree, his mother would wave a finger under his nose and say, "You bring *this* one home. I'll get out the good china."

Too bad he wouldn't be bringing her home. How could he? Any attraction to the daughter of a thief was a no-win situation for him. And if she turned out to be involved in this mess, he'd have to send her to jail. Even if she was innocent, when he proved that her father was guilty, she'd never forgive him. And if she were hurt or killed, he'd never forgive himself.

A gun had been pointed at Desiree once already, and she'd come through whole, no thanks to her self-defense techniques. Next time she'd better have more than a pillow for protection, or the outcome would be different. Tony had seen too many corpses in his lifetime. The thought of seeing Desiree injured or worse…

No. He had to protect her. Even if that meant putting her behind bars.

Five

*D*esi checked again to make sure her briefcase contained everything she needed, then snapped the lid shut. As she left the house, she locked doors behind her and set the alarm system. Since the feds were ogling her from on high, along with whatever rodent might be peeking from the sewer, Desi kept her expression neutral during the brief walk to the detached garage beside the house. The balmy air tasted of sunshine and budding flowers after yesterday's gloom.

Her stomach fluttered nonstop.

Sliding into her compact car, Desi exhaled a long breath. She lowered her head to the steering wheel. *God, help me.* That was all the prayer she had in her. It had to be enough.

The commute to the office passed without incident. If anyone had followed her, they didn't give themselves away. She wasn't fooled though. They'd grown cagier since her mad dash toward the federal building the other day. Besides, Agent Lucano wouldn't have rookies on an investigation that involved a murder and millions of dollars of missing art. After checking in with staff about various projects, Desi took Max with her and headed for Boston Public Museum to conduct the employee interviews.

"How are you doin', hon?" Max fitted two coffees into the holders between them.

And just what do I say to that? Desi let seconds pass while she merged into hectic freeway traffic.

"Better and worse than I expected." She settled the car into a lane. "I can function, which surprises me, but I've got big-time jitters, Max. I wanted more responsibility, but I never wanted the whole load. Not yet! What if I can't keep HJ Securities afloat?" She glanced at her passenger and then returned her attention to the road.

Why is she looking at me like her coffee's been spiked with lemon juice? "Look, Max, just say it. And don't soft-pedal what's on your mind because I'm the newly bereaved. I don't have time for coddling. Too much is on the line here."

"All right. Here it is." The Texan let out a long breath. "HJ Securities is a great company, and I love my job, just like you do. But it's a business, not a monument to Hiram. You can make it yours now, do things your way. Or even try something new. You would do great at anything you chose."

Desi opened her mouth, but no words came out. She did *not* treat the company like a shrine to her dad… Did she?

"But you've got bigger problems." Max looked away out the side window. "I think—no, I *know*—you need to do everything you can to help Lucano solve this case. What happened with that guy breaking into your house nearly scared my hair straight, Des. We've lost your dad, and that's awful, but I don't think I could take it if something happened to you, too."

"Way to make me cry again, Max." Desi picked up her cup, then set it back down again. Her hand shook, and she couldn't drink.

"Well, hey, you told me not to soft-pedal."

Desi let out a thick chuckle. "You don't always have to do what I say." Good thing she hadn't asked her friend to get involved in her little game of now-you-see-me, now-you-don't today. It was clear that Max didn't understand. Desi would never be able to look herself in the mirror if she panicked and left her father's name in the dirt.

You're on your own, kiddo.

Desi and Max gathered their paperwork after a morning of interviews with museum employees. A throat cleared at the conference room door. Desi looked up. Curator Plate smiled and rubbed his head in a familiar gesture. Desi returned a nod.

Plate stepped across the room with his usual bounce. "How did everything go?"

"Just fine." Max came up with the smile Desi had been unable to muster. "We made good progress this morning."

"Let me walk you ladies to the door." The curator reached toward Desi's briefcase.

Heart thumping, Desi lifted the case away from his fingers. Plate frowned but didn't say anything as she and Max led him out the door.

"How well do you know Paul Dujardin?" The curator fell into step with them in an exhibit hallway.

"My father counted him a close friend."

"Ahhh. But how well do *you* know him?" The man gave her an owlish stare.

"Why do you ask?"

Plate's gaze danced away. A muscle flexed in his jaw. "Art

critics, movie and book reviewers—those sorts of people—they wield great influence without the matching responsibility."

Desi looked away to hide her smile. So Paul *had* given the museum a hard time in his reviews. "Many would agree with you. However, the best critics hold themselves accountable to the patrons of their particular art form."

Plate sniffed. "So, you'll be back after lunch?"

They stopped at the exit doors.

"Not me." Max held up her case. "I'm gonna hunker down in my office and go over these schematic drawings the security chief gave me."

"I'll conduct the final interviews," Desi said. "Then I want at least three hours uninterrupted to go over the data and determine if I need any callbacks before I leave for the day."

Plate nodded. "I'll make sure my people know that heads will roll if you're disturbed."

Desi gave a short laugh. "I haven't seen any guillotines around here, Mr. Plate."

"Sanderson." The man beamed. "Or Sandy, as my friends call me." Color filled his round cheeks.

"Thank you, Sanderson." She offered a smile and her hand. "I'll see you this afternoon."

They shook hands all around.

"Hoo-wee!" Max chuckled when they were out of earshot on the way to the car. "You must have charmed the socks off that guy after you stole his painting the other day. Jealousy *and* flirtation in one sixty second conversation."

"Jealous of Paul? That's ridiculous. The man is more than twice my age."

"Paul, is it?" Max rolled her eyes. "He's rich and good-lookin' and single. For some women, that's all it takes."

"Now I know you're teasing."

"You've got that right, girlfriend, but I don't hear you deny-ing that our escort was fishin' for a little encouragement. You handled him like a pro. Discouraged him without antago-nizing him. Your daddy would have had a laughin' fit. In private, of course."

"High praise, lady, but don't think it's going to get you a thousand dollars and a day off." Desi pushed the remote on her key ring to unlock the car. *Oh, Dad, if only you were here to laugh with us.* Those dratted tears started to get the better of her again, but she battled them back and had herself under control by the time they settled in and shut their doors.

Max buckled her seat belt, still grinning like a nut. "You're neither a gold digger nor desperate, so that leaves out one critic and one curator. But if we could get this sorry mess behind us, I could sure see you on the arm of a certain dark-eyed agent. Mm-hmm."

Desi shot out of her parking space, earning a few honks as she careened into traffic. "Max, your fantasies could give J. R. R. Tolkien a run for his money."

Her friend laughed. "Just call me a visionary."

Desi ignored her. Dangerous territory. Nobody needed to know that she'd not merely been *on* Tony's arm, but wrapped in them, not many days ago.

Or that she liked his eyes.

Desiree stepped out the main door of the Boston Public Museum of Arts and Antiquities. She looked at her watch. A little after 2:30 p.m. That gave her two hours to be back where she was supposed to be. She trudged down the steps.

Two men sat inside a nondescript sedan parked at the curb. They eyed her up and down, then looked away, no recognition on their faces.

She knew exactly what they saw—a middle-aged woman with graying hair dressed in a shapeless long-sleeved dress and carrying a small handbag. An utterly forgettable human being.

Desi smirked beneath her makeup and turned right. A few blocks later, she reached the bus stop. She sat alone on the bench, her handbag on her lap and her ankles crossed. The bus pulled up with a squeal of air brakes. Desi climbed aboard, paid her fare, and found a seat at the back.

She looked through the rear window. Lots of people scurrying around, but no one she knew from the museum or the surveillance team. She'd shaken her tails. The young agent stationed outside the door of her private workroom would get quite bored this afternoon.

Desi sat back and rubbed her shin. It still stung from barking it on that ductwork. She crossed her legs and counted bus stops. One. Two. Three. Four. Time to scoot out the door.

"Wait!" She lunged to her feet and hurried down the aisle.

The bus driver gave her a dirty look and reopened the door.

Desi hopped out and watched the people in the windows as the bus pulled away. None of the passengers returned her look with interest or alarm. To make extra sure, Desi made two more abrupt bus changes. Not a soul showed any interest in her movements.

Satisfied, she hailed a cab.

Seagulls wheeled in the air at Pier 1 of East Boston Harbor. Their screams greeted her as she stepped onto a sidewalk skirting a line of sheet metal–covered buildings. Beyond the buildings, whitecaps played on gray-green water. Smells of fish and brine and diesel fumes fought in her nostrils. In recent years many of the old waterfront warehouses had been converted into upscale condominiums with amenities to match. This section, however, was a working shipyard.

In the distance, laborers unloaded cargo with shouts as raucous as the gulls'. Close by, burly men in jeans and stained jackets stepped around her still figure. Desi shivered. The air was much cooler on the waterfront than in the city.

"Excuse me, sir." Desi addressed an older worker before he could hustle past. "Could you tell me where I might find Dock B, Warehouse 5?"

The man squinted at her, the lines around his eyes making deep furrows. "Right over there." He lifted his arm and pointed to an area a little apart from the rest. The spot contained several large warehouses fronted by a dock that berthed a variety of midsize ships.

Desi thanked the man, who touched his fisherman's cap and then strode on. She stared at the dingy buildings, a choking sensation squeezing her throat.

Feet, you're not going to run. You're going to go in there and do it now.

The sidewalk up to the front door of the Dock B warehouse office was cracked, but someone maintained a pair of trimmed bushes on either side of an opaque glass door. Inside the reception area, the smells of the wharf lost the battle with a citrus air freshener and the scent of cheap perfume.

Desi's stomach knotted. Stepping across a worn linoleum floor, she approached a woman seated behind a desk and tapping at a computer keyboard. The perfume smell got stronger.

Pale gray eyes looked up at Desi through a pair of trendy glasses. "May I help you, ma'am?"

Ma'am? Desi almost turned to see who might be standing behind her. Then she remembered her altered appearance. *Yikes! Senior moment!* "Yes, please. I'm here about Container 1193."

"Container 1193? Hmmm. Let's see." The woman's fingers flew over the keyboard. She read something, then looked up at Desi with an inquisitor's stare. "Name, please?"

"Desiree Jacobs."

"Do you have identification?"

"No driver's license, but I brought a raised seal birth certificate. Will that do?" Desi produced a tattered document from her small handbag.

The secretary studied the paper. "The birth date is smudged."

"I know. The certificate got wet a while back."

The woman frowned. "All right. I'll ask the verification questions and see what happens."

"Verification questions?"

"While Desiree Jacobs is listed as the only person besides the lessor to be granted access, the lessor provided four questions to ask if anyone shows up claiming to be her." She returned her focus to her computer screen.

Desi answered four questions that only she would know about her father—the name of his sixth grade teacher, who first inspired him with the love of art; the date and place he first met his wife; and the restaurant where he took Desi on her last birthday. The secretary smiled, placed a brief phone call, and soon a lanky young man in baggy jeans emerged from the warehouse area to escort her to the container.

"One moment, Ms. Jacobs. You'll have to sign in." The secretary thrust a log sheet at her.

So close and now this added risk. Her disguise ensured that she couldn't be identified by sight, but if the federal agents or a murderer found this place, her signature would condemn her. Desi signed anyway. She had no choice.

The young man whistled as he guided her between towering aisles of shelves stacked with crates and boxes. She was lost by the time they reached a wall of plastic containers, each taller than Desi and wider than her arm span. The teenager stopped at one labeled 1193 in big block letters.

"I'll come back in fifteen minutes to see if you're ready to go." He shuffled off.

Desi glared at the container. *What secrets are you hiding?* A familiar electronic keypad leered back at her with numbered teeth. Moistening her lips, Desi punched in the code. She held her breath until an airlock exhaled, and the door swung toward her. An automatic light came on. Pulling the door wider, she peered into the smooth-sided vault.

Her gaze traveled over six wooden-slatted crates of varying sizes. All were flat rectangles—the shape of paintings. None of the pieces were stacked on top of one another but stood on edge, ringing the wall. A fact that showed meticulous care for the contents.

Bile rose in Desi's throat. She swallowed hard. *Get a grip, Des. There must be a logical explanation.*

A small black book caught her eye. The slim volume sat atop one of the crates. Desi crept forward on shaking legs and entered the container. Inside, she was able to stand upright, but not by much. The enclosed space smelled of packing materials.

Just get it over with. Surely there's a logical explanation. She snatched up the book before she could talk herself out of it.

The leather cover bore no title. A snap held the book closed. She pulled and the snap released with a loud click— like the cocking of a gun that might blow her to smithereens. She opened to the first page and found words written in her father's large-lettered scrawl.

My Dear Daughter,

If you're reading this journal, it's because I'm no longer in a position to tell you these things myself. Not that I ever meant to say a word if I could fix this without involving you. The fact that you hold this book in your hands means my good intentions have come to nothing, and you're left with the mess I never meant to create. I have no idea how you will ever forgive me, though I hope that in Jesus you might someday, somehow find a way.

But first I must confess all.

Why are these precious pictures hidden away in a container on a dismal wharf?

Because it's true, my darling daughter: I stole them. To my everlasting pride and shame, I may be the best art thief the world has ever seen.

Desi slammed the book shut. Tears blurred the crates into surrealistic shapes. Her breath came in gasps. Where were strong, warm arms when she needed to collapse again?

What? She wanted Tony here now? Was she insane? Her father had just confessed to theft.

She sank to the floor, clutching the little book to her chest. Tony Lucano must not find her father's journal or this container. And she would never surrender the contents to a murderer. She needed time to figure out what to do. And she'd be doing it alone. Not only couldn't Max help; now even God couldn't help her because she was protecting a criminal.

Her father.

King of thieves.

A man she had never known.

Six

S he'd better be where she's supposed to be!

Tony strode toward the private room where Ms. Jacobs should be hard at work evaluating interviews. "Don't disturb me all afternoon," she'd said. Yeah, well, it didn't take a rocket scientist to know something was up with that. He could *kick* the station agent on duty outside her door for not reporting the suspicious request sooner.

With closing time near, museumgoers drifted toward the main exit. Tony gritted his teeth and dodged the flow of people. He was swimming upstream in more ways than one. Desiree Jacobs kept throwing out obstacles when she should be scrambling to cooperate.

"One moment, Agent Lucano."

Tony pivoted at the male voice and watched the museum's curator hustle toward him.

"May I walk with you?"

Tony jerked a nod. "You can keep me from getting lost in this rabbit warren."

"My pleasure." Plate's chuckle was brief. "I need to talk to you about a troubling matter."

"Our request to study the last few hours of camera tape?"

Tony started off again with the curator by his side.

"Not at all. Happy to help. Your partner explained how concerned you are about protecting Miss Jacobs from whoever killed her father."

"That's right." *Now that's a shocker! Stevo, you can be tactful when you want to be.*

At their last squad meeting, word had come down from on high that Desiree Jacobs was to be treated as equal parts suspect and potential victim, with the public emphasis on protection.

Plate went silent.

"You had a concern?" *Spit it out and move along, man.* He needed to deal with whatever he found—or didn't find—in the room up ahead.

"I don't mean to second-guess you," Plate said, "but that *art critic,* Paul Dujardin, was skulking about at Hiram Jacobs's funeral. He seemed extra attentive to Desiree, and I didn't like it. He's not a man to be trusted. You should look at him closely."

Tony stopped and stared down at the curator. That hard edge didn't come from casual suspicion. More like bitter rivalry. "Are you saying Dujardin has a romantic interest in Ms. Jacobs? Or is that you?"

Plate spluttered. "Oh my, no. Dujardin is older than her father was. She would never be interested in... What I mean is, my concern is professional."

Sure it is, buster.

Tony narrowed his eyes. The curator looked away.

Maybe he should remind the plump little weasel that he wasn't much younger than Hiram Jacobs had been. Desiree would have no interest in this prissy specimen of masculinity either. Would she?

What did he know of her taste in men? She was so enamored of her father that maybe she went for older guys. The FBI had psychological profiles on women like that.

No, not this woman. He couldn't make that picture fit. And not just because he didn't want to.

Tony forced a smile. "Nothing personal? Okay, if you say so. Then give me your *professional* reasons for distrusting Dujardin."

Plate looked away. His hand skimmed the top of his head. "The man has no appreciation of true art. He's about buying and selling. I'd put my money on him as a black market dealer."

"That's quite a stretch from attending the funeral of a friend."

The curator scowled. "You'll be making a big mistake if you overlook him."

"We aren't about to overlook anyone." *Not Dujardin and not you, pal.*

Plate lifted his chin. "Very well. I'll leave you to escort Desiree from the building. I have closing time duties." The man walked away, polished leather shoes flashing beneath his creased pants.

Tony stared after him, then went on toward the door he wanted. He knocked.

"Entrez," came the singsong answer.

Good girl. You're right where you belong.

He stepped into a rectangular room that held a long table, boardroom chairs, and not much else. Desiree sat at the end of the table, laptop open in front of her. No sign of her briefcase. Her cheeks were pink, and her breathing seemed too hard for someone who'd been caught up in paperwork for hours. Maybe she'd been working the kinks out with aerobics. *Yeah, right!* The face that looked back at him, wide-eyed, wore no makeup.

Attractive even without it. Attractive—and guilty as sin. Wherever she'd gone, whatever she'd done, she hadn't had time to reapply her cosmetics.

Please, Lord, just let me shake her until she confesses. But even the Bureau wouldn't give him the go-ahead on that.

Pain shot up his arm. He released the door handle; he'd about squeezed it off.

Tony walked toward her. *Let the stare do the talking.*

"Um, hi." Her fingers raked through disheveled hair. "What are you doing here?"

He prowled the room. Dust on a large vent cover had been disturbed. Fresh tool marks scratched the screws. He looked toward her, then at the vent, then back at her. She paled.

"Let's go." He jerked a hand toward the door.

"Wh-where? I'm not done here."

"Yes, you are."

Her knuckles turned white around the arms of her chair.

If he had to pick her up and carry her out of here, he would. He was done cutting this woman an inch of slack.

No, son. Be her friend.

Tony frowned. He looked away from Desiree's pale face. *Okay. I hear You, Lord.* He paced toward the other end of the room, keeping his back toward the woman that was making him half-crazy. *What's going on? Why are You taking the side of a thief?*

A picture popped into his head. Three crosses on a hill. Thieves had hung on two of them. "Today you will be with

Me in paradise." That's what Jesus said to one. *Sure, but that guy repented.*

He looked back at Desiree. She was closing her laptop, her movements sluggish, her face ashen.

So far, a hard line had gotten him nothing but more of the same back from her. A change in tactic couldn't hurt. Last time a woman had clouded his judgment, he hadn't known how to listen to good advice. Time to wise up.

He stuffed a hand into his pants pocket and jingled the change in the bottom. "I'm going to drive you home. You're too tired to be safe on the road."

Desiree's lips quivered. "You have no idea." She bent and pulled her briefcase from under the table. The laptop slid into a zippered outer compartment.

Tony pulled the case away from her, and she pierced him with a glance. He just smiled and opened the door.

What flickered across her face? Surprise? Gratitude?

They walked through the empty museum without speaking. The briefcase was heavy, but that didn't mean much. Paperwork weighed a lot.

Edgar Graham, the security manager, waited by the exit door. "You done for today? Okay to fire up the alarms now?" He grinned big at Desiree.

"Of course." She returned a half smile.

Tony glanced from one to the other. *Does every man adore this woman?*

He led her out the door. Rush hour was over, but vehicles and pedestrians flowed past in a steady stream. When they reached Desiree's car, Tony held out a hand. "Keys, please."

She gazed up at him. "Are you sure? I'll be fi—"

"You're already making it next to impossible to protect you from a killer. I'm not going to lose you to an auto accident I can prevent."

Desiree ducked her head. "Oh." The word came out in a huff. Lips compressed, she rummaged through her purse. She slapped the keys into his palm.

He closed his fingers around hers. "Why don't you trust me? I can help you."

Her hand trembled in his, but the stubborn set of her jaw did not relent. "I trust you to uphold the letter of the law. I don't expect you to help me personally. That's not your job."

Tony sighed and released her. He opened the passenger door and held it while she got in.

"Thank you." She settled into the seat, back stiff, eyes ahead.

He bent close while she fastened her seat belt. "I would, you know."

She halted in her task. "Would what?"

"Help you in any way that didn't violate the law. I want you to live through this, Desiree. I want to see your business prosper and your family name cleared. If that's not possible, I want to see you find a new life away from danger."

He shut the door on her wide eyes and open mouth. Had she noticed his use of her first name? He'd enjoyed saying it. Maybe too much.

He drove. She said nothing.

Tony glanced at her still figure and frowned. The woman was asleep. Her head tilted toward him, that beautiful hair a soft curtain over one side of her face. Those full lips were parted, not clamped shut with her usual guarded control.

Dark stains underscored the thick lashes that rested on a pale cheek. She had a wounded beauty, like a flower with some of its petals crushed.

Tony's heart turned over in his chest. He fixed his eyes on the road.

Desiree stirred as they rolled into her driveway. Her eyelids fluttered open at the rumble of the garage door.

She smiled at him, the intriguing mix of gold and brown and green in her eyes clear and frank. "Thank you."

"No problem."

He pulled into the garage and turned off the engine. Desiree gathered her purse and briefcase off the floor, but didn't move to get out. They sat in the cool shadows—and he caught the increased rate of her breathing.

Tony stayed still and quiet. *Make the right choice, Desi. Let's work together.*

She angled her body in his direction. "What would you do if you discovered that someone close to you was into something bad and dangerous—something way out of character? But you never got to find out why because they died."

Tony gripped the steering wheel. "Hurt like that takes a long time to heal. Mainly because the questions don't go away." *Like it ever heals.* But he couldn't tell her that.

Her wide eyes drank him in.

He cleared his throat, forcing the words out. "At first you concentrate on getting through the next minute, then the next hour, then a day at a time. For a while you do your best to forget it ever happened. Work is great for that." He laughed, but there was no humor in the sound.

"Think about the good times. Everything couldn't have

been a lie. Let some distance come. Maybe some perspective. While you're waiting for your life to turn right side out again, you pray. A lot. Because when the rubber hits the road, God's the only one who won't ever play the hypocrite."

A smile quivered on her lips. "Sounds like you've taken that journey."

"Oh, yeah."

Soft fingertips brushed the back of his hand. Heat jolted up his arm. Desiree had never gazed at him with tenderness before. Maybe…

He squelched the idea before it could form. Ms. Jacobs could be cut from the same cloth as Meranda, and he couldn't go there again. Not ever.

He slipped his hand away.

"Want to talk about it?" Desiree's gentle gaze slipped past his defenses.

Tony chuckled through a thick throat. "You're an amazing lady. You know that? Here you are in a world of hurt yourself, and you think you've got time for someone else's problems."

She made a face and looked out the window. "My father would have been surprised, too. Pastor Grange's teaching on the characteristics of Christ in us, the hope of glory, has really spoken to me. I guess I've always had to work on mercy. I never felt I had much need of it myself…until now. Guess that lands me in the hypocrites' club, huh?"

"Don't be too hard on yourself. It's hard to see our own complacency. God'll help you walk this through."

"You're really a believer."

"Sure. What did you think?" He chopped the air. "Never

mind. I know what you thought—I attended church to keep an eye on you and your father. Can't say that aspect didn't occur to me, but mainly I was checking out churches near where I live and ended up liking that one."

"You live around here?"

"Ten blocks over. Those new condos behind the stone walls and iron gates."

"Swanky."

Tony shrugged. "Enclosed neighborhoods like a few law enforcement types living there, so I got a special deal. Besides, I prefer my privacy when I'm off duty. But here." He pulled his notepad and pen out of his breast pocket. "Let me give you my home phone number and address. I'll put you on my approved visitor list." He scribbled on the paper, ripped it out of the pad, and handed the sheet to Desiree. "You can call me anytime, day or night. If you think about anything pertinent to the case, or even if you just need to talk."

She tucked the page in her purse, her expression unreadable.

They both got out of the car. Desiree pushed the button to close the garage door, and they headed toward the house. On the porch, Tony returned her car keys.

Desiree laughed.

She had a great laugh, warm and thick, like rich cocoa on a winter day. He'd never heard it before. "What's so funny?"

"Do you realize we just had a regular conversation?"

He put his hands in his pockets and rocked on the balls of his feet. "Yup. Just what the doctor ordered."

She lay her hand on his chest, over his heart. On purpose? Did she know that organ was about to pump right out of his rib cage?

Her lashes lowered. "Then I guess it's thank you again."

"Anytime."

Desiree went inside and closed the door.

Tony stood for long seconds. Then he turned away and strode up the block toward his condo. Stevo had picked him up for work this morning, so his car was still at home. He could go next door and get someone in the surveillance house to drive him, but he needed a good walk right now.

Call him an idiot, but those last few minutes hadn't been about a case. Just a guy and a gal who liked each other despite the junk standing between them.

Dangerous thought.

But then he'd always welcomed a certain measure of danger.

Desi leaned against the closed door. The buffer of Tony's presence faded. The house rang with emptiness. A chill crept through her pores and into her marrow.

You've turned everything you ever taught me into a dirty joke, Daddy. Why?

God, how could You let this happen?

She was whining, and she didn't care! God answered Job in the middle of his mess. He could answer her, too. If He didn't, she would…

What? What would she do?

Run away. Just run away. Go anywhere where she didn't have to look at her larcenous father's confession. Or watch the business they'd built swirl into the sewer. Or face the hurt on her employees' faces. Or hear the outcry from betrayed customers across the globe.

If only she could have told Tony what she found today. A killer lurked out there, unpunished. Thieves prowled uncaught.

Desi's fingernails chewed into her palms.

Before she'd left the container on Dock B and all of its infamous contents, she'd made herself reopen her father's journal and finish the note on page one. The last paragraph marred every relationship in her life.

I took the paintings. Me alone. But I dare not tell a soul where they are. No one in the office. No law enforcement agent. No member of government. He has people in all these places. Anyone can belong to him.

Anyone? A too-beguiling Italian-American agent? A laughing redhead who liked to watch old movies with her? If her dad had been sucked in, no one was above suspicion.

Her purse and briefcase thudded to the floor. She pressed her palms to her temples.

Maybe Dad was mistaken. Perhaps, along with his thievery, he'd fallen into some kind of sick paranoia at the end of his life.

No. His murder said otherwise. What had Tony said? It was a professional job. One done in a far-off country. Whoever her father had feared, it was someone real.

Someone with tentacles everywhere.

The phone shrilled. Tony groaned and rolled over, away from the sound. The phone clamored again. Grumbling, he sat up and reached for the handset.

This had better be good. He'd been strolling along the beach on a sparkling summer day with Desi's hand in his. In his dreams, of course.

"'lo?"

"Hey, pard, caught you sleeping on the job." A brief cigarette-hoarsened laugh.

Tony squinted at his digital alarm clock. 3:54 a.m. "Stevo? It's my weekend off. Yours, too. Or did you forget?"

"Nah. Couldn't sleep. You know me. I've been down at the office going over those videotapes from the museum. We got her, pard."

"Got who?"

"Desiree Jacobs. No question. I'll show you when you get here."

A jolt shot through Tony. He wasn't sleepy anymore. "Can't this wait until the sun clears the horizon?"

"Not unless you want to miss the interrogation."

"The what?"

"You must still be out in la-la land. Go back to sleep. I can handle this myself."

Not unless snowballs freeze in Hades. Tony was out of bed, wriggling into his pants one-handed with the phone pasted against his ear. "I can be there in thirty minutes."

"Don't get a speeding ticket." The harsh chuckle again and the pop of a wad of gum. "The night duty guys just left to haul her in. They're not burning any rubber, so they won't be over in your neck of the woods that fast. Hey, maybe you want to give them a hand—"

"No! I mean, yes. I'll meet them over at the Jacobs place. What's the charge?"

"No charge. Yet. Just suspicion."

"Suspicion of what?"

Long seconds of harsh breathing on the other end of the line. "You know the kind of people we're dealing with here. We've got a lot of latitude when it comes to terrorist activity."

"Ms. Jacobs is no terrorist!" Tony winced. He didn't need to let his emotions show in his volume.

"Maybe not, but the people dancing around her daddy's grave are."

"Don't you think we should tell her that? She should know we've got something a lot more serious going on than a few missing pieces of artwork."

"Nix on that. The SAC will have us for lunch if he thinks we've tipped our hand to a suspect."

Says the man thinking about his pension. Tony juggled the phone to pull on his shirt.

Yes, the Special Agent in Charge of the Boston Field Office would bust a gasket if they messed this one up, but Stevo was making a big mistake in his approach to Desiree. "The information might scare her into coming clean if she's told who's profiting from the thefts."

"Assuming she doesn't already know."

Tony stopped buttoning his shirt. "Nothing in all of our months of investigation suggests she does. Or even that her father did."

An exasperated noise answered him. "Just get down here if you want to join our chat."

Tony sat on the edge of his bed. He didn't like Steve Crane, not a bit, but the man had a solid track record as an agent. Professionally, Tony owed his partner the truth. Personally?

Well, laying something on the line might be a good litmus test as to how far he could trust the guy that had his back.

"Stevo?"

"Yeah?"

"I already knew she'd been out on the town without an escort, but I couldn't prove it."

"Didn't want to prove it?" The gum snapped.

"Maybe."

"Be careful, pard. A pretty face almost got you killed once before."

An old pain flared through Tony like rheumatism of the soul. "I don't repeat my mistakes." He broke the connection and headed for his car.

Crane's words grated him. Would his fellow agents ever give that case a rest?

Would *he* ever get past it and move on with his life?

Seven

See this?" Steve Crane's laser pointer circled a tiny mole on the close-up of a woman's hand on the left side of the wall screen and then did the same for the hand on the right side of the screen.

Tight-lipped, Tony glared at the PowerPoint image. He took a sip of last night's coffee and grimaced. The two of them sat in a small briefing room, surrounded by rows of plastic chairs and technical gadgets. Not his idea of a good night's rest.

Crane clicked off the pointer. "One picture is Ms. Jacobs going into the museum yesterday. The other is Ms. Jacobs leaving the museum around two-thirty disguised as someone else."

Tony nodded. Stevo had done good work. Too bad Tony was in no mood to be impressed. Maybe he *was* losing his objectivity.

People never seemed to learn that playing games with the truth ended in disaster. What was Desiree thinking? They'd find out soon enough. She was sitting in an interrogation room, left to wait and wonder.

"Now watch this." Crane advanced the film to the next set

of pictures—close-ups of two different female faces. "One of the forensic techs cross-matched the shapes and positions of the eyes, noses, mouths, and cheekbones. She assured me these are the same person." Crane switched to full body shots.

Tony sat forward and leaned his arms on the molded chair in the aisle ahead of him. No obvious resemblance between the people.

"Here's the best part." Crane exited the computer projection and pushed the play button on the video machine.

On the screen, a frumpy-looking woman in a shapeless dress and scuffed loafers stepped across the museum lobby. She appeared and disappeared between knots of people, always moving with slumped shoulders and a flatfooted gait. No trace of the confident stride of Desiree Jacobs, businesswoman. She was swallowed up in another persona altogether.

"Remarkable!"

Stevo let out a harsh laugh. "Told you this babe was a piece of work. Too bad she isn't on our payroll instead of working for the lowlife who's got her on a short leash."

Tony stood. "Let's go find out who that is." He crumpled his foam coffee cup and tossed the remains into the garbage can by the door.

"Not you, pal o' mine." Crane got up and stretched. "Cooke wants you front and center in his office right after we leave this room."

Tony's gaze dissected his partner, trying to read beneath the cool, almost cocky exterior. What did the second in command of the Boston Field Office want to see him for? Tony rubbed between his eyes. The headache that had begun at 3:54 a.m. grew larger by the minute.

❖ ❖ ❖

Bernard Cooke, Assistant Special Agent in Charge, closed a manila file and set it on his desk. The light-skinned African-American sighed and drummed the top of the file with his fingertips. Tony stood in front of the desk, hands at his sides, feet planted apart—braced for a blow.

Cooke frowned up at him. "I understand you were aware of Ms. Jacobs's duplicity last night and took no action. Would you care to explain your reasoning?"

"A judgment call, sir. She knew I knew. I'm trying to gain her confidence. Get her to see me as an ally, instead of an enemy. But when I had to roust her out of bed at four-thirty this morning and haul her down here, that strategy got blown out the window."

Tony didn't bother to disguise his irritation. One person besides Desiree knew that he'd let her escapade slide, and Stevo had wasted no time informing the powers that be. He'd even rousted a top bureaucrat out of bed and into the office by seven on a Saturday morning. Crane had just crossed a line with him…but why?

Tony gritted his teeth. He should have filled out that report on his partner instead of giving him the benefit of the doubt.

Cooke tapped the folder. "This report claims you've developed a romantic interest in the suspect that's clouding your judgment. Your partner is worried you won't be able to follow through if hard choices become necessary."

Tony hid fisted hands behind his back. "I have no idea what would give Crane such a poor opinion of my professional capabilities. Or a clue about my so-called romantic inclinations."

Wry amusement passed over his superior's face, only to be doused by a stern look. "The counterterrorist squad is very interested in this case. They're about a half step away from taking it over. Any hint of mishandling and that's what will happen. Ms. Jacobs won't be treated like a lady if they move in. To satisfy them, the kid gloves come off today."

Tony opened his mouth to protest.

Cooke pointed a finger at him. "Crane's handling the interrogation. Solo. If he gets nothing, you'll have your turn—your way. I've studied your file. Female suspects tend to like you. To trust you, just like you want with the Jacobs woman. Even that case five years ago, the one where the wheels came off and things got messy. You did your job, and the case was closed to the satisfaction of the United States government."

"Not to my satisfaction." Tony clamped his jaw shut on further comment.

Cooke shifted in his chair and looked away. "Understandable." He bobbed his chin at Tony. "Nevertheless, I'm betting national security that you'll do your job…whatever the cost. Do you understand?"

Tony stared at a place on the wall above his boss's head. "Does Lourdes agree with your assessment of my…skills?"

The ASAC couldn't possibly have cleared this off-the-books procedure so fast with his direct superior, the top dog at the Boston office. No way was he going to become a government gigolo, or even look like one. That other time happened by accident and people got killed, even though the outcome looked good on paper. Bad guys—and one traitorous woman—dead at each other's hands. Nothing for the FBI to do but take the glory.

Some glory! He'd survived by God's grace. If anything like that happened again…

Cooke cleared his throat. Tony looked down. The man held out a fax, and Tony took the paper. The header identified it as from Special Agent in Charge Jason Lourdes's home fax, timed an hour ago.

Give Lucano his head with this one. He's got good instincts.

A neat way to authorize what no one wanted to be accountable for. But nothing there about romancing a woman under false pretenses, so he was basically free to follow the lead of his true Superior. *Good deal, Lord.*

He smiled at Cooke. The ASAC smiled back.

"I can live with this," Tony said.

"Thought you might feel that way. I'll put the sheet in your personnel jacket. It's a nice commendation." He shot Tony a sharp look. "As long as you live up to it." Cooke stood. "Let's go watch an interrogation. Crane has his…ah…skills, too. Yours may not prove necessary."

A knot jerked tight around Tony's insides as he followed Cooke out of his office. Crane's *skills* had their roots in the rough edges of his New York street cop beginnings. Just like Tony had been given his head with this case, no doubt the powers that be had given Crane carte blanche to throw the full force of his abrasive techniques at Desiree.

Stevo was smart and slick and had never demonstrated a conscience. Case in point, his speed in filing a negative report on his partner in order to protect himself. The man was starting to be a menace. He must have suspected that Tony was less than happy with his behavior, and by filing a report first, he'd done an end run around any possibility that Tony could take *his* concerns to their superiors. A counterfiling would look like retaliation.

Tony was stuck juggling a sociopathic partner, a sneaky suspect, and a murder/theft case that showed no signs of turning out well. He took a long, deep breath before stepping into the observation room. Talk about walking by faith. This was it.

Big-time.

Desi had never been claustrophobic, but the walls of the stark white interrogation cubicle closed in more each second. Her lungs expanded and contracted, but oxygen didn't seem to reach her arms and legs. A creeping numbness had taken over her fingers and toes.

"What time I am afraid, I will trust in Thee." The verse from a favorite Psalm whispered inside her.

All right, Lord, You've got me pegged. I'll follow Your advice…or try anyway.

She took her elbows off the battle-scarred table, sat back, and wiped her palms on her slacks. Maybe this wouldn't be so bad. Tony—Agent Lucano—had been all business when he picked her up this morning, but she could stomach him. At least he'd be around to curb his partner's rabid instincts.

A noise at the door brought her heart into her throat. *Here goes!*

Steve Crane entered the room. The door swung shut. No Tony.

Desi's gaze swiveled to the opaque window that covered the upper half of one wall. Was Lucano just going to watch?

Crane walked to the other side of the table, between her and the observation window. She stared up into pale, unblinking eyes.

Desi gulped. Should she spill what she knew? A viselike pressure closed around her chest. No! Trusting the wrong person would be worse than keeping her counsel. More lives than hers hung in the balance.

The agent walked around the table, shoving chairs in as he went. He came all the way to her side and invaded her space. His bulk towered over her.

Don't give him the satisfaction of cranking your neck backward to look at him. But her eyes had a mind of their own. They traveled up the buttons of his shirt, found his bull neck, then jumped up to meet his cold stare.

"Ms. Jacobs, are you aware that withholding information in an FBI investigation is obstruction of justice and a federal offense?"

She cleared her throat and pulled her rebellious gaze away from him. "Now that you told me, I am. What leads you to believe I'm withholding information?"

Was that *her* talking? How had she managed that cool, calm tone?

Crane pressed a rough-knuckled hand onto the table and leaned toward her. She smelled stale coffee, cigarettes, and the barest hint of spearmint. He cracked gum behind a set of large teeth. The sound of bones breaking. She shuddered.

He grinned.

"You wandered away from your surveillance team yester-

day dressed up as someone else. Not the action of an innocent woman...or one that needs protection." He eyed her up
and down, like she was lower than roadkill. "If you're so sure
of your safety out there on your own, you must be in bed
with this load of thieves and murderers. Now you're gonna
tell us how, when, where, and why so we can catch the guy
who killed your papa. Or maybe a woman like you doesn't
care about that."

An icy burn spread through Desi's insides. "You have no
clue about me or about my father." No matter that she wasn't
so sure of her father anymore. "Your job has stuck dirty
glasses on your face. You see everything ugly."

An odd expression—surprise? dismay?—ghosted across
Crane's face. He whirled and stalked to the other side of the
table. Pulling out a chair, he flipped it around, then straddled
it and leaned his arms on the back. His upper lip curled.

"All right then, Daddy's Girl. Why don't you paint me a
pretty picture? What was a creepy crawly like Leone Bocca
doing in your papa's apartment?"

"I've answered that question a dozen times. Looking for
something." She left the *duh!* off, but he got it.

His face reddened. "And what might that something be?
You know. You tell. 'Cuz if we find out later that you're keeping
secrets, you'll go from designer clothes to an orange jumpsuit in
a New York minute. Might have a hard time salvaging that
precious business of yours from a suite at the Iron Hilton."

Silence draped the room.

Beyond weary, Desi hugged herself. She didn't want to
disrespect her faith by lying—especially to the authorities
that Scripture said were ordained by God. But what was a

citizen to do when honest answers might put lives in danger? Maybe it was a good thing Lucano wasn't present. She might be tempted to let down her guard.

"Stolen art." There. She'd told the truth. He could take her statement any way he liked.

"Now ain't that the newsflash of the century." Crane shook his head. "You can do better. Like telling me where you went yesterday afternoon."

Desi arched her brows and lifted her chin. "I wasn't aware that dressing up and avoiding a tail was a crime. I've just become an orphan. That hits hard at any age. I needed to be alone, away from prying eyes and listening ears, to commune with my father."

He chuckled. "You're a spiritist now? What did you do? Hold a séance?"

"I'm a Christian. We don't talk to the dead. Grieving people sometimes need to get away by themselves to relive their memories. Or don't they teach that in Fibbie Psych 101?"

Crane slammed a meaty palm onto the table. Desi jumped. He half rose from his chair, face aflame.

"So you're saying you went to all that trouble yesterday in order to take a walk down memory lane?"

Desi fought back tears. Her hands shook. She gripped them together. *Don't act pitiful. Don't act pitiful.* She clenched her teeth and sucked in a breath.

"Look. I rode lots of buses yesterday afternoon. Not only do I need to deal with my father's murder, but I have to face the idea that he might not have been the man I thought he was. If that makes me act a little strange, then so be it. Now, if you're going to charge me with something, go ahead.

Otherwise, I'm leaving." Back stiff, she stood.

Crane's lunged to his feet. "One step, and we'll find a reason to hold you." He pointed to her chair.

Desi hesitated and then sank back down. "Do a lie detector test. You federal guys like that sort of thing, don't you? Ask me this: 'Miss Jacobs, have you ever stolen works of art from homes or museums?' I will say, 'Yes, of course I have.'"

Crane's head jerked backward. Then his eyes narrowed, and he rasped a laugh. "That's a trick answer, Ms. Jacobs. We all know you've walked off with plenty of pieces that came right back in the door after you proved to the owners you could take them. Try another question, and give me an answer that means more than spit in the wind."

"All right." Desi spread her hands on the table. "How about this one? 'Miss Jacobs, have you at any time conspired to steal art for personal gain?' Answer: 'No.' 'Were you aware that your father might have been involved in such activities?' Answer: 'No, and I want to deck you jerks for suggesting it.' 'Do you have any idea who might be involved in this theft ring or who might have killed your father?' Answer: 'Absolutely not, but I wish I did so I could turn them in so fast their heads would spin...after I draw and quarter them myself, of course.' Is that enough Q and A? I guarantee the detector needle will show negative on every one of them."

Veins stood out in Crane's fists.

He wants to hit me. Chills chased themselves up her spine. What held him back? The watchers behind the one-way mirror?

The agent's fingers loosened.

Her insides melted, but she held her spine straight. She stared at the mirror. Who was back there, and what did they think of this waste-of-time interview? Had they even noticed how close one of their agents had come to abusing a suspect?

Did they even care?

Standing in the observation room, Tony suppressed a chuckle. Desiree turned the tables on Stevo like he was some first-office agent fresh out of Quantico. If Tony didn't want to throttle the truth out of her himself, he'd cheer her performance.

Beside him, Cooke let out a long groan. Sweat beaded the man's forehead, and his hands trembled—as if he'd been the subject of the interrogation.

"You all right?" Oh, great! He could top off the morning by calling an ambulance for the ASAC.

Cooke pulled out a handkerchief and mopped his brow. "Sure. I just get jittery if I don't eat breakfast. I'd better go grab a bite. Doesn't look like Crane is going to pull any useful information out of the suspect. Too bad. Your turn now. Report straight to me and no one else as soon as you know anything." The man left like his shoes were on fire.

Blood sugar problem? No way. Tony knew that brand of sweat. High anxiety. Someone with a lot of clout must be leaning on the agency to solve this case by any means necessary. Oh, joy! Politics had to be in play if he was being ordered to report to one of the professional paper pushers instead of his squad supervisor.

Tony turned back toward the interrogation room. Desiree was on her feet, sweeping up her purse. She moved toward the door like a queen on the way to a state banquet. Stevo growled something about watching her step.

Tony waited thirty seconds and then left the room. Desiree was just boarding the elevator. She didn't look at him.

Crane stood in the hallway. He ran a hand through his hair. "I'm going home to get some rest." He went for the next elevator car.

Tony shook his head. How many six-packs would his partner slurp down to put himself out?

Tony turned in the other direction and took the stairs double time. As soon as he hit the ground floor, he spotted Desi's petite figure heading for the exit. A few male agents coming on duty followed her with their eyes but made no move to approach. No doubt she'd fry them with a look. He strode after her.

"Ms. Jacobs. Desiree, wait!"

A marginal pause in her step; then she hurried on. He caught up to her at the doors. She stopped and turned her face toward him. Oh yeah, fire all right. He could be incinerated for talking to her, but a man only lived once.

"Let me give you a lift home since I'm the one who dragged you here."

Desiree shook her head, mouth flat. "I don't care for any more FBI company today. Thank you, but I'll take a cab."

Tony watched her go. Right back out into the danger zone. And if she wouldn't cooperate with the law, not a soul in the world could protect her from herself or any other menace out there.

Like a cold-blooded killer.

❖ ❖ ❖

The poor cabdriver must think I'm crazy.

Another sob snuck past Desi's clenched teeth. She wrapped her arms tight around her middle.

So she won that round. They let her go. Big deal. She was still alone. How could she tell friend from foe? What if her silence today was a fatal mistake?

"Miss?"

She blinked at the driver.

"I got something for ya." He held something small and round and flat over the side of the seat.

Desi took it from him. She looked down at the coinlike object in her palm. A bus token?

What? Why?

Blackness edged her vision. She grabbed for breath.

"Why did you give me this?" She shot forward and clutched the seat between them.

"Take it easy, lady. Some dude stopped me down the block from where I picked you up. Said to give it to my next fare. And there you were on the curb, flagging me down. Thought it would be a kick to follow through. I sure don't need a bus ride." He laughed.

Steve Crane? Of course! That goon wouldn't be happy if he didn't get the last word.

"Was this man built like an ape with ice-blue eyes?"

The driver frowned at her in the rearview mirror. "Naw. Small guy. Kinda scrawny. Hoarse voice. Didn't really see him good."

Not Crane? Then who? Desi wilted back into her seat.

No one but me knew about the bus rides until less than an hour ago in that interrogation room. Unless... The token burned in her fist. *Someone followed me from the museum!* Her heart sped up.

Did they stay with her all the way to the warehouse? Not possible! By the time she quit the buses and took a cab to the wharf, she'd doubled back and turned around enough to make a bloodhound dizzy. What was she missing?

"Did this man say anything else?"

"Oh, yeah, almost forgot." The cabdriver gave her a back-handed wave. "The guy said, 'Tell her I want to know where this takes her.'" He shrugged. "Don't figure that token would get you out of downtown. Weird, huh? I've driven cab in Chicago, Minneapolis, and now here, and I'm tellin' ya, there's lotsa nuts in this world."

He had no idea.

Eight

*L*ook, the guy can't just drop off the planet. We're all missing something."

A sniff answered Tony on the other end of the phone line. "Interpol shares the FBI's concern. I assure you, even if Bocca is on Mars, *we* will find him."

Tony stopped twiddling the pen between his fingers. *Implication: The Bureau isn't up to the job. Sure! Why not add a little interagency hotdogging to an entertaining week?*

"Keep us in the loop, okay?" Tony hung up the phone, leaned an elbow on the workstation counter, and rubbed his chin.

That went well. Why couldn't anyone get a whiff of Bocca? Five days since Crane's bust of an interview with Desiree and nothing to show for all the cages they'd rattled since.

He needed to get through to that stubborn woman, and fast! If she'd just break down and give them some hard evidence against the mastermind of this operation, she'd get a good deal—witness protection, the whole nine yards.

I'd never see her again. A vise clenched around his gut. *Better than watching her buried beside her father.*

"Hey, pard, you look like you could use a shot of java."

A mug of black coffee appeared under his nose. He inhaled the steam, then took a cautious sip.

"Where'd you find fresh-brewed around this sludge factory?"

Crane heaved his bulk into the chair at the station across from Tony. "If you want it, you gotta make it yourself." He frowned into his mug. "About the only thing hot going on right now."

And maybe you're still putting on a show like Saturday never happened and you didn't shaft me to the big bosses. Tony let more coffee slide down his throat. Just like he'd let the incident slide for now—but he wouldn't forget.

He set the mug on his desk. "We know that this shadow boss must be someone with deep connections in the art world and a grudge against Western society—enough to make him approachable by terrorists looking to traffic in art for cash—and with a gifted forger on his payroll. Why can't we get a line on this mastermind through the forger? Forgery's not a broad field of expertise."

Crane shook his head. "He's gotta be new. And better than good. The trail's always cold before the substitutions are spotted. Nothing smash and grab. Sophisticated all the way. Hard to say if we even know the half of what's missing yet."

"It all comes back to Bocca." Tony picked up the smuggler's file and flipped it open. Not that he'd find anything he hadn't already memorized. "This guy's a mercenary. He'll do a deal in a heartbeat to save his miserable hide. Maybe even give us something to leverage information out of Desiree, and the dominos'll start to fall."

"Ah, *Desiree* is it? So what's your next move with little Ms. Jacobs?"

Tony scowled.

Crane grinned and waggled shaggy brows. "You two make a cute couple. You know, when this case shakes out, I hope we're all wrong, and she turns out to be innocent. I doubt it, but I can hope. Just call me a dreamer."

Tony stared, then barked a laugh. "The day you're a dreamer I'll hand you a toga and a bow and arrow, Cupid."

Crane guffawed.

"Hey, you two," someone called from a neighboring workstation. "Sounds like waaaay too much fun happening over there."

Tony grabbed a small handful of hard candies from the dish on his desk and chucked them over the partition. A ragged clatter sounded on the other side.

"Oooh, gifts from on high," the voice shot back.

"Do not despise the benevolence of the Lord, my son." Crane folded his hands over his stomach, tucked in his chin, and set his mouth in a grave line.

"Now I've seen it all." Tony laughed. "Father Steven, is it?"

So old Stevo had a respectable vocabulary *and* a sense of humor. His partner must save his lighthearted side for his drinking buddies. Maybe he ought to smell the guy's breath.

Crane's head jerked up. He looked past Tony's shoulder.

"Squad meeting. All you wiseacres into the task room now!"

Rachel Balzac.

Tony turned. His squad leader bored a hole in him with her eyes; then her gaze moved on. He slapped Bocca's file onto his desk and stood. "Looks like we're done spinning our wheels for the day."

Crane came up behind him as they followed the herd. "If

you were a bug, she'd step on you, pard. Guess she's still torqued you edged her out of the martial arts championship last fall."

Tony stopped and stared at his partner. "That explains a lot."

"Like why you got stuck with me." Crane's grin stretched his mouth, but didn't enter his eyes.

Tony opened his mouth, shut it, and walked on. Stupid was nowhere in Stevo's employment record. Too bad winning personality wasn't either.

After the brief, touch base meeting, Tony threaded his way back toward his desk through the end-of-shift nuthouse in the bull pen. He lost Crane somewhere along the route. Not a bad thing. The guy had stuck to him like superglue all day, not even taking time out for a smoke break. Lack of nicotine usually made Crane as irritable as a goaded wolverine, but all week he'd been Mr. Sunshine. What was up with this change in behavior?

And why is Half-Pint Henderson from OPR skulking by my desk?

Tony increased his pace. The skinny agent from the Office of Professional Responsibility looked around, his gaze meeting Tony's. The man's nostrils flared; then he turned and hurried away. Tony reached his station. A file drawer stood open an eighth of an inch. The pen he'd been playing with was on the floor. Sloppy job—or maybe just rushed.

A boulder weighted Tony's stomach.

He'd pegged himself as the chump who pulled the assignment to put up with Crane until the man's retirement. But that didn't jell with recent history. On Crane's say-so, Tony had been called on the carpet. Who was really babysitting whom?

Was this search more of Crane's doing? Or was he still high on Balzac's radar? And for what? Internal affairs needed more than a lost trophy to go gunning for a fellow agent.

"So you never answered my question."

Tony turned and watched Crane step up and start shoving paper clips, pens, and files into drawers.

"What question?" *Cool it, Lucano. Could you snarl any louder?*

Crane gave him a hard look and rippled his shoulders. "The Jacobs woman. What's your next move?"

"No moves. I'm going with the flow." He clinked the cover onto his glass candy dish. "Our church is having a bowling party tonight. She signed up. I signed up. You want to come?"

Tony squared a stack of papers and ignored his partner's pop-eyed stare. *Let's see how deep this reformed character goes.*

"You gotta be kidding." Crane slammed a drawer shut. "When I bowl, I wanna throw down a few brewskies and tell jokes my mama wouldn't appreciate, not guzzle lemonade and holler 'Hallelujah' with every strike."

Ah, back to normal. The weight in Tony's stomach eased.

"Hey, most of my group guzzles the hard stuff—good old root beer. And we don't yell 'Hallelujah.' It's 'Praise the Lord.' No high fives either. Just hold hands and pray before every ball. No other personal contact allowed. Get your details straight, Stevo. Where did you get your strange ideas about Christian social behavior?"

Crane lifted his hands. "All right. All right. I'll quit stereotyping. You sure don't fit, anyway. Maybe that's why you bug me so much sometimes. I want to be able to figure you out so I can write you off."

Tony laughed. "Let me know when you get the job done, Stevo. Maybe then I could see walking through this crazy life without faith in something bigger than me." He walked away, headed for home.

So, Lord, You ready to take on the Bureau's internal machinery? Looks like something's up, and I need answers fast.

Better yet, could You let me in on the questions first?

Desi finished lacing her bowling shoes and sat up. She scowled in Tony's direction. He chatted and laughed with another guy in the lane next to hers.

What's next? He asks to rent Dad's apartment and moves in downstairs?

It could be worse. He could've drawn the same team she did.

Get over it and move on, girl.

Tony had just been doing his job when he dragged her down to FBI headquarters. She knew that. But what she couldn't figure was why he'd abandoned her to his partner's mercy—or lack thereof?

Maybe he didn't have a choice.

Desi considered the thought. Tony wasn't a one-man show in that gargantuan organization. Maybe they told him he had to do it that way.

Or maybe that was the dressed-up explanation. Maybe he'd just been playing mind games with her—the old good cop/bad cop thing.

So ignore him already.

Kind of like turning a blind eye to the pink elephant stomping around the living room.

The man looked way too good in a polo shirt and jeans. He stepped up to the lane, swept his arm back, and let the ball fly. It sped straight for the center pin.

Desi's breath caught. *Oh, dear Lord, that's me everywhere I turn. About to get bulldozed.*

A hand passed in front of her face.

"Earth to Desi." Max chuckled. "Or should I say *Dizzy*? You're up."

"Uh, sorry. I was daydreaming."

"Moonin' is more like it." Max laughed again. "Not that I blame you. If I hadn't already snagged Dean, I'd give you some competition. That man doesn't just look nice; he *is* nice."

"Don't even go there." Desi groaned. "How did I let you talk me into this?"

Max pulled her to her feet. "You're both on the same side now—eager to catch the bad guys. Right? It wouldn't hurt to be friends."

"Hey, Max! Des! You two going to talk or bowl?" Dean Webb put an arm around his wife's waist. She poked him in the belly with her elbow, and he rubbed his paunch but didn't release his hold. They grinned at each other.

Friends. That's what they are. I sure haven't found that yet.

Desi waved at them and went to the carousel. The ball slipped from her fingers, crashed to the floor, and careened toward another group of bowlers. A large foot shot out and clamped down on the runaway. Cheeks burning, she stared up into Tony Lucano's grinning face.

He pointed toward the far end of the bowling lanes. "The varmints ya wanna shoot are thataway, miss."

Her heart sped up. *Don't think you'll get on my good side with that to-die-for grin, mister.*

Max hooted. "He could pass for a Texan any day."

Tony touched an imaginary Stetson.

Fine. Two could play at this game. "Now, suh—" Desi batted her lashes—"you may be mistaken. Puhhaps I connected with the right vahmint aftah all."

Everyone within earshot laughed. Color rose on Tony's face.

Take that, Mr. Good Guy. How I do love flustering the master of control.

Tony bent and picked up her ball. He held it out to her, but didn't let go when she tried to take it.

"Do be careful, Desiree."

Her name whispered from his lips, caressing her nerve endings. And that look. Like he cared.

She wobbled off to take her turn, but she might as well have sat on the sidelines. The ball made a beeline for the gutter. She sank into a seat and watched Max bowl.

A hand tapped her shoulder. Tony smiled at her from the set of chairs back-to-back with hers. He held out a plastic cup.

"Go ahead. It's orange soda. Your favorite."

Blast the man! Did he know *everything* about her. It wasn't fair. She knew zilch about him. Maybe it was time to change that.

She took the offering.

"Pax." He held up two fingers. "I was against hauling you in last Saturday."

She studied him. He'd never lied to her yet—that she could tell. "All right. You're on probation, Agent Lucano."

"Call me Tony. We should get past titles and last names."

She took a pull on her soda straw. The fizz burst into her mouth.

Scary territory. This man was all about exposing secrets. He could find her out if she let him burrow close enough. But if she didn't, how would she ever know if his inside was as real as his outside?

She put the glass into the cupholder. "Desiree is fine, but Desi is better."

"Deal." He nodded. "I like seeing you like this."

"At church functions?"

"Sure, that. But I meant just being yourself. Relaxed. Having fun."

"Those moments are hard to come by." She looked away from him. No doubt he thought he'd touched her raw grief. But right now her biggest problem was her ridiculous, galloping attraction to the man sitting behind her. *What a time to fall for a guy, Desi. And why this one?*

If she were smart, she'd say something polite and go talk to someone else. But smart would blow her "get to know Tony" quest.

"So, tell me about the last movie you saw."

"What do you like to do in your spare time?"

Their questions overlapped each other. They both laughed.

"You go first." Tony waved her on.

"No, you."

"If we're not careful, we'll be arguing like Chip and Dale over who can be the most polite."

"The Disney chipmunks! You like cartoons, too?"

"Sure, when I was a kid. Don't tell me you still watch

Saturday morning 'toons."

"No way! Wouldn't touch the new stuff. I like the old ones. You know—Road Runner, Bugs Bunny, Speedy Gonzales. *Arriba, arriba! Andele, andele!*"

"You do that well." Tony pointed at her. "You should try out for voice-overs."

"Riiiight. I'll add that to my short to-do list. I'm really more into grown-up classics."

Tony groaned. "Then you'd hate my DVD collection."

"Not necessarily. Classics were new releases once. What makes them timeless is how well they've aged. People never outgrow the characters that make us love them, the themes that speak to our souls. *Casablanca. The Sound of Music. Brigadoon.*"

"Hey, I'm hooked. Where do I buy a ticket?"

Desi laughed. "My house. Friday night. Max, Dean, and I are watching Orson Welles's *The Stranger.*"

A shadow passed over Tony's face. He looked away and frowned.

Desi's heart squeezed. Did he recognize the title? *Daddy said someone in the FBI was in the theft ring. Did you send me that note and video, Tony? Are you the one? Oh, please don't be.*

His gaze returned to her face. "I don't know, Desi. It's one thing to run into you at a church event, but it's pretty much a no-no for us to socialize in private. When this investigation is over, I—"

"Hey, no problem. You'll just have to let me know when I'm off the suspect list. Of course, you could justify Friday as close surveillance. Bring the whole team if you want."

Tony laughed. "I'll think about it, all right?"

Someone's call alerted him to his turn. He stood. "Go jogging with me in the morning. We'll talk about Friday and...other things. The surveillance unit will be nearby, so it'll be like an informal interview. Good health, clean conscience. Who could ask for a better offer?" His gaze pierced through her.

"Jogging it is. If you think you can keep up." She grinned.

Tony stepped toward his carousel, laughing.

Max slid into the seat beside Desi. "Oh, girl, I sense progress here."

"Maybe."

What kind of progress? Was she working on a friendship that might become more? Or had she just baited a trap for an enemy?

Nine

"You're going to…have to decide…who to believe in…pretty soon." Tony puffed out the words in rhythm with his stride.

His tennis shoes thumped in unison with Desi's along the dirt path in their neighborhood park. Dawn was only a hint on the horizon, but the birds were up and singing. Blooming lilac bushes laid scent along the way. But the best part of the new day ran beside him, looking downright cuddly in her Boston Red Sox sweat suit. The lady had good taste.

"Let's keep this…recreational. When I have…something to say…believe me…I'll say it." She increased the pace and struck out ahead of him.

Tony grinned. Fair enough, but she didn't want to challenge him. She really didn't.

He matched her speed, then stepped it up another notch. She was game—too game for her own good. Another cause to worry about her.

They passed into a grove of trees and started an uphill climb. Desi's stride hitched. Her breathing rasped. Tony eased the pace, and though she didn't object, she didn't say thank you either. Tony kept his grin to himself.

At the top of the hill, they burst out of the trees onto a

grassy hillside. Tony stopped, jogging in place. Desi bowed her head toward her knees and puffed.

"Don't miss the sunrise," he said.

She pulled herself upright and walked back and forth on the grass. Then she stopped and stared east. Tony moved alongside her and stood still.

"Ahhhhh, Tony. This is awesome! Do you do this every day?"

"Every day I can."

He watched the rising sun play across her face. Parted lips. Wide eyes. The first rays haloed her features in gold. *I've sure never seen her this way before.*

Desi took his arm, resting her head against his shoulder.

Tony swallowed. *Don't you move, Lucano. The woman doesn't know what she's doing. And you're not going to mess up the moment.*

Minutes got lost. The birds sang their throats out.

Desi stirred and let out a long sigh. "Thank you. I can't believe I sleep through this." She looked up at him and smiled, then moved several yards down the hill, stretching her arms and working her legs. She stopped and turned.

"So last one down the hill is a rotten egg." She grinned at him, backpedaled a few feet, then whirled and ran.

"Hey!" Tony ran after her. *Did she even realize she snuggled up to me all on her own?* "Watch out below, lady!"

Longer legs were a good deal in a foot race with a sneaky female. The distance between them narrowed. He swept past her at the bottom and didn't bother to slow down.

No quarter, babe. You did it to yourself.

He waited for her at the exit to the park. She tore up to

him, face red—then socked him in the shoulder and ran past. He laughed and fell into stride beside her.

"Okay, we've both proved…we can run like idiots. Let's…walk it out from here."

"Gladly."

"In fact—" they slowed to a walk—"we can grab a ride back to your house." He nodded toward the surveillance car inching along behind them.

Desi threw him a look that could have boiled water.

"Just a thought." He chuckled.

"I think…I'll make it home…just fine."

Tony believed her. Minimum of three workouts a week at the gym. No exceptions. The lady was in shape.

Physically fit. Brilliant. Daring. A mistress of disguise. Privy to the security details of billions of dollars in art. Perfect profile for the burglar substituting fakes for masterpieces all over the globe. The scenario made total sense, except for one thing.

He didn't buy it. At least not when he was with her. When they were apart… Well, two plus two was hard to keep from adding up to four. Was his cop sense being influenced by her obvious charm? Or was he getting a true reading of her character when they were together? If only he dared trust his instincts, but he'd been fooled before.

Tony studied her from his greater height. Her glossy head barely reached his shoulder.

Okay, let's assume for a minute she's not the thief. Then who is? Did that part of the operation die with Hiram?

They stepped up onto Desiree's porch, and she turned to face him at the front door. Tony brushed a thumb across her flushed cheek. *What are you hiding, beautiful?*

He put his hands in his pockets. "See you at the movies on Friday."

"I'm glad you decided to join us."

Glad? Then what put the white around your lips and the panic in your eyes when you said that?

Desi opened her front door, and Max hustled in.

"Dean's going to be late, but I brought the beverage." She held up the two-liter of ginger ale and started up the stairs. "Nothing else goes as good with popcorn. And I hope you got some of that, because if you didn't, we're sunk. The kids ate the last of ours the other night. What was the movie you said we're going to watch? An Orson Welles? I saw *Citizen Kane* once, but—"

"Whoa, girl. Rewind, and go slo-mo. You've left me in the dust." Desi looked up at her friend from the bottom of the stairs. *What's up with you, Max?*

Her friend turned around on the third step from the top. "Well, get on up here, girlfriend. This is your place, your party."

"Tell you what. You come back down and let Tony in. He should be here any second. I'll go up and put ice in the glasses. That way, neither of us has to bounce up and down these stairs like a yo-yo."

"Makes sense to me." Max clomped back down.

Desi took the soda. "What's wrong? And don't tell me nothing."

"It really is nothing." Max shook her head. "Just the life of a charter pilot's wife. Other than bowling three nights ago, I haven't seen hide nor hair of my husband. Then he calls to tell me he won't make it on time for our date." She sighed.

Desi hugged her. "You do have it bad when you call watching a movie with a third wheel like me a date."

"Oh, come on. We like being around you. Besides, Dean takes me out on the town lots when he's home. Some real nice places, too."

"Exactly."

Max laughed and planted her hands on her hips. "Now you went and spoiled a perfectly good pity party. I hope you're happy."

"Ecstatic."

"Did you say your hunk with a badge is gonna join us?"

"No, Tony Lucano is."

"One and the same."

Desi held up the bottle of soda. "Max, if I didn't like you so much, I'd dump this over your head."

"Naw. Go dump it in the glasses. I'll cover for you here."

The doorbell rang.

Desi's heart thudded. She clutched the bottle to her chest. *Easy. Keep your cool. It won't be anything like last time I stood here and he came through that door.*

Max opened the door, and Tony stepped over the threshold. Jeans and a T-shirt replaced the suit he'd worn last time...and Desi's heart rate slowed.

It really is different.

He smiled and held out a box. "I brought microwave popcorn. Hope that's all right."

"A man after my own heart." Max laughed. "Let's get to this thing."

Desi led the way up the stairs and headed for the kitchen with the soda and popcorn. When she came back with full glasses, Tony had taken one of the easy chairs, and Max had commandeered the sofa. Still hoping for hubby to show up. Desi grinned at her; Max winked back.

"Let me help you with those." Tony jumped up and took two of the glasses. He passed one to Max.

Desi set hers on a coaster on the coffee table. "I have to go back and get the popcorn out of the microwave."

"Let me." Max headed for the kitchen.

"In that case, I'll get the movie ready." Desi crossed to the TV. She looked down at the VHS video lying on top. Acid burned the back of her throat.

Do it. Give it to him. Let him look at it while you look at him.

"Here." She turned. "Open it for me, will you?"

"No problem." He smiled at her. "Um, you have to let go of it."

"Oh, sorry." She snatched her hand away.

He had the shrink-wrap off in seconds.

Not a flicker of an eyelash. He really doesn't know what it is or where I got it. Thank You, Lord. Desi wiped her palms against her jeans.

"I'll put it in." She took the video back from him. "You know VHS tapes are pretty much obsolete."

"So why'd you buy it in that medium?" Max rounded the corner of the sofa and set a big bowl down on the table. "I'm sure you could've found it on DVD."

Max, you're going to wind up with that soda on your head yet. Desi thrust the cassette into the player. She sat down in the easy chair opposite Tony's. The introductory credits rolled. Desi shut her eyes.

Who are you, and why did you choose this movie? Is it the scenario? Did my dad stumble onto your identity, so you silenced him? Or are you hinting that someone I would never suspect is a monster?

"Hey, what's this, Des? Are you riding the bus these days?"

Desi opened her eyes. Max was holding up the token Desi had left on the coffee table in plain sight.

"Someone handed it to me one day." Desi shrugged. "I just haven't gotten around to throwing it away."

"Don't toss it. There's an old guy at our church who uses these all the time. Give it to him."

"Good idea."

She looked toward Tony. His eyes were turned toward the television.

But an ear was pointed in her direction. A sure bet he was testing her as much as she was testing him. For different reasons. He couldn't be all that sure she wasn't a thief. She understood that. And not a thing she could do to prove her innocence.

Not yet.

Still, just because Tony's behavior tonight indicated that he wasn't the accomplice in the Bureau, that didn't mean she was going to hand him her father on a silver platter. And there wasn't a thing Agent Tony Lucano could do about that!

The doorbell rang, and Desi just about jumped out of her skin.

Oh, get a grip! Wound like a spring, and you don't even know it.

"That's for me." Max leaped up.

"You're quiet tonight," Tony said. "Not enjoying the movie?"

Desi forced a smile. "Most activities I used to enjoy fall flat these days. Guess it'll take a while for anything to seem normal again."

Tony nodded. "Sure, I know what you mean."

Maybe he did. He'd dropped hints. Stuff from his past. "Bowling was fun. Jogging was torture."

"Want to run with me again tomorrow?" He grinned.

She laughed. "You're on."

What was it about this guy…? The way he sat—feet planted on the floor, not crossed, hands relaxed, not clenched—said he had nothing to hide. *Lucky him.* He leaned toward her, gaze searching her face. He cared. He didn't trust her, but he cared.

Not that it mattered. As long as Dad's murder remained unsolved and a killer could strike more of those she loved, she had no hope of connecting with Tony. Or any other human being. Not unless she wanted them to end up like her father…

Sorrow erupted inside Desi. She didn't want the tears to pour down her face any more than the residents of Washington State had wanted Mount Saint Helens to blow. But she couldn't stop the disaster.

"Hey, hey, hey." Tony hunkered down in front of her chair.

She melted toward him, and he pulled her into his arms. Kneeling on the carpet, she clung to him and sobbed. One of his hands made calming circles on her back. She surrendered to his touch, his gentle murmurs—

"Whoa! What's going on here?"

Desi jerked from her fog and pulled away from Tony. Dean Webb stood over them, glaring.

"You insensitive clod!" Max swatted her husband's arm. "He's just comforting her."

"Looks more like a con job to me. Leave her alone with him for a few minutes, and this long arm of the law has his paws all over a vulnerable woman." He pointed at Tony. "Don't think I didn't notice you putting the moves on her at the bowling alley."

Tony stood rigid. "I'd rather have my hands chopped off than hurt Desiree."

"Tell that to the judge. Hah!" He glanced at his wife. "I've always wanted to say that."

Desi scrambled to her feet, scrubbing at her wet face. "Would you two put a muzzle on it? Dean, I can take care of myself. Tony, thanks for the hug, but don't read anything into it. Am I clear, you two?" She glared from one to the other.

Tony jerked a nod, eyes narrowed at Dean.

"Crystal." Dean thrust his chin in Tony's direction.

Max blew out a long breath. "Cut it out you guys. We're here to have fun and relax. The least you can do is make this pleasant for Desi."

Dean looked at his feet. Tony lowered his shoulders.

Beep! Beep! Beep!

Tony pulled his pager from his belt and looked at the screen. His lips thinned. "My turn to use the kitchen. I need to make a phone call." He tugged out his cell phone as he strode for the back room. "Restart the movie. Don't wait for me."

Desi fussed around filling individual bowls with popcorn and rewinding the movie. Dean and Max settled on opposite ends of the sofa. *Great! Now we've got a family feud going over a case of mistaken chivalry.*

Tony came back into the room. "Got to go."

Desi caught her breath. "A break in the case?"

He shook his head. "Can't say." His gaze passed through her to whatever had his mind a million miles away.

So this is what his wife would have to look forward to. She'd need to be one special lady. *What is your problem, girl? Tony and marriage in the same stray thought?* Someone should put a leash on her imagination before it got clean away from the pound.

She mashed her thumb on the remote control's play button. The crunching of popcorn sounded loud in the uncomfortable silence.

Desi stared at the screen. She heard and saw nothing. If Tony's emergency had to do with her father's murder, she wanted to be with him, not curled up in an easy chair, gawking at someone else's fictitious problems. He'd better believe he wouldn't get away with that tight-lipped act when they went jogging tomorrow.

Pretty hypocritical considering you're being less than honest with the guy.

Oh, shut up! I just need a little more time.

Time—and one more shot at that storage compartment on East Boston Harbor. Then she'd have to decide. Knuckle under to threats—or put her faith in a man who thought she was a crook.

Great set of choices there, Des.

The body wasn't pretty, and the stench could gag a maggot. Agents had opened all the windows to air out the basement laundry room where the body lay.

Tony stretched his fingers in the tight rubber gloves and adjusted his air filter mask as he squatted beside the huddled remains of Leone Bocca. A team of crime scene investigators moved around the room. Unofficial cause of death: an FBI SWAT team bullet fired twelve days ago.

Ironic that the man had bled to death within a few blocks of Desiree's house. Frustrating that Bocca had chosen to break into the basement of a home where the owners were on vacation and then collapse onto the cement floor and die. The older couple had opened their doors this evening to discover a rank smell filling their house.

"Bled out mostly on the inside." Crane's mask-muffled voice commented over Tony's shoulder. "And it was drizzling that morning. No wonder we didn't find a blood trail to lead us to him."

Tony rose and stood beside his partner. "I hope we get some fresh leads off this guy's body. If not, our case is about as cold as he is."

Crane scowled and crossed his arms. His aggressive stance held intimidation value for no one in particular. The man on the floor was beyond such tactics.

Tony shoved his hands in his pockets and closed his eyes. He saw Desiree's hope-charged face when he'd left her apartment. She wanted her father's murderer caught, no question about that.

And no question that she was hiding something.

But did that mean she was guilty of a crime? A truckload

of suspicious circumstances screamed yes, but there wasn't a shred of court admissible evidence. What if all the suspicious circs turned out to be smoke and mirrors?

Tony's heart leaped. He wanted that. Almost as much as he wanted other things…things he didn't have a right to want from her.

"We're calling off the surveillance on Desiree Jacobs as of this morning."

Cooke closed the file in front of him and leaned back in his chair. "If no further leads come in soon, we'll refer the case to the art theft division in New York. Lourdes, Balzac, and I agree this is best."

Give me a break! Tony bottled a snort. He and Crane were front and center in the ASAC's office to get news their squad supervisor should have told them. And now they were planning to pass a hot potato case off to another division? Someone around here was covering their hind end.

"Don't you think we're getting ahead of ourselves?"

Tony hid a chuckle at his partner's bald comment. *Way to forget about your pension, buddy.*

Cooke sat forward and tapped a finger on his desktop. "With Bocca dead, we have no reason to believe Ms. Jacobs's life remains in danger or that she was ever involved with her father's illegal activities. The evidence—"

"—isn't all processed yet." *Guess my pension can go on the line, too.*

Cooke's nostrils flared. "I was going to say that the evidence of complicity needs to be a lot stronger than circumstantial before this office will waste any more time, money, or manpower on a dead-end lead. Is that plain enough for you?"

"Perfectly, sir." Tony clenched his teeth. *Surprise! Surprise! The budget gets the last word.*

They left the ASAC's office and headed down the hallway.

Crane frowned. "I don't like this, pard. We're dropping the Jacobs angle too soon. She can lead us to something good. I know it."

Tony jabbed the down button at the elevator door. "We're on the same page there. And Desi's not safe by a long shot. I figure the bad guys have been lying in the weeds, waiting for us to get out of the way."

"You know it, pal. We need to find a way to keep an eye on this bird."

"How? Drop our other cases and quit sleeping?"

A soft ping sounded, and the door glided open. They stepped into the empty car.

Crane cracked the gum he'd kept silent in Cooke's office. "I know some retired agents who'd give their eyeteeth to get back in the action. They'd do it for the thrill, nothing more."

"Lonely hours of surveillance are a thrill? These guys *must* be bored."

Tony grinned. Crane grinned back.

What do you know? Stevo wasn't *always* a headache waiting to happen.

Ten

*D*esiree stared at the clothes in her father's closet. She touched a sweater…a jacket…a pair of pants. How could she pack away his life? She pulled her hand back and went to sit on the bed. An empty box tipped off the edge and thumped to the floor. Hollow. She knew the feeling.

Tony had called earlier to say he had to miss their jog together, and she couldn't help wondering why. A new lead on the theft case? Something that would implicate her father? Her blood pumped faster. A clue pointing to his murderer? Her fists clenched.

Maybe it was something to do with another case. *It's not as if Daddy was involved in the only crime in town.*

Her gaze traveled around the room. Every object hit her like a fresh good-bye.

So, Dad, what am I supposed to do with this mess you left?

She flopped back on the bed and covered her eyes with her forearm. Blank, black darkness. She couldn't see her way.

I miss you like a hole's been dug in my chest, but if you were here, I'd probably hit you!

Whatever she chose to do, someone would get hurt.

If she confessed everything to Tony, he'd have to enforce

the law. Bye-bye, HJ Securities. Her staff packed off to the unemployment line. Museums mortified for displaying undetected forgeries. More heads on the chopping block. And Tony might or might not catch the murdering monster that instigated the thefts. So where was the good in that?

If she handed the booty over to a killer, he might back off and leave jobs and lives intact. She'd have everything but justice for Daddy—and the murderer would take the high road to riches—a road paved in her father's blood.

"Aaaagh!" Desi bounded from the bed and paced the room, empty boxes scattering before her feet.

I could just pull a Sergeant Schultz and "know nothing." Who could say what she'd found? Or even if she'd found anything at all? Oh, Mr. Monster might hope, Tony might suspect, but no one *knew* except her.

And God.

She went still, shoulders slumped.

Okay, Lord, You're not the author of confusion. What am I missing?

There had to be a way to save lives and jobs and catch the crook at the same time.

The doorbell chimed. *Now what?*

Desi went to the foyer and eased the door open. Shafts of sunlight dazzled her over someone's broad shoulders. She blinked and focused.

Tony?

No! Don't tell me any more bad news. Last time he wore that expression, he brought tragedy to her doorstep.

"Good morning, Desiree."

Desiree? Had they lost ground since last night?

"Ms. Jacobs." Lounging against a porch pillar, Steve Crane nodded to her. She'd seen a friendlier expression in the eyes of a caged cobra.

She frowned at Tony. "What's this all about?"

"We've found Leone Bocca."

"Oh, thank God. Did he tell you anything that might lead to my father's killer?"

A muscle jumped in Tony's cheek. "I'm sorry. Mr. Bocca was dead when we got to him."

Desi grabbed the edge of the door frame. "Another murder?"

Tony shook his head. "He died of a gunshot wound inflicted the night he invaded your home. He'd been dead for some time when he was discovered."

Blackness swirled through Desi's vision. Tony's arm came up, then fell back to his side. His hands jammed into the pockets of his slacks. "The FBI deems you no longer in danger, and we have no proof that you knew anything about your father's activities, so the surveillance has been dropped. You're free to resume your life."

Resume my life? Why was he acting like a detached detective from a *Dragnet* rerun? Hadn't his arms been around her just last night? What changed?

Her lungs froze.

Of course! How could she have been so gullible? Tony cozied up to her as long as he thought she might lead him to Bocca and whoever was behind him. Now that she was no longer some kind of missing link, he had no more use for her. That's what she got for reading personal interest into strictly business.

Desi drew herself up straight. "Thank you for updating

me on the latest development, Special Agent Lucano. I trust you will continue to pursue the case from other avenues."

Steve Crane took a step forward. "You better believe we'll be on the job. We're gonna find out everything about everyone in on this caper." His stare pegged her as one of the guilty parties.

Desi matched the man's steady look. At least Crane didn't play games. "I'm pleased to know you aren't giving up. I won't either." She parted her lips in a smile she didn't feel. "Good day to you both."

Desi closed the door and leaned her forehead against the wood surface. Long seconds passed; then footsteps retreated from her porch. Lucano the Louse had had the gall to look angry when she dismissed him and his partner. The man relied too much on his charisma to let him wind women's hearts around his little finger.

Not this woman's. No way. No how.

She straightened, then marched back into her father's bedroom and began to strip items from coat hangers and fold them into boxes.

That headstrong woman is going to drive me to drink. Wouldn't that make Stevo's day if I bellied up to the bar with him?

Tony gritted his teeth as he drove away from Desiree's house. He'd had to be on his professional behavior for their little talk. How could she not know that? Unless she was through with him now that the Bocca threat was gone.

A chill bit deep into his bones. That made sense. Too much sense.

He veered around a corner, and his shoulder hit the door.

"Hey, pard, keep it below the speed limit." Crane scowled at him. "We're not on emergency call."

Tony eased his foot off the accelerator.

Maybe the innocent sincerity he thought he'd seen in Desiree was an Oscar caliber performance, even better than Meranda. He smacked the steering wheel. *Am I always going to be some conniving female's patsy?*

No. As a matter of fact, he wasn't. He gritted his teeth. "How soon can you have your guys on surveillance?"

Crane chuckled. "Testy, are we? The damsel didn't seem to be in distress."

"Drop it!" *One more word and I'll knock the grin off your face, boyo.*

With a grunt, Crane pulled out his cell phone and punched in numbers. "Watchdogs, coming up."

A half hour later, they were ready to start an interview for an unrelated case and still had no one lined up to keep an eye on Desi. Retired FBI agents must have better things to do than sit by their phones on beautiful Saturdays in May.

"I'll try again as soon as we get through this." Crane's gum cracked and popped as they headed for the interview room. "We can't leave her to her own devices for long. No telling what mischief she'll get into."

You can say that again, Stevo. A woman who'd take on a killer with a pillow might try anything, and they needed to be right on her tail when she did.

The phone rang, and Desiree dropped the shirt she was holding. Forcing her heart back into its proper place, she picked up the extension just as the second ring started. She stopped with the handset halfway to her ear. What if this was one of the crooks? Maybe this was her call with "instructions." How had they known to reach her in her father's apartment? Or that the FBI surveillance was over?

"Hello?" A deep voice at the other end. "Hello?"

Relief swept Desi. "Dean, you're home this weekend."

Max's husband chuckled. "Don't be so shocked. Just because the big cheeses like to fly to the hot spots on weekends doesn't mean I never get one off. I've got a pickup in New York on Monday, but my feet'll be on the ground until then."

"I'm sure Max is happy to have you around."

A deep groan. "She went to get groceries, and I'm here with Luke and Emily and a honey-do list as long as my arm. But say—" he cleared his throat—"I didn't call to complain. I called to apologize. I was out of line last night. It's just that—"

"Don't worry about it. Your heart was in the right place."

"Even if my mouth wasn't?"

"If it makes you feel any better, I think you were right about Lucano. We were supposed to go jogging this morning, but he cancelled before I even went to bed last night. Then he showed up at my door a little while ago all business. It seems I'm no longer of interest to the Federal Bureau of Investigation."

"What! Of all the—They're not going to protect you from that dude who broke into your place? Max is *not* going to want to hear that."

"Bocca's dead."

Sharp intake of breath. "Dead? Are you sure?"

"Well, I didn't see the body, if that's what you mean. But

Ton—Agent Lucano says the SWAT team didn't miss after all."

"Yeow! Well, I guess all that's left to say is thank God you're safe and it's over."

Over? No surveillance? Why am I putzing around with Dad's clothes? Nuts! Wicked crazy, as the dockworkers would say. "Dean, I need to go now. Thanks for calling. Apology accepted. See you and Max tomorrow at church?"

"Sure thing. I'll give her your good news."

Desi returned the phone to its cradle and then raced up the stairs. She assembled the things she needed and left the house, briefcase in hand. Just like she was headed to the office for a quiet Saturday of catch-up work.

The FBI might have packed up and gone home, but evil eyes could still be watching.

At the deserted headquarters of HJ Securities, she changed into her drab persona and slipped out the back door into the alley. Her rapid bus changes went without incident.

At the warehouse, a sleepy-eyed weekend staffer offered a mumbled greeting. Nothing like the suspicious secretary she confronted the first time. He signed her in and sent her back with no escort. She lost her way a couple times, but at last arrived at the container.

Desi's pulse throbbed in her throat as she punched the code and stepped inside. Everything appeared to be as she had left it. Six thin crates and a black leatherbound journal. Desi grabbed the book and curled into the corner of the storage bin to reread her father's words. No new clues popped out at her.

With a sigh she shut the journal and rubbed a hand across the back cover.

What's this? The leather had an odd bulge.

She flipped the book open and explored the seam. A slit on one edge gave access to a folded white envelope. Her shaky fingers ripped the stitching further as she worked the envelope free. It was addressed to her and dated the day before her father left for his European tour. This letter had been in the journal the whole time, but she'd missed it in her hurry the first day.

Her mouth went dry.

Maybe she was about to discover the identity of a criminal mastermind.

Who killed you, Daddy?

She tore the envelope open, drew out several sheets of paper, and unfolded them. Her gaze fell on the familiar script. She blinked away tears and forced herself to read. No preamble, just a sentence bolded by overwriting several times.

I think you should trust Lucano.

Desiree gasped. Her father said *that*? There was more.

The man is way too earnest about doing right to be a dirty agent.

Bull's-eye, Dad. She could almost hear her father's dry chuckle.

I know he's been a thorn in the flesh to you. Me, too, though from the guilty side. But you need to turn the masterpieces over to the authorities, and I strongly suggest Special Agent

Lucano. In an honest agent's hands, they may stand some chance of being returned to their owners. This has always been my goal. I will never surrender these priceless works to the black market. I took them to protect them…and you. (More on that later.)

Do NOT handle this matter on your own, baby girl.

Again the script in bold.

I know you think you can save the world if you just make the right move. You're too much my daughter. Please, don't be a fool like your old man.

A tear hit the page. Dad knew her so well. "You were never a fool, Daddy." The words fell from her lips in a whisper. Her fingertips caressed the page that her father, warm and alive, had so recently penned. A sob left her throat. Laying the journal and papers aside, she searched for a tissue in the scruffy purse her alter ego carried. She wiped her eyes and blew her nose, then returned to the letter.

Run from this problem, hand it off to someone else, even if it costs the business. Everyone will pick themselves up and go on, including you.

Now, I need to share with you how this travesty came about…

Desiree devoured two more pages. Her father spoke with passion and sorrow about a time of weakness in his life right after Desi's mother died—before he came to rely on the Lord as his Rock. A time when he was desperate for money to support his little girl and not thinking clearly. He had pilfered a small but valuable painting from a museum client—a classic low-tech theft—and sold it to Paul Dujardin for enough money to keep the business afloat.

As soon as the theft was accomplished, they were both horrified by what they had done and made a pact never to steal again. Her father put the painting back at the earliest opportunity but kept Paul's money as a loan, which he later repaid.

Desi had known about the loan and had accepted the monetary bargain as a part of the closeness between the two men. To find out now that there was so much more to the story... Her breath hitched.

At the time, the theft and then sudden reappearance of the picture created a media sensation. You can imagine our relief when the case went cold, and no one came knocking at our doors. But we congratulated ourselves too soon. Someone knew about Paul's involvement—someone crafty and patient. He kept the knowledge hidden until he could use it to his advantage.

This person has a long history in antiquities theft. I know that much. He started by blackmailing Paul into participating in more burglaries of priceless objets d'art. Then he made Paul tell him who took that first piece for him. I think it was me he wanted along. I have access and know-how few people possess.

So do you, which is why I made sure he never went

near you, honey girl. I agreed to cooperate instead.

How I wish I could name this faceless monster, but he remains hidden. I think Paul knows, but he refuses to say. He's terrified for his son's sake. Such a scandal would ruin Senator Dujardin's career. As if the loss of HJ Securities would be any less a tragedy for you and me!

But I begin to sound pitiful and lose my focus. All my desire is for your health and happiness, dear daughter. Please do not let bitterness poison you.

Tomorrow, I leave on my business tour through Europe. If you never read these words, then I was successful in freeing Paul and myself from this web of treachery, successful in securing the return of the paintings in this crate to their rightful owners. If you hold this journal in your hands, then I failed us all, and my dangerous legacy lies in your hands.

Be brave. Do as I have instructed. Never forget how much I love you.

A moan rose from Desi's heart. She squeezed her eyes closed. Tears seeped down her face and plopped onto the paper. *I'm not mad at you, Daddy. I'm not.*

Her father was a good man. He'd just made a mistake in a vulnerable moment all those years ago—a mistake that came back to haunt him. He should have told her everything as soon as the blackmailer showed up. She would have helped. Together they could have—

Desi's throat tightened. Exactly why he hadn't told her. Were their positions reversed, she would have kept him out of it as well—would have given her life, just as he did, to keep him safe.

Love meant sacrifice freely offered. No regrets. Just like Jesus.

Oh, Daddy, you loved me so much! And you, too, Abba Father. Thank You for helping me find this, for letting me know that my dad died a man of integrity, at peace with You, determined to stand up for the truth. With such an example, can I do any less?

She opened her eyes and wiped the wetness from her cheeks. The letter was signed *Dad* in her father's large scrawl.

One more page remained, a formal note to the authorities.

To Whom It May Concern:

I took these paintings over the course of the past six months, but have avoided turning them over to the mastermind behind the theft ring, a person who calls himself The Chief. I convinced him the items were in safe storage until a sale was made. In reality, I have been searching for a way to expose this Chief. But now a man named Leone Bocca has approached me to say that a buy has been arranged, and I am under lethal pressure to relinquish the pieces—a thing I will never do. So I must act.

My plan is twofold. During the course of my European tour, I will use my many contacts in the art world to uncover the name of the person in charge of this operation. Then I will come home to turn him in to the authorities, even as I surrender myself and the stolen goods.

Should I not discover my unseen blackmailer's identity, I shall begin returning the pictures to their owners using much the same methods as I employed to take them. During that process, I expect this Chief to attempt to stop me, and it is my intent to be sure he is caught doing so.

Following is a list of the paintings, as well as the names and addresses of the private collectors and organizations that own them, in case I am unable to complete my self-imposed assignment.

Desi scanned the list and whistled through her teeth. The value of the masterpieces in this crate could set someone up as king of their own Caribbean island. And wealth certainly seemed to be the main objective. Whoever ran this organization treated priceless art like common commodities to be dealt away for mere money.

Not Paul Dujardin. Paul had to be as reluctant a burglar as her dad. Paul's fierce reputation for protecting art and antiquities was well-known. Yes, he'd been a party, perhaps an instigator, in that smaller theft a quarter of a century ago, but Dad's confession indicated sincere remorse and reparations on both their parts. Not an excuse for what they did, of course, but who in the human race had any excuse for their sins?

Desiree slapped the notebook shut. She rose to her feet, jaw firm.

Paul Dujardin might not be the mastermind behind the thefts, but he involved his friend in a scheme that got him killed. Desi's blood raced hot.

Coward! To think I was so charmed by you at Dad's funeral. You were only there to make sure nothing happened to smirch your precious reputation.

Desi paced the container.

No doubt Dujardin justified his conduct as protecting his offspring, the same way her father had protected her. But that wasn't apples to apples at all. Dad stood between the thieves and his daughter, while preparing to do the right thing at the right time. The dapper millionaire, with all the power of wealth and position, closed his eyes and washed his hands like a modern-day Pontius Pilate.

Well, Mr. Pilate, you're about to be confronted by an avenging angel.

Desiree left the warehouse, her father's journal and letter in her purse. Her strides destroyed the image of a middle-aged frump, but then her makeup job had been washed away by tears and tissues anyway. Who cared! Not the warehouse attendant snoring on the ratty couch in the front office.

Outside, in the salt-laden air, Desiree brushed past rough-hewn dockworkers. The way she felt, she could power walk home. And nobody better get in her way.

She reached the street and stepped off the curb—

Brakes squealed. A flash of dark blue and a Yukon Denali just missed her toes. The mammoth SUV rocked to a halt in her path, and Desi looked into the driver's face.

Her knees turned to gelatin.

Eleven

We're back in business on the Jacobs case." Tony towered over his partner, who sat hunched and glum at his desk.

Crane glared suspicion up at him. "What? How? I haven't managed to connect with anybody to watch our little suspect yet."

Tony waved the sheets of paper in his hand. "These came in by fax. The Italian polizia have arrested a professional hit man caught in the act. Ballistics matched the bullets in their new case with the ones they found in Hiram Jacobs's body. We have our shooter, the best link to the one who hired him."

Crane beamed—a rare toothy smile. "When can we get our hands on this dirtwad?"

"They're allowing one of us to come over to Rome and interrogate, but extradition is unlikely. This guy is hot property throughout Europe on multiple counts."

Crane scowled. "I don't suppose I get the minivacation."

"Sorry, Stevo. I speak the language. You don't."

"So you're leaving me in charge of the Mistress of Disguise? That might not be so bad."

"Don't let the assignment go to your head."

Tony's gut clenched. So Stevo got another run at Desiree.

The man wouldn't play any nicer than last time.

Why do you still care? She used you, man.

Well, she was on her own until Tony got back.

"When do you leave?"

"Mañana."

Crane stood and poked Tony's chest. "*That* is not Italian."

Max leaned over and thrust open the passenger door of her blue SUV. If she turned a shade redder, she'd burst into flames.

"Get in!"

Desi backed up a step. "Are you friend or foe?"

"What in the Sam Houston is *that* supposed to mean? Get your sorry behind in here so we can talk."

Desi hesitated, then climbed in. She wanted to talk. No, she *needed* to talk to someone, even if that someone turned out to be on the wrong side. Desi glanced at Max's stony profile. "How did you find me?"

The redhead snorted and pulled away from the curb. "Since movie night at your place I've had homing devices on your briefcase and that ugly handbag you use with your favorite disguise. If a sharp cookie like Tony Lucano thinks you're hidin' something, then I reckon your best friend can see the signs, too."

Desi looked down. Her knuckles were white around her purse strap. "I didn't want to get you involved. It's too risky. You've got family—"

"Even the Lone Ranger had a sidekick, woman. You'd best come clean with Tonto so we can figure out what to do."

Desi swallowed.

This is your friend, not a conspirator. Stop being so suspicious.

"All right. I'll tell you, but you have to promise not to breathe a word to anybody else, not even Dean. This is dangerous stuff. The fewer people who know, the better."

Max stopped at a red light and stared at her. "I won't tell Dean anything as long as I figure he and the kids are safe."

"Fair enough." Desi pointed ahead. "The light's green." They pulled out, and Desi took a deep breath. "All right, here goes." She told Max everything. The whole sorry story. "But I was holding it together, barely...until I ran across this from Daddy today." She took the letter from her bag. "You'd better pull over, because neither of us is going to be able to see straight if I read it to you."

Max found a lonely spot in the corner of a business parking lot and shut off the engine. Gray edged her lips. Every freckle stood out. "Put those tissues here." She patted the seat between them. "I'm about on overload and ready to spill over the edge."

Desi started to read, choked, then tried again. She didn't get much farther. "Here!" She thrust the letter at Max.

Shouldn't the well run dry pretty soon? She ruined another tissue and dug out a fresh one.

Max finished reading and lowered her head to the steering wheel. "I never imagined...I couldn't... Oh, Des, I'm so sorry."

"Me, too." Her whisper was the last word for a long time. Finally, she let out a ragged sigh. "I don't know who to believe in anymore. Dad's best friend betrayed him to a criminal. Plus my father kept major secrets from me, his only child. And he tells me that people in high places are corrupt, but he doesn't know who."

Max shook her head. "Girl, you've had a heavier load than anyone should carry, but you're takin' a chance on me, aren't you? You made that decision when you got in this vehicle. And Tony Lucano. Your father said to trust him, so do you?"

"Yes and no." Desi shrugged. "I think he's an honest agent, but I'm not sure he'll do right by Daddy. The FBI wants to catch crooks, and technically what my father did was against the law. But Hiram Jacobs should be remembered more as victim—maybe even tragic hero—than villain."

Max started the SUV. "Sounds like you'll just have to take a chance, hon. You can't go on this way, that's for sure."

Desi stared out the passenger window. It would be so nice to have someone take the choice out of her hands. Then she wouldn't have to feel responsible for whatever happened. But not making a decision was as bad as leaving it to somebody else. *Talk about cowardly! I've got Dujardin beat.*

They left East Boston and turned onto the freeway headed west.

"You'd better take me to the office. I left my car there."

"Nope. We're going to the federal building. Isn't Tony on duty this weekend?"

"I know you're giving me good advice, Max, but I'm not ready yet. There's something I need to do first."

"You are *not* going to pay a visit to that Frenchman."

Desi pressed her lips together and looked down.

Max shot her a glance. "You're not thinking this through. If you alert Dujardin that his secret is out, what's to stop him from destroying evidence before they can arrest him? This is one time my take-charge boss had better back off and let other professionals handle her business."

"All right. All right. Just not now." Desi rubbed above her eyebrows. "I feel like I've been dragged through a knothole backward. Give me tonight to process all this and pray. I'll see you in church in the morning for a stiff dose of the Word of God. Facing Tony is going to be one of the hardest things I've ever done." Her gaze pleaded with Max. "What can one more day matter?"

Max's expression told Desi what she already knew.

One day could mean plenty.

Desi's chest hurt from so much crying. She lay in her darkened bedroom and stared at the ceiling.

She knew what she had to do—what her father would want her to do. Why couldn't she accept it?

The future lay before her as dense and dark as a black hole. What she did tomorrow would change her whole life, even more than it had changed with her father's death. And not only she, but also countless others, would feel the force of her choice.

But was it even a choice? Wasn't she backed into a corner with only one right way out? Then why did that way feel so wrong?

God, is there no reprieve for me? Some kind of alternative?

No answer spoke to her out of the night.

Desi sat up, turned her pillow, punched it, and flopped down on her side. She closed her eyes, but they popped open again. She glared at the wall.

Fine. She'd do what she must. She hadn't caused any part of this situation, so she shouldn't feel guilty for the consequences.

Then why did she?

This time she knew the answer. Because exposing her father's guilt, even with his well-meant motives for what he did, made her feel like the lowest form of traitor. She might as well walk up and spit on his grave. A completely unreasonable gut reaction, but real in her heart.

Might as well face the fact that her feelings didn't matter. She'd committed to going to Tony with her information tomorrow, and Max the Faithful Friend would hold her to it.

Her father's letter was her guide and maybe someday, if she could ever get her aching heart around it, her absolution.

Full circle. Max and I back in a vehicle. Mine this time. And no more excuses to put off the inevitable…except one.

"Call first." Desi handed Max her cell phone. "I don't want to get all the way to Government Center, and then discover Tony is out on a case."

"Fair enough." Max took the phone.

Desi leaned her head back against the passenger seat and closed her eyes. Max had the wheel again after sending her family home from church in their SUV.

Desi's head throbbed. Why couldn't she just go back to her darkened bedroom and curl up with soothing music on the CD player? *Why do I have to go downtown and betray my father?*

Max let out a growl.

"What?" Desi lifted her head.

"I never should have let you talk me into waiting. All I got was a pinch-nosed receptionist. 'I'm sorry, but Special Agent Lucano is unavailable. He left this morning on assignment and won't be back for several days. Would you like to speak to Special Agent Crane?'"

"No!"

"Exactly what I said." Max gave the phone back. "Now what, Kemosabe? No, forget the sarcasm." She raised a hand. "I'm just crabby because I wanted to get the pressure off you."

"No pressure? That sounds heavenly."

"Speaking of heavenly." Max touched Desi's shoulder. "I know this place where they make the most divine blintze soufflés."

Desi let out a short laugh. "You could eat any time, any place."

Max drove out of the parking lot. "Well, you need to eat, too. You don't look like you're doing enough of that these days."

"But your family—"

"Can get along without me for one meal. Besides, I told Dean I was taking you out to a girls only lunch after you saw Agent Lucano for an update on the case. But I promised to be home in time to take the kids to the zoo later this afternoon. Wanna come along?" She paused and blinked, then grinned. "Skip the question. You *are* coming with us. The last thing you need is more time to mope."

The pressure in Desi's head eased. All right. She'd been swept along by forces beyond her control for days now. Might as well be swept along by a force of nature called Maxine Webb.

At least she knew she'd be safe.

"Auntie Desi, come wook."

Emily tugged Desi's hand and pulled her over to a small

cage. "They gots baby bunnies. See? I wike that one." She pointed to little black and white rabbit sitting by itself in the corner. "It needs a fwiend." The child turned away from Desi and threw her arms around her mother's legs. "Mommy, can I have the bunny?"

Max bent to her daughter's level. "Oh, sweetheart, if we take the bunny home, he'll miss his mommy and daddy. Why don't we go over there by Luke and Dad and feed the pygmy goats?" She looked toward a nearby corral.

"Piggy goats?" Emily grinned, showing dimples like her father. "I want to see piggy goats." She skipped ahead of the adults, brown curls bouncing.

"Whew! Dodged the bunny this time." Max laughed. "Sometimes the attention span of a three-year-old is a blessing."

Desi smiled. "I think it's sweet that she was worried about the rabbit having friends. She's got a good heart, like her mama." Desi nudged her friend. "Thanks for making me come along today."

Luke galloped up to them, a miniature version of his mother with his red hair and freckles. "Dad says we can go see the tigers as soon as he's done helping Em pet the goats." He bounced from one foot to the other. "Aunt Desi, are you coming to my graduation?"

"Wouldn't miss it!"

Luke flashed his teeth, then bounded off to join Dean, who approached them, Emily riding on his shoulders.

"I guess it's off to see the white tigers," he said.

They headed out of the farmyard area and on up the walk. The sun's warmth seeped into Desi's muscles. *Better than a massage.* She inhaled the scents of spring.

"Children have a way of putting adult problems into perspective." Desi nodded toward Luke, who kept pace with his father by taking two steps for the man's one. "Graduating from kindergarten is a real milestone in Luke's life."

"That's for sure." Max chuckled and shook her head. "He talks constantly about 'after I graduate,' like he's gonna start a whole new life once he's headed for first grade. And this kid's a planner. Would you believe he dictated a guest list to me the other night?"

"And they better attend or else."

"You got that right!'"

They both laughed.

A whole new life. God, what I wouldn't do right now for a fresh start. It would take one of Your miracles.

Emily squirmed, and Dean let her down from his shoulders. The little girl ran back to her mother and took Max's hand; Luke appropriated his father's. Desi fell back a few paces.

What would it be like to have a family—a husband and children of her own? To not trail around after someone else's family, a beloved outsider, but an outsider nonetheless? If she wasn't careful, she could almost imagine that a man's hand held hers—

Wait a second! A man's hand does *hold mine!*

She whipped her head around just as the hand let go, leaving something compact in her palm. She glimpsed the profile of an aquiline face wearing opaque sunglasses, but before she could get a good look, the stocky blond figure shoved through a knot of people and strode away.

"Hey!" She took off in pursuit. Good thing she'd changed into jeans and tennis shoes.

The man ahead picked up his pace. Desi dodged clumps of zoo-goers. Her foot caught in an uneven spot on the sidewalk, and she pitched forward. Hands grabbed her shoulders from behind and steadied her. She whirled.

Dean stared at her, brow furrowed. "What's going on?"

"That man gave me something." She looked in the direction of the chase, but her quarry had vanished.

Dean paled. His face went slack. "What did he give you?"

Desiree looked down at the folded slip of paper in her hand. She opened it up and read the message.

All pleasure leaked from the day.

"He is arrogant, and he grows careless." Detective Raoul Gaetano jerked a nod at the man seated in the interrogation chamber. "He thinks we know little about him, but Interpol has an extensive file on this one under many aliases. We even know his birth name."

Tony stood beside the detective, hands in his pockets. He gazed through the one-way window and studied the assassin.

Adolfo Zambone was of medium build, though well-muscled. Ordinary brown hair and a smooth Mediterranean complexion. Not handsome, not ugly, he would go unnoticed in most situations. Dressed in a one-piece jail uniform, Zambone leaned back in his chair, body still, face without expression.

But your eyes betray you.

Zambone's gaze darted from one side of the room to the other, sometimes up toward the ceiling, sometimes down toward his cuffed hands.

"Terrorist connections?"

"Not specifically." Gaetano shook his head. "He deals with anyone who can pay his price. If we follow the money trail, then we will find his clients. Even the one who hired the death of the American, eh?" The detective slapped Tony on the shoulder. "We hope you have luck in getting him to reveal his most recent address. We think there we will find important clues to the money."

Tony pulled his hands from his pockets. "Whatever he tells me won't be due to luck. More like the grace of God. Indulge me on a little inspiration." He grinned at the Italian detective. "Zambone's file says his alternate language in his travels is German and he speaks very little English. I want him to think I don't speak *any* Italian. Go in with me and pretend to translate between us. We may work an advantage if he thinks I don't understand what he says." He outlined the rest of his plan to Gaetano.

The detective pursed his lips and nodded. "It will indeed be an act of providence if this strategy succeeds." He led the way into the interrogation room.

Zambone's shoulders stiffened. "So you are the American agent?" He looked Tony up and down then turned his head away, lip curled.

Tony raised an eyebrow at Gaetano.

The detective translated. "He doesn't like Americans," he added.

Tony lifted one side of his mouth. "I gathered that much." He walked behind the suspect, but the Italian detective remained in front of Zambone. The assassin's foot tapped the floor.

"Do you remember a man named Hiram Jacobs?"

Gaetano translated for Zambone, whose head swiveled back and forth between his interrogators. "Never heard of him."

Too fast, too smooth.

"That's odd. You shot him in the Hotel Savoy on April 25. The bullets we found in Mr. Jacobs's body came from your gun."

Zambone scowled while the detective repeated the statement in Italian. Then the assassin glared over his shoulder at Tony. "I do not know this Jacobs person. The gun the polizia confiscated is not mine. I found it a few days ago. You have nothing to connect me with the shooting of an American." The foot tapped faster.

"On the contrary, we're certain you committed the murder. There is other evidence."

I'm not lying. There is other evidence. It'll just take a little help from you to find it. He stared down at Zambone.

Tap. Tap. Tap. The foot ticked like a metronome.

Tony began to walk clockwise around the table. The Italian detective followed, keeping the same distance from Tony. Zambone's gaze twitched from one to the other.

"Give us the name of the person who hired you," Tony said, "and perhaps things may go easier for you."

The suspect barked out a foul word and crossed his arms over his chest. *Tap. Tap. Tap.*

Tony walked faster. "If you aren't hiding anything, then why don't you tell us your home address? What could it hurt?"

At Gaetano's translation, Zambone's face flushed red. He leaped to his feet. "If you had other evidence, you would not make me dizzy with children's games. I have no more to say."

Tony waited for the English version, then held up his hands. "Get him out of here."

Frowning, Detective Gaetano opened the door. He motioned the suspect to follow him, then continued many paces ahead. Tony fell in step beside the assassin.

Zambone muttered personal slanders against Tony's parentage. "My friends at Rocco's will laugh and raise their glasses to me when I tell them of the stupid American who likes to play 'Ring Around the Rosie.'"

Rocco's. No doubt some dive where lowlifes brag about police interrogations and other interesting things.

Tony smiled at the assassin. "*Molto grazie,* Adolfo. I'm sure Rome's finest will have little trouble squeezing your address out of these fine friends of yours."

Zambone froze. Cords stood out in his neck. Spewing curses, the assassin launched himself at Tony.

Twelve

*T*ony sidestepped the attack, and Zambone's head grazed his chin. Tony's jaw snapped shut.

The assassin hit the wall.

Bet that rattled more than his teeth.

Zambone whirled and lunged again. Tony put him to the floor with a chop to the neck and a leg sweep. The assassin lay on his back, gagging.

Gaetano and the guard holstered their weapons. The detective smiled while the guard gathered up the winded prisoner.

"That one is good at shooting unarmed people from safe cover, but very bad at hand-to-hand fighting. He will not do well in prison." He cocked a brow at Tony. "You learned something?"

"A raid on a place called *Rocco's* could be a gold mine."

"You would like to come with us?"

Tony grinned. "Wouldn't miss it!"

Tony pressed his back against the wall next to the rear exit of *Rocco's* and breathed through his mouth.

From a similar position opposite Tony, a member of the

Roman polizia made a face. "Do the alleys of America smell so bad?"

Tony gave a low chuckle. "Garbage stinks the world over."

"*D'accordo!* The rest of the team will enter by the front soon…we hope."

Muted sounds of wild laughter and loud conversation carried from inside. The evening was young, the party just getting started. Glass clinked. Someone started to sing.

The noise dimmed and died. *No different than in the U.S. when a bunch of badges walk into a hole-in-the-wall.* A voice of authority spoke. Tony couldn't make out the words, but he knew what Gaetano was saying—anyone with information about Adolfo Zambone should speak up.

Let's see what sort of scum flushes through the woodwork.

A shuffle sounded on the other side of the door, then a small thump and a curse. The door inched open and a squatty figure slipped out, looking over his shoulder. Tony's companion grabbed the man and whirled him against the wall.

The smaller man squawked. "I did not do anything!"

Do lowlifes share the same script internationally?

The Italian officer snapped on the cuffs. "I think when we get to the station, we will find some nice outstanding warrants. And what is this? A gun! This is no good."

Tony heard a thud behind him. He spun in time to see a thin man dash away from an open window. Tony sprinted after him.

"Run, Turtle! Run!" The prisoner shouted.

Turtle's feet grew wings as he leaped over a set of boxes. Tony stayed with him. The thin man's hand went into his jacket pocket.

torture rack for months—ever since the FBI began lookin' at Hiram as a suspect. It's about time we get some answers. I'm going. And I'm just as capable of hoppin' a commercial flight as Desi if you won't help us."

"You're pushing my buttons, Max, but all right, all right." Dean heaved a long sigh. "If we leave early tomorrow morning, I'll have time to make an extra stop."

Max pumped her fist. "Yesss! We'll beard the rat in his den."

Desi smiled. "I think that's beard the lion."

Max humphed. "Not when we're dealing with a rodent in a monkey suit."

Dujardin as a rat in tailcoat and top hat? Too fitting. Desi let out a laugh.

The children stirred and murmured in their sleep.

"You're going to his house? I don't think that's a good idea," Dean said. "You'll be on his turf, and he'll have the advantage."

Desi looked at the note in her hand. *I have to talk to this man!* "What do you suggest?"

"Uhhh. Skip the country, and let the FBI sort out the mess?"

His wife socked him.

"Sorry. Bad joke." Dean shook his head. "Well then, call Dujardin when you get to Washington. That'll be your element of surprise. Set up a meet under the public eye, but private enough to talk. A park. A café. Max, bring along some of your electronic doodads that'll warn you if he's packing heat or wearing a wire."

Max slanted him a look. "Packing heat? Wearing a wire? Hon, your cop lingo is getting out of hand. I could see the gun—or maybe a bodyguard with a gun—but why would

Dujardin want to record our conversation?"

Several heartbeats passed.

Dean cleared his throat. "Have either of you considered the possibility that this man might be working for the law? I don't know what you're up to, Desiree, but I know when my wife's not telling me everything. And I don't think either of you have been forthcoming with the feds. You two could stroll in there and implicate yourselves like crazy." He glanced at Max. "I'm not wild about having a jailbird wife."

Desi slumped. "Max, you are soooo not coming along."

"Try leaving without me." Max turned and scowled. "You never know where I might've stuck one of my homing devices."

"Cool it, ladies. How about I tag along, too? I'll find someone else to fly my—"

"No!" Desi's protest sounded in unison with his wife's.

"We don't want to scare the guy off," Desi said. "He's got old-world attitudes that might lead him to underestimate the fairer sex. Women have turned that ignorance to their advantage for centuries."

Dean hissed out a breath. "I know when I'm whipped. But don't sell this joker short by counting on your feminine wiles. Run like mad if you catch a sniff of danger."

Desi didn't respond.

This whole business was like standing in the middle of a minefield. *All we have to do is figure out which direction to move without getting blown sky high...*

The hotel phone rang as Tony zipped his travel bag. He stepped over to the nightstand. "Lucano."

"Guess where our little bird and her main chicklet are flying off to this morning?"

No mistaking a crow in that voice.

Tony glanced out the hotel window at a brilliant blue sky. Early morning in Boston, but it was past noon in Rome. "You tell me, Stevo." He sat on the edge of the bed, his stomach a lump of stone.

"I've had the guys all over Ms. Jacobs since yesterday afternoon. One of them followed her and the Webb family to the zoo, where she took a sweet handoff from an unknown male, who disappeared into the crowd. Our tail opted to stay with Jacobs and company. He was kind of disappointed when all they did was drive home. But around 5:00 a.m. today, our suspect made a trip to the office. The Webb woman and her husband were there, too. The Webbs grabbed some funny-looking gadgets out of the company van, loaded them into their car, and took off. The tail let them go while he watched to see if prime suspect number one would leave the office. No sign of Jacobs for a full hour, so our guy gets antsy, starts taking a stroll around the building, and do you know who he passes flat-footing toward the rear entrance of HJ Securities?"

Tony's heart stuttered, then rammed into overdrive. "Dowdy little Myra, who likes to ride buses."

"Give the man a cigar! Myra, huh? Name suits her." Crane snickered. "And our private agent, he's smart enough to sneak himself a digital photo to prove his sighting. Got the picture right in front of me, and Myra's clutching her briefcase to her chest like it's made of gold. Wonder what our little quick-change artist crept out the back door to retrieve? Stolen goods, maybe?" Stevo's gravelly chuckle echoed through the international connection. "Might be enough suspicious behavior to net a fresh search warrant."

"I wouldn't count on it." Tony ran his fingers through his hair and resisted the temptation to pull some out. Contrary to public perception, federal judges held the FBI to higher standards of cause than local cops.

"Well, whatever." Crane's gum snapped. "I'm gonna try anyway. Meanwhile, we keep watch. Dean Webb is scheduled to make a pickup in New York this morning, but he altered his flight plan to accommodate a pit stop in Washington. Desiree Jacobs and Maxine Webb got on the plane with him carrying some equipment and that solid gold briefcase. I'll give you three guesses who they're going to see in Washington, and the first two don't count."

Tony let out a breath. "Paul Dujardin."

"I'd bet my pension on it."

"They could have a legitimate contract in Washington. HJ Securities does business all over the globe."

"Well, we'll just see, pard. We've notified some guys there to follow Jacobs and Webb wherever they go. If those two meet with Dujardin—who we know is dirty but just can't prove yet—then I want you to wake up and smell the coffee about Desiree Jacobs. It's too late in my career to break in a new partner if you go and shaft your future in the Bureau over a two-timing thief."

"Warning noted." Tony gritted his teeth. *Desi, you better not do anything stupid. Don't make me arrest you.*

"How did the suspect interview shape up over there?"

"What? Oh, yeah." Tony got up, tucked the receiver under his chin, and finished zipping his bag. "We played a little game, and he said more than he should have." Tony paced back and forth by the bed while he relayed the details.

"So the guy jumped you? *Dumb-da-dumb-dumb!* He do any damage?"

"I've got a little bruise on my jaw where his head butted me, but he's got a big pain in the neck and more trouble than he can handle."

Crane barked a laugh. "Any results from the suspect's blabbing?"

"The Roman police let me help with a raid. Pretty standard sweep in some dive, but we rounded up some lowlifes with outstanding warrants only too eager to deal in information. We located the assassin's apartment this morning. They've got Interpol hacking the guy's computer to find the money trail. We'll be informed of anything they find."

"Great! You get home now so we can bust some chops on this end. I've got a good feeling we're about to collar the head cheese of this whole operation. Could even turn out to be a female, you know?"

Tony held his peace. *Not going there, Stevo.*

Crane popped his gum. "Look on the bright side, pard. You'll get a promotion, and I'll retire a hero."

"Yeah, the bright side." Tony hung up the phone, then grabbed his bag and hustled out of the hotel. The cab ride to the Rome Fiumicino Airport took forever. Once through security and into the waiting area, Tony located the terminal's wireless hot spot and booted up his laptop. He had two hours before his flight left. Time to take another look at the famous art critic.

Three cups of coffee and a pair of blurry eyes later, Tony

clicked on a link to the archives of a prominent literary journal. A decades-old issue contained Dujardin's review of a young artist's show. He read a few lines and jerked to attention: *"Sanderson Plate hasn't an original bone in his body. He should return to imitating the masters. He might make a world-class forger one day."*

Tony whooped, then grabbed his computer as it slid off his knees. People gave him 'what nuthouse are you from?' looks, but Tony just grinned them down.

Months of worthless leads, and now bingo! Paul Dujardin and Sanderson Plate have a history. No wonder none of the denizens of the forgery underworld knew of this forger's existence. He was a respected member of the international art community.

Tony's chest constricted. *And once again, Desiree, you're smack in the middle. Both these guys have an unnatural interest in you.*

He returned to the article and read it again. Something still didn't add up. Plate had reason to resent the art critic. The man had shafted his fledgling career as an artist. But if Plate was working with Dujardin in the thefts, why did the curator point an accusing finger at the Frenchman that day at the museum? Dujardin's arrest would lead to his own.

Unless he's not planning to stick around long enough for that to happen. Plate could get his revenge and disappear before his betrayal of the critic came back to bite him.

Did Desiree plan to run off with the officious little man? Tony's insides curdled. He couldn't picture them together. Wouldn't.

Shades of his past jeered at Tony. *Sucker!*

Tony bookmarked the page and shut down his laptop. He went to a more secluded spot to use his cell phone. When

Stevo came on the line, he didn't even say hello. "Any news from Washington?" Tony leaned a shoulder up against the wall and checked his surroundings. Habit.

"Inconclusive. The ladies and their equipment are in the city, but they've made no contact with Dujardin or anyone else yet."

Good girl, Desi. He turned to face the wall. "I've linked Sanderson Plate and Paul Dujardin. It seems Plate is our mysterious forger." Tony shared the contents of the web page.

"All right! Now we have a direction to probe. I'll get on it."

Tony's flight was announced over the intercom.

"Got to go. I'll call for an update from my London layover."

"You do that. If those two ladybirds meet up with our light-fingered art critic, I'll be on my way to Washington in a heartbeat. The front desk will know my whereabouts when you call."

"Shouldn't be a problem to change my ticket from a Boston destination to DC."

"Not necessary, pard. I've got it covered."

Tony slammed an internal door on his emotions. "If Desiree Jacobs is going down, I plan to snap on the cuffs."

Crane's laugh raised the hairs on the back of Tony's neck. "There's the right attitude. I just love when a case breaks wide open. Not a feeling in the world like it."

Heart hollow, Tony boarded the plane.

"Yes, Mr. Gambel, this visit is included in the regular service you've already paid for." Desi rolled her eyes at a glowering Max seated on the other bed in the hotel room. "We need to run a systems check on your security apparatus at least every six months."

The voice at other end barked another question.

"Yes, I realize it's only been five months since the last check, but my chief technician and I are in town on other business, and we thought—" More growling.

Desi crossed her eyes and stuck out her tongue at Max. The woman lost her scowl, tipped over sideways, and buried her face in the pillows, shoulders shaking.

"That sounds good, Mr. Gambel. We'll come to your house at 8:00 p.m. sharp."

A brief snarl.

"Yes, of course your security man can follow us around."

Max peeked up from the pillow. Desi made rabbit ears with two fingers behind her head. Max buried her face again.

"Mm-hm. Mm-hm. Very good then. We'll see you tonight." She hung up the phone.

Max glared at her, cheeks aflame. "Don't ever make me laugh like that when you're talkin' to a client."

"You've been such a sourpuss all day. Then Mr. Rottweiler starts snapping in my ear. Time to lighten up."

Max canted her head. "I don't read you today, girl. We're already in as much trouble as a polecat in a gunnysack. Now you've got this half-baked scheme to return one of the paintings. And you seem downright cheerful about the whole thing."

Desi looked at the Postimpressionist Vincent Van Gogh that lay in the middle of her bed. The painting was pulled tight over its stretching frame, but missing its outer frame. Presumably this would be found around the forgery that had been left as a replacement at Mr. Gambel's palatial home.

She'd give an arm and a leg to know who was doing the forgeries for this theft outfit. The work must be outstanding to hold up under day-to-day scrutiny for so long.

She stroked the edge of the Van Gogh. "Dad was going to start returning paintings to draw out the mastermind of the theft ring. I'm just following his plan. It's a relief to finally take action."

She walked over to the mirror and began brushing her hair. "I've felt helpless. I hate that. Now, with your help, I can move toward finding my father's murderer and right a wrong at the same time."

Desi turned and pointed her brush at Max. "By the way, my scheme isn't half-baked. We've done this one many times. We're just going to reverse the results. I'll leave the client's house with the forgery and let the real thing stay behind. No one the wiser."

Max shook her head. "Let's hope things turn out that way."

"Snap out of it, Mrs. Doom and Gloom. It's almost showtime with Paul Dujardin."

Max heaved a sigh. She got up, nudged Desi over, and started refreshing her makeup. "You're doing what Dean said not to do, walkin' straight into the guy's lair."

"It's not a lair. It's an estate."

"Whoopi-de-do. It's a lair if you get eaten."

Desi took Max's arm and turned the redhead to face her.

"All right. Look. What's Dujardin going to do? Kill me in the library with the candlestick and blame Colonel Mustard? You've got my back, girlfriend. And I trust you with it 100 percent. I'll be wearing a wire, and you can call in the National

Guard for all I care if things start to go bad. If I confront him in an environment where he feels the greatest margin of safety—"

"I know. I know. He might speak freely, and that's worth the risk." One side of Max's mouth drifted upward. "If I didn't know better, I'd say you're more of a rootin', tootin' cowgirl than I am."

Desi grinned. Cowgirl? No. But a Jacobs, her father's daughter? You bet! And that beat a cowgirl all hollow.

Thirteen

*D*esi braked her rental car to a stop by the call box of the Dujardin estate—home of the famous art critic, his senator son, and family. The mansion was located in the prestigious subdivision of Georgetown. Enclosed by a high brick wall, the imposing four-story Federal-style mansion dominated a lush green lawn dotted with shrubbery and flower gardens. Afternoon sunshine glinted off spike-tipped bars guarding the entrance to the driveway.

This is it, Des.

A female voice answered her buzz at the gate intercom. Desi inhaled a deep breath. *No turning back now.* "Desiree Jacobs to see Paul Dujardin."

"Is he expecting you?" The electronic transmission gave the question a tinny echo.

Desi sucked at her tongue, trying to work up a little saliva. "I doubt he'll turn me away. Why don't you ask him?" Now she was the one who sounded odd, like some gangster with a raspy voice out of a bad B movie.

"Very well." The tone dripped disdain.

Desi waited several minutes; then the iron gates swung soundlessly inward. A well-oiled trap.

Calm down, girl. This is for Dad.

She drove up the cobbled drive to the timber-framed double doors. White-flowered viburnum shrubs lined the walk. Their spicy scent enshrouded her as she stepped out of the car. She trod up the steps and raised her hand to knock. The door opened, and a tall, hatchet-faced woman stared down at her. The woman's uniform proclaimed her a household staff member.

Desi lowered her arm. "Ms. Jacobs to see Monsieur Dujardin."

"Follow me." The same voice as on the intercom. The woman turned and walked away without a backward look.

Desi stepped under the rounded fanlight and into an oval foyer. A child's laugh greeted her, followed by the sprite herself scampering out of a nearby room and up a broad staircase. The housekeeper's face softened.

At least she doesn't look quite so much like Dr. Frankenstein's assistant. A warm flush spread over Desi's skin. *And thank You, Lord, for reminding me that this is the home of an innocent family, not a den of criminals.*

Desi followed the housekeeper into an octagonal library that smelled of wood polish and old books. Heavy velvet curtains were drawn across tall windows. A single lamp glowed in one corner. What had she said about Colonel Mustard and a candlestick…?

The housekeeper withdrew and closed the door.

Dujardin rose from a high-backed armchair near the cold fireplace. He came to meet her, leaning on his cane. *How has he aged so much in less than a month?* The art critic took her hand and bent over it.

A shiver traveled up Desiree's arm and she pulled her hand back.

"Come, make yourself at home." Dujardin turned toward a sofa and easy chair in the corner near the lamp. "May I offer you some refreshment? A seltzer water or perhaps some tea?"

"Nothing, thanks." Desi took a seat on one end of the sofa.

He lowered himself into the chair. A nonthreatening start. The art critic studied her beneath bushy white brows. Desi smoothed the wrinkles from her pantsuit and laid one arm across the back of the sofa. She waited, head cocked, eyes wide.

He needs to see me as a lamb, easily led.

The Frenchman grimaced and lowered his gaze. "I apologize for the terse note, and for the unusual method of delivery, but your every move has been watched by the authorities for quite some time."

"Not true anymore. The FBI decided I'm no longer in danger, and they've dropped me far down on their suspect list."

"Excellent." A gleam sparked in the old man's eyes.

"I'd appreciate an explanation. Just when I thought life might get back to normal, you start some spy novel intrigue. Do you know something about Dad's murder?"

Dujardin thumped his cane on the Oriental carpet. "This conversation is not about what I know, but about what you know. The death toll has risen quite high enough."

Desi caught her breath. "You *do* know something. You need to cooperate with the auth—"

"As you are?" His words ended with a snap of teeth, like a hound reaching the end of its tether.

She stared at the older man, a chill snaking up her spine.

He leaned back and expelled a breath through his nose.

"Let us not continue to toy with one another. A clever woman like you must have discovered your father's cache of pictures and his journal. He told me he left clues that only you could decipher. Since you have not turned these items over to the federal agents, I must assume you share my loathing of scandal."

So much for this pseudogentleman underestimating the fairer sex. Dujardin was the last person her father visited before his death. Was that fact more significant than she had thought? Her heart rate tripled.

The Frenchman laid both hands on top of his cane. "Now then, if you wish things to return to normal, you will give me everything Hiram left behind. I will dispose of the items in a manner that will restore both of our lives."

"Dispose of masterpieces? You must be joking!"

Her host tipped back his head and laughed. The sound held no merriment. "You are indeed your father's daughter. You worry about the fate of color on canvas when your future teeters on a precipice. Save your concern. No harm will come to the pictures—or to you—if you tell me where to collect them." Dujardin leaned toward her, nostrils flared. "The destruction of the journal is paramount. When Hiram visited me, I tried to tell him he was making a mistake. He would not listen."

The stuffy air gathered around Desiree like thunderheads. Her palms dampened. "Should I be afraid of you, monsieur?"

The old man's mouth dropped open. He closed his eyes and shook his head. "You do not understand. How could you? You have no family." He lifted his cane and pointed to the end table by the sofa.

She turned her head. A happy, healthy group smiled at her from a framed photograph—the senator, his wife, and three children.

"You see, I have much at stake."

Desi's ears burned. How *dare* he! "No family, Monsieur Dujardin? Who should I thank for that? I have already lost far more than you and could lose the business my father entrusted to my care."

"I understand." The Frenchman nodded. "I have been insensitive because of my own concerns. Forgive me. Let us make arrangements, then, to help each other keep what matters most to us."

"I'm afraid you've miscalculated. What matters most to me, and what mattered most to my father, has nothing to do with paintings, or a business, or even our own lives."

"Ah, you speak of the faith Hiram clung to. It did not save him in the end."

"You're mistaken about that, as well. And such faith believes in powerful intangibles like justice and truth. Matters that evidently mean little to you." Heart pounding, Desi stood and stared down at the man Hiram Jacobs had considered a friend. "Did you kill my father?"

Her host struggled to his feet and matched her glare. "I did not."

"But you know who did."

His gaze fell away, and he frowned at the empty fireplace. "I cannot help you there."

"And I cannot help you. Our talk is finished until you have a better answer for me." Desiree walked toward the library door. *Don't run. Walk.*

"You are making a foolish mistake."

Desi's hand closed around the doorknob. *Eyes forward. Don't let him see your fear.* She opened the door and let out a squeak—the only sound that got past her closed throat. A man towered over her. The man who passed the note at the zoo? Was he also a murderer for hire? Somewhere in the library, a clock ticked away what might be the last seconds of her life.

"Let her pass, Jenson." The Frenchman sounded every year his age.

The man stepped aside, and Desi forced her knees to unlock and her feet to move.

Dujardin's voice followed her into the hallway. "Think over our conversation, dear Desiree. You know where to find me when good sense prevails."

Desi fled the house. Her hands shook as she headed out of the driveway. "God…God…God!" His name was the only prayer she could manage. *I might have stood eye-to-eye with Daddy's killer.*

Was this Jenson capable of cold-blooded murder? Dujardin could have ordered the hit on her father. He had as much motive for murder as any unseen boss of a theft ring. And why couldn't the art critic *be* that boss and not the victim of circumstance he pretended to be?

Desi drove around the corner onto the next block. She spotted the rented van where Max waited with her listening equipment.

Oh, no!

A police car sat beside the van, lighted bubbles wheeling.

❖ ❖ ❖

Desiree paced the hotel room.

When they concocted their game plan, she never should have agreed to cruise on by and let Max handle it if the authorities showed up. What had she been *thinking*?

The lock clicked on the door, and it swung open.

"Max!" She wrapped her friend in a bear hug. "I have never been so happy to see anyone in my whole life. The police didn't detain you?"

"Naw. The officer succumbed to my Texas charm." Max laughed. "I explained that I was with a security company and named off several clients. I even handed him my cell phone and invited him to call some of them. I was outta there five minutes after I saw your car go by."

Desi planted her hands on her hips. "Five minutes! What took you so long to get back here? Didn't you know I'd be worrying my head off?"

"Aw, girlfriend, I'm sorry." Max's smile disappeared. "I should've called, but I guess I didn't think about it or how much time was passin'. Too busy gettin' back on the right road after I missed my turn." She shook her head. "Whew-ee! DC's a bear to navigate."

"Still...oh, never mind." All was well. What was she fussing about? Desi sighed and flopped backward onto her bed. "I feel like a limp noodle."

"Well, Miss Noodle, I'm starved. Want to order room service? Then you can give me your impressions about your afternoon adventure. Mine turned out to be pretty tame."

Desi sat up. "Deal."

Max went down the hall to get bottled waters from the vending machine. Desi phoned in the orders. When Max returned, she handed Desi a bottle, then sat by the table, one leg curled under her.

Desi hung up the phone and leaned back. "Dujardin makes a Vegas cardsharp look like the soul of honor. He's desperate and he's dangerous. Dad so trusted this man. His good friend. Hah! He should have had a clue when Dujardin put him up to that first theft all those years ago."

"I hate to point this out, hon—" Max frowned—"but your father was as much a part of that deal as Dujardin."

Desi lowered her head. "I know. I know. I'm still struggling to understand that side of Dad. But he didn't know the Lord then." She took a sip of water. "So did you get a good recording of our conversation? That's what counts right now."

The redhead laid a CD case on the table. "Clear as a bell and twice as incriminating. You confessed to nothing. Dujardin is in trouble up to his aristocratic neck. Someone like Tony could take this and get a warrant to turn the man's life inside out."

"We need to give the recording to him."

"Yep."

A knock sounded at the door. "Room service."

Max jumped up. "I'll get it."

Desi heard the door open. The smell of turkey melt sandwiches invaded the room, and her stomach rolled, but not with hunger. Would food ever appeal to her again?

Max returned with a laden tray and a pale face.

"What is it?" Desi took the tray and set it down on the table.

"There's a man spyin' on us from the next corridor. He peeked around the corner when I signed the room service bill. And that's not all. I've seen him before. After you drove by me and the police officer this afternoon, this guy cruised past in a little gold economy job. He had to slow down to get by my van and the police car. I got a real good look at him."

"Is he tall and husky with blond hair?"

"Nope. About medium height and ash gray hair. He's a senior citizen, for Pete's sake. What do you make of that?"

"You are one observant lady, Max." Desi leaped up and paced a familiar route through the room.

"Thanks. I trained with the best."

"My father?"

"You and him both."

Desi stopped and leveled a steady gaze at her friend. "That was a nice thing to say. Thank you. I've always wanted to measure up to my father. Never thought I could. But maybe…no, never mind." She shook her head.

Did she even want to be compared to her father anymore? Was that healthy? The thoughts whispered through her mind, but Desi thrust the questions away.

Max looked at the plates on the table. "You gonna eat this sandwich, or can I have it?"

Desi laughed. "Let's eat while I figure out a trap for our shadow man. I think we need to ask him who he's working for."

Desiree drove the car out of the hotel parking garage. She turned in the direction of a local mall. Within a block, she spotted the gold compact model behind her. The rental van,

Max at the wheel, was nowhere in sight. Excellent! No need to crowd their quarry.

She turned into the mall lot and slipped into a parking space facing out into the drive lane. Her tail did the same one row back and a few cars down. Desi sat and people-watched. Lots of coming and going. Plenty of witnesses to deter a violent reaction from the unknown factor in the little car.

A brown van entered the lot and cruised between Desi and her watcher. When the van stopped smack-dab in front of the gold compact, Desi peeled out of her parking place and circled into the lane behind the car.

The small car started to back out, but Desi braked to a halt behind him. The compact squealed to a stop.

Gotcha!

Desi leaped out of her car and dashed for the passenger side of the little car. She whipped open the door and slid into the seat. Her feet plunged into a sea of empty fast-food containers. The interior smelled of stale coffee and old French fries. "Hello, there. Please leave your hands where I can see them."

The man's fists wrapped around the steering wheel. He stared at her like a startled owl.

Oh, man, the guy must think I have a gun. Maybe that's for the best when I have no idea what he might be carrying.

A tap on the driver's side window brought the man's head around. Max looked in on them, smile wide as Texas. She waggled her fingers. The guy closed his eyes and let out a long groan.

"Chat time," Desi said. "Who are you, and why are you following me? Better yet, who hired you?"

"It's not what…I mean, I'm not… Hey, get out of there!"

Desi ignored him and continued digging through the glove compartment. She found his name on an insurance card. No clues there. But...

"Bingo!" Desi waved an envelope at Max.

The man grabbed for it, and Desi let him have his property. He scowled and clutched the envelope. The return address made the contents a statement from a retirement fund. A government retirement fund.

She studied him. "Ex–federal agent, I'm guessing."

He returned a stony stare.

Desi tapped her fingers on the dashboard. "The million-dollar question is are you dirty, or did Tony lie to me about withdrawing the surveillance?"

"Dirty?" The man snorted. "I'm not the one that's dirty, lady. Your stupid stunt just proved it."

"I don't think so. In a way, I'm disappointed that you're on the side of the law. I was hoping to corner a louse who could point me toward my father's murderer."

"Look in the mirror." Her watcher sneered. "Someone's bound to get hurt when greed puts you in bed with terror networks. Crane was right. You *are* a piece of work."

Desi recoiled against the door. "Terror networks? But how—"

"Like you didn't know where a good chunk of that black market money goes."

"No, I didn't. I—"

"Get out. The filth on you is messing up my car."

Desi staggered out onto the pavement, slammed the door, and backed against the vehicle in the next spot. Max jumped into the van and moved out of the way. The retired federal agent drove off like he was being swarmed by bees.

Desi walked to the van and climbed in beside Max. "This whole thing is way worse than I ever imagined."

"You don't look too good. Maybe we should cancel tonight's project."

Desi wanted to. Oh, how she wanted to. What she wouldn't give to walk away…go back home…hide there forever. But she shook her head, squeezing her hands into fists. "Not a chance." She met Max's gaze, new determination filling her.

None of the masterpieces would ever be used to fund bombs and guns. She would see to that. And she wouldn't rest until they were all back where they belonged. Just as her father had wanted. "We're doing this. Just like we planned."

Max's frown deepened. "I hope you know what you're doing, girl."

"Sometimes you just do what you can. And we're trained for this."

If only Desi were as confident as she sounded.

Fourteen

*T*ony hustled off the plane at London's Heathrow airport and pulled out his cell phone. *Blast!* He *knew* he should have traded it in before he left. This one had been losing its charge too quickly.

All right, find a telephone.

People congregated three deep around the first set he ran across. Tony continued down the concourse. There! He spotted a lone unit on a support post. A stout elderly lady jabbered and nodded with the handset to her ear. Tony set his bag down and planted himself next in line.

The woman's pale blue eyes widened. "I need to go, dearie. There's someone waiting."

Tony forced a smile at her stage whisper. "Please don't hurry on my account."

She brightened and bobbed a nod. Turning her back, she chatted on.

Tony sighed and began a visual dissection of the area. He'd had a bug-under-glass feeling while he stood in line to board the plane in Rome, and the funny feeling hadn't let up since. Paranoia wasn't normal for him. If it *was* paranoia.

How did the saying go? *Just because I'm paranoid doesn't mean they're not out to get me...*

This section of Heathrow wasn't quite as crowded as the customs area and passenger gates. But a fair number passed by or patronized the refreshment vendor fifty feet up the concourse. A group of laughing college kids meandered down the hall. "On holiday," as they said in England. Near a book kiosk, a woman sat engrossed in a newspaper. The pages blocked her head and upper body from view. Tony's gaze halted on her.

He recognized the dark green knee-length skirt from his flight out of Rome. He hadn't seen her face then and couldn't now. Her legs were crossed, feet encased in low-heeled pumps that matched the suit. She had a small tattoo of a red rose on her ankle. Slender, toned calves indicated someone who kept herself in good physical condition. A business professional of some type judging by the expensive clothes. Dark spots on the backs of her hands betrayed mature age. Not a young woman.

Someone tapped Tony's arm. He looked around.

The elderly lady from the phone blinked up at him. "Your turn, love. I'm through." Then she waddled off, trailing a small wheeled carry-on.

Tony snatched up the phone receiver as a man in a sport jacket darted for it. The man gave a tight-lipped nod and turned away. Tony recognized him from the Rome flight as well. Any number of people from his earlier flight could be killing time waiting for a connection.

You're losing it, Lucano. Dreaming up surveillance out of an itch between your shoulder blades.

As he punched in the numbers for the office, Tony glanced toward the seats near the bookseller. The woman was gone.

Crane grunted hello.

"You're still in Boston?"

"Don't let that little fact make your day." He growled like a bear with a toothache. "Word trickled down from Cooke's office that a file audit was in the offing, and all case paperwork needs to be completed with every i dotted and t crossed. Oh, and he wants expense accounts and requisitions no later than yesterday. I've been chained to a desk all afternoon. Forget investigating actual cases. You owe me big-time, pard."

Tony chuckled. No mention of a trip to Washington. *Atta girl, Desi. Just keep on behaving yourself.* And a bonus, too! A dreaded housekeeping chore would be done by the time he got back to the office. What more could a guy want? "My flight lands around 9:50 this evening. Then I'm heading home to take a long, hot shower and get as much sleep as jet lag allows. I'll see you in the morning."

"You'll see me tonight. I'll pick you up at Logan International, and we'll drive to Washington. Should be there by early morning. We can roust our pretty little suspect out of her beauty sleep. What do you want to bet we find some real nice evidence in her belongings?"

Tony's gut nose-dived.

"You will not believe what Thelma and Louise have been up to," Crane continued. "And they're still at it. They just left their hotel room for some unknown destination."

Thelma and Louise? The movie about a pair of housewives who go joyriding and end up on a crime spree? Tony listened as Crane filled him in on Desiree's stop at the Dujardin mansion, an encounter between Max and a local police officer, and the entrapment of one of their surveillance men.

"We lucked out that the Washington guys have been working in pairs just in case the ladies split up. The other one is still with them."

"Good work." The commendation tasted sour on his tongue. "I'll see you tonight."

"Gotcha." The receiver slammed down.

Tony rested his forehead against the cool metal of the phone box. Desiree had never promised him anything. Not like the other woman who tore his heart out and threw it in the trash. Why did he feel twice as betrayed?

He headed for the boarding lounge of his flight. People gave him wide berth.

Vengeance is mine, saith the Lord.

Well, sometimes God left vengeance in the hands of the law. Right now that assignment suited him like a holy calling.

Desi rang the doorbell and waited with Max in front of Victor Gambel's mansion overlooking the Potomac. She recognized the stocky man who opened the door. Their client's private security agent, Abel VonHolten. Stone-faced, VonHolten admitted them into the majestic foyer. A vaulted ceiling soared over their heads. Antiques and priceless sculptures lined the walls. An original Matisse hung over the refectory table.

Max lugged a metal box that looked something like a mechanic's tool chest, only bigger. Desi carried her usual briefcase, from which she removed the standard permission form for the procedure, while Max set her burden on the marble floor and started to dig out her equipment.

Desi left Max to her business and followed the security agent to Mr. Gambel's study. The multimillionaire sat in front of a wide screen showing a news station.

"Well, at least you're on time." Gambel poked a button on a remote control, and the sound muted. "I suppose you have some form or another for me to sign. The computer age was supposed to reduce paperwork. Hah! Just made it easier to produce more."

"Right on both counts, Mr. Gambel. I have a form for you to sign, and the wisest man on earth has yet to explain how electronic records transform themselves into mountains of paper."

Gambel poked the remote in her direction. "I'll tell you where a good bit of it comes from. All those infernal government regulations, that's what. A man can't even run his own business without being told which hoops to jump through and how high."

"Or a woman either." Desi laughed. She set the permission form on the side table, along with an HJ Securities pen. "This is one of my hoops, but I'll let you keep the pen."

He gave a rusty chuckle. "I suppose if a person has lots of papers to sign, he should have lots of pens."

Desi took the signed form. "Thank you for your time, and have a good evening, Mr. Gambel."

"Be better if those stock prices would rise." He pointed the remote at the TV, and the sound came to life. Desi headed out of the room. VonHolten opened the door.

The TV went silent. "You're as personable as your father, young lady, but you've got your own style. My prediction?

You won't need to fill his shoes. You'll be a success in your own right."

Desi's breath hitched. She stopped and looked back.

"And we have more violence in the Middle East," the news anchor blared. The multimillionaire sat with his back to her staring at the screen.

"Thank you, Mr. Gambel." He didn't move, so she left him with his gruff pride intact.

In the hallway, she turned to the security agent. "Can you walk me through the house and point out any acquisitions made in the past six months? We want to make sure that safeguards for those items are up to HJ Securities' quality."

"Follow me then. The boss bought a few sculptures."

They moved from room to room. Desi took notes on each piece. "No paintings?"

VonHolten shook his head. "Not since Mr. Jacobs was here last. There's only been one new picture in the last year. Your father was especially impressed with it. Want to see?"

"Of course."

He led her to the main dining room.

My apartment would fit in here twice over. She spotted the fake Van Gogh hanging at the far end of the room.

Desi stepped toward the piece. Video cameras mounted under the cornices watched her progress. She stopped in front of the picture, a careful foot distant. Any closer and the motion detector would sound off.

"Beautiful."

"One of the boss's favorites." VonHolten spoke over her shoulder. "That's why he had it hung where he could look at it over every meal."

If only she could ask Gambel who did the work, but he had no idea it wasn't Van Gogh. The forgery was superb.

She turned away from the painting and set her briefcase on the table. "If you want to find Max, I'm sure she'd like access to the control room. I'll stay here and polish my notes."

"Very good. Ah, miss?"

She looked up.

The security agent shifted from one foot to another. "Just wanted to say that I was sorry to hear about your dad. He was a good man."

Desi's heart twisted. She glanced away, then took a deep breath and met his gaze. "Yes, he was. I miss him a lot."

The security man nodded and left the room.

Now, Max, just keep him busy, and do your thing. We'll set matters to rights here.

Desi sat down to her paperwork. Mr. Gambel would chuckle over this stack of forms. Funny how a few minutes of conversation could change a person's perception of someone else.

The red operation light on one of the cameras blinked off. Desi checked the others. They were all dark. She leaped up and went to the painting, then waited. The alarm shrilled. Desi unhooked the hidden sensor in the back of the frame, and snatched the Van Gogh. The clamor ceased and then started again in a different room.

Now I've got two minutes to switch canvases before Maxie-girl finishes the alarm check. She had to have the real Van Gogh back on the wall before the last alarm sounded and Max switched all the security devices on again.

Desi held the painting by the outer frame with one hand

and pulled at the stretching frame with the other. *Aaagh!* Neither moved a millimeter. She laid the painting on the table and used her thumbs to try to press the outer frame away from the stretching frame.

Wedged tight!

She flipped open her briefcase and pawed through it. What happened to her screwdriver? It must have fallen out some… No! She left it in the storage vault when she pried the crate open to get the Van Gogh. An acrid taste rose in her throat. *Now what?*

Her gaze darted about the room. Nothing…nothing… there!

She ran to the sideboard, where a butter knife had apparently been left behind from the morning's cleanup. She snatched it up. The blade bore traces of grease. She wiped it on her blouse in a spot under the blazer where the stain wouldn't be noticed and hustled back to the picture.

It didn't matter two hoots whether she ruined the thing. She had to get it out of there and the real Van Gogh put back.

Her breath whistled between clenched teeth as she fitted the blade between the outer frame and canvas and pried. *That's it! That's it! There! Thank You, God!* Desi wiped her brow, then lifted the fake from the frame and fitted the genuine Van Gogh into its proper place. Not quite so tight this time. The forger must have been off an eighth of an inch or so on his measurements.

Alarms still wailed in steady sequence. Getting closer. Closer. Almost full circle. She thrust the fake into her case.

Keep it going, Max. Just a little longer.

She whirled and raced to the wall. The house went still.

Desi froze. She glanced up at the nearest video camera. *No light yet. I've maybe got five seconds before all systems are go.* She hung the painting and reattached the hidden sensor. *Rats! The painting's crooked.* She gripped the frame and tugged it straight.

Whaaaaah! Whaaaah!

Desi staggered back and tottered on the heels of her pumps. *Think! Think!* She glanced up. No camera light. *The shoes! All right!*

She swooped a pump from her foot and wrenched off the heel. *Red light! Red light! Who do we see tonight?* She showed the camera a sheepish smile and held up the broken shoe.

God grant that the security agent believed her "accidental" bump against the frame.

"What a rush!" Max settled into the driver's seat of the van. "When that alarm sounded out of sequence, I figured our goose was burned to a crisp. Then when the monitor went on and I saw you hold up that broken shoe, I just about passed out. That look on your face! VonHolten laughed. I've never heard him make that sound before. The guy doesn't even crack a smile."

Desi groaned and slumped in the passenger seat. "I think I've exceeded my excitement quotient for one day. That one was a little closer than I like. Plus I ruined a new shoe, and one of my favorite blouses has a grease stain on it. Not to mention my hose." She lifted a shoeless foot to display runs in the stocking.

"Cheer up. We got away with another caper."

Desi let out a shaky laugh. "We did, didn't we? To think, we choose to do this sort of thing as part of our living. A good shrink would have a heyday psychoanalyzing us."

"Let's have a little wind-down music." Max turned the radio on.

Desi closed her eyes. The sounds of worship washed over her. Tension leaked from her muscles and bones. She'd sleep well tonight.

Desi lay awake, staring at the shadow play on the ceiling. The bed beneath her might as well have been a block of granite and her pillow a stone.

What she and Max had done this evening was against the law, even if they were righting a wrong. The owner hadn't given them permission to tamper with his possessions. She'd even told a lie of misdirection with the broken heel ruse.

Foolish to keep doing this.

Five more pieces of stolen art cried to her from the hidden vault. Her father paid for their preservation in his blood. A lump rose in her throat.

Would she be a coward to turn the paintings over to the authorities? To Tony? What a relief to move this weight onto someone else's broad shoulders.

But what of her father's reputation? The business? The threat of reprisal from the thieves? They might carry out their threat if they discovered what she and Max had done with the Van Gogh. Should she turn the remainder of the cache over to them and hope for their mercy?

Never!

As if you didn't know where a good chunk of that black market money goes.

"But I didn't!"

She bit her lip and listened. Max's breathing continued strong and even from the other bed. *Yeah, Max, you always brag that you can sleep through a Gulf Coast hurricane. So let's test the claim.*

Desi sat up and clicked on her bedside light. She opened the nightstand drawer and pulled out the Gideon Bible. *Wisdom, Lord. I'll take a whole bunch, please.* She propped herself up against her pillow and opened to her favorite book—Ephesians.

She'd read it time and time again. Could there be something—anything—for now?

This mess wasn't getting any less tangled. She had to know which thread to pull in order to set matters straight.

Flow into me, Lord, Your words eternal.

She read through one chapter. A second. A third.

What's the matter? No connection. As if God's speaking to anybody but me.

Desi sighed and closed the book. When Scripture didn't communicate, the problem was never with God. It was always with people. With her.

She bowed her head. "Lord, I'm ready to do anything you show me. I don't want to try and figure this out by myself any more."

She went to Ephesians again. Chapter 4. Verses passed beneath her finger. She sighed. Verse 14.

We should no longer be babes, swung back and forth
and carried here and there with every wind of teaching

that springs from human craftiness and ingenuity for devising error; but telling the truth in love, we should grow up in every way toward Him who is the head—Christ…

Desi sat up poker straight. Every hair on her scalp prickled. *"Tell the truth in love."*

Too simple. Totally right!

Sure, the passage referred to false teachers of the gospel, but she was dealing with plenty of craftiness and error here. And God's solution was to tell the truth. Every day she held back, she let the wicked swing her back and forth on a pendulum of indecision. In God's eyes, she was behaving like a child.

All this fussing about reputation, worries about preserving a business—nothing but a smoke screen for her own insecurities. She didn't want to step out from under her father's shadow. Max told her she could do something different with her life. Mr. Gambel said she could succeed in her own right. But she hadn't believed them.

Maybe she hadn't *wanted* to believe. Because if she did, she'd have to stop scrambling to restore status quo.

She wasn't responsible for her father's choices or their impact. She was responsible for her own. Could she believe that God could make a way for her and all the innocent people to survive the fallout once the truth was known? Who better to believe in?

Desi set the Bible on the nightstand, turned off the light, and settled against her pillow. *Thank You, Father. I'm always Your little girl, but I will stop being childish.*

Sleep came. Comfortable as a warm bath.

❖ ❖ ❖

Vise grips squeezed Desi's arms. Hands!

Her eyelids popped wide. A rag stuffed between her teeth bottled the scream in her throat.

Shadows hovered. Masked figures.

Her heart flailed against her ribs. She bucked. Arms pinned her flat.

Maaaaax!

Something pricked her arm. Desi thrashed, then plunged into nothing.

Fifteen

Steve Crane leaned over the hotel front counter, eyes slitted, nostrils flared. "We're federal agents with a warrant and we expect your cooperation." He angled a glance at Tony. "Roast beef him."

The hotel night attendant backed up a pace, mouth half open.

Stevo, what are you doing? Tony gave his partner a disgusted look. Scaring the guy was counterproductive. "What my partner means is I should show you my badge." He flipped open the black case. "Desiree Jacobs is checked in here, and we need a key card to her room."

Crane slapped the counter. "Today!"

The attendant jumped and blinked. His cheeks reddened. "Um. Ah. May I see the warrant?"

Crane pulled a folded paper from his jacket pocket. He pointed at the signature on the warrant sheet. "Federal judge. Now let's have the key."

The attendant cleared his throat and got busy. "Here you go." He laid the card on the counter. "May I ask what this is about?"

"Federal investigation. Keep your head down, and stay out of the way."

The man paled. "This has been one strange night."

Crane turned toward the elevators.

Tony grabbed his arm. "Hold it a second." He looked at the attendant. "Strange how?"

"Cats!" The man shook his head. "Somebody's idea of a joke, I suppose, but we had an infestation of stray cats. About a half dozen running around. Took us two hours to catch them all."

"Didn't you call animal control?"

The man's eyebrows soared into his hairline. "Do you have any idea how long it would take them to get here? Our guests would be out and about, tripping over mangy felines before animal control stuck their heads in the door. No, no, our night staff handled it with gloves and laundry sacks." The man gasped. "You're not going to call the SPCA are you?"

Crane snorted. "Nah! We're not interested in your cats."

"Yes, we are." Tony glanced around the deserted lobby. It was a nice place, but then Desiree had good taste. "Was the front desk ever vacant during your cat hunt?"

The attendant straightened a stack of forms. "Only for a few minutes. I assure you we do everything in our power to remain available to our guests."

"I'm sure you do. Thank you." Tony walked away.

Crane fell into step. "So someone could have come or gone unseen." The older agent shook his head. "Am I losin' it? I don't normally miss juicy stuff like that."

"I don't think you want me to answer that, Stevo." The man was acting like he had fleas. Why was he so nervous?

Crane pushed the elevator button. "What do you wanna bet our little distraction has something to do with the *guest* we're dropping in on."

"All bets are off where Desiree Jacobs is concerned."

They stepped into the elevator car.

"You can say that again, pard. We have no idea what we're going to run into. I say we go in prepared for the worst."

"Negative. No guns. Whatever else she is, Desi's not violent."

"What do you call swinging a lamp at a burglar?"

"Self-defense."

Crane chuckled. "I'll give you that. Nobody ever said Jacobs didn't have guts. But I wasn't thinking about *her* having a gun."

Tony rubbed jet lag grit from his eyes. "Now *I'm* the one not thinking straight. If someone snuck in here and got to her room, *they* might be armed."

They walked up the hall and stopped in front of the right door. Tony listened.

No sound.

Crane jerked a nod. "Be my guest."

Tony banged the side of his fist on the panel. *If they're just catching their beauty sleep, that ought to wake them up.*

Crane put his face close to the door. "FBI! Open up!"

Seconds ticked past. No response.

Tony used the key card.

Crane's hand went to his gun butt. He backed against the wall. Tony pushed the door open, and Crane darted through in a crouch, gun extended. Tony followed, weapon ready— stomach churning.

The room was dim and quiet. Predawn light hazed the edges of the drawn window shade. A human-shaped lump lay curled in the farther bed. Soft snores sounded from beneath the covers. The sheets of the nearer bed were rumpled, but empty.

Crane slunk in a crouch toward the still figure. Tony flipped on the bathroom light and peeked inside. No one there. He moved deeper into the room. His partner halted near the bed. He took one hand off his gun and shook the body. "FBI! Wakey, wakey!"

The figure screeched and sat up. A mop of red hair fell around her face. She brushed it aside and stared at the gun in her face.

Maxine Webb accounted for. Where's Desi?

Crane rose out of his crouch. "Where's Jacobs?"

"Don't you *ever* sneak up on a person like that! And get that gun away from me." Webb bounded to her feet and brushed past Crane. A nightshirt draped her from neck to knees. She gazed down at the empty bed beside hers. "Where *is* Desi?" She furrowed her brow at Tony.

Crane growled a curse. He shoved the woman facedown on Desiree's bed and pressed the barrel of his weapon into the back of her neck. "I am sick to death of the games you women play. Now, where's Desiree Jacobs?"

"Whoa!" Tony held out a hand. "We don't do it like this, Stevo." *Don't slip any further over the edge on me, Crane. You've got to come off the street, but let's get you out of here without bloodshed first.*

Veins in Crane's neck stood out. He breathed like a man fresh from a race. Maxine whimpered.

"Ease up," Tony said. "We'll search this place. The evidence will speak for itself."

Crane's shoulders lowered, and the gun inched back. He took a step away, then holstered his weapon. "All right. Let's get to it."

Webb scrambled across the bed and stood with her back to the wall. Tears wet her cheeks. She glared at Crane. "You gentlemen knock yourselves out searchin'." She hauled in a breath. "I'll be in the li'l lady's room."

"Not until we check your belongings in there," Tony said.

Maxine slumped on the edge of Desi's bed and rubbed the back of her neck. "All right, but make it snappy. After this kind of a wake-up call, I need to use the facilities."

"Stevo, you check the bathroom. I'll start going through the luggage."

Crane walked around Tony without looking at him. Tony started on the luggage, then turned toward Maxine. "Where's Desiree's briefcase?"

"Aren't you going to read me my rights?"

"We're not arresting you...yet."

Webb crossed her arms. "I'm not sayin' a word unless you read me my rights."

Tony sighed. *All right, humor the woman.* He recited the Miranda warning.

She put her bare feet up on the bed, crossed her ankles, and leaned against the headboard. "I plead the Fifth."

Bravado on the outside. A bundle of nerves on the inside. One pudgy bare foot waggled a steady rhythm.

"Suit yourself, but you may soon wish you'd been more cooperative. Things don't always have to be done the hard way."

"Hah! Seems like it with you guys. You're sniffin' up the wrong trail. You should be ransacking Paul Dujardin's house."

Tony examined a wrinkled blouse with a grease stain on it. "Mind telling me why?"

"Yup. Desi needs to be the one to speak up if she wants."

"She visited Dujardin yesterday."

"Yeah, what of it? She's lookin' into her father's death, since you and Mr. Chuckles in there—" she jerked her head toward the bathroom—"don't seem to be makin' any headway. Right now, you need to quit rummaging through women's clothes and find Desi. Unless that's too big an assignment for you."

"You don't know where she is?"

"Not a clue. She was here last night when I fell asleep. I have this bad feelin' she needs help."

Tony's insides twisted. *Too bad I have the same feeling.*

Stench awakened Desiree. She opened her eyes to blackness. The air was cool, close, and sticky. Her tongue felt like she'd been eating cotton balls. She lay on her back, and something slimy reeked under her nose. Bile rushed to her throat. She fought it back and tossed her head. The foul item fell away and the smell faded. But not by much. Pain gouged through every pressure point on the underside of her body, as if she lay on pebbles.

Where am I? What happened…? Oh! I was kidnapped out of my hotel room!

She held her breath. Where were her captors? Where had they taken her? Traffic sounds carried to her ears.

Desi flexed her arms and legs. *Shouldn't I be tied up?* She groped in front of her and knocked something solid. The object tumbled away.

She gazed up into a deep purple sky sprinkled with fading

stars. On two sides, tall buildings loomed upward. She lay in an alley next to a dumpster if her nose was telling the truth. She appeared to be alone. Whoever her kidnappers were, they'd covered her in trash and left her to rot. She turned her head and spotted a cardboard carton. That was what she'd knocked away.

Desi bounded to her feet—

Big mistake. Her brain whirled like a leaf in a windstorm. She staggered, then bent over and clutched her middle. *Slow, easy breaths. Stomach, get back down there!*

She eased into a standing position. A wall beckoned. *So nice to lean on.* She tottered toward it.

"Ow! Ow! Ow!" Bits of who-knew-what poked the bottoms of her bare feet. Damp morning air hung heavy around her. She shivered. Pajamas were not meant for an outdoor junket.

Okay. First things first. Find out where she was and then get back to her hotel. She could speculate later about who had done this to her. And why.

The twilight alley had grown a little brighter, so she glanced around and spotted a door. She eased toward the entrance. Faded letters were painted on the face, and her mouth fell open. She'd been dumped in the alley behind her hotel? What was going on?

At least I can get back inside and find Max. She'll help me— Max! Had the kidnappers done something with her, too? *Oh, no! Please…*

Desi jiggled the doorknob. Locked out.

All right, just walk around to the front door. It's too early for many people to see me walk in wearing Bugs Bunny pj's. And what do I care about that anyway? If anything's happened to Max, I'll—

Music sounded from the direction of the Dumpster. The "William Tell Overture." A cell phone? Desi's mouth went dry. Someone wanted to talk to her. Three guesses who.

She baby-stepped through noxious detritus back toward the Dumpster. The overture repeated, pulling the knot in her gut tighter.

She lifted the Dumpster lid and recoiled at the stench. *No way am I diving in there.* Her grip faltered. The lid slammed down. The overture started in once more.

"Oh, shuut up!" Her blood raced, and a steady roar filled her ears as her mind tried to make sense of what was happening. What if her abductors had Max, and this was a ransom demand? She *had* to find that phone!

Okay. Calm down and listen. She held herself still, settled her breathing.

The sound was coming from under the Dumpster, not in it.

She dropped to her hands and knees and pressed her cheek to the pavement. *Whoever you are, this garbage deal is not a smidgeon funny.*

Desi spotted the phone tucked behind the right front wheel. The overture began another rendition. Desi snatched it up. *Stop shaking. You have to answer, and you have to sound in control.* She licked her lips. "Hello?"

"Good morning, Miss Jacobs." The voice was electronically altered. "I trust you had a nice rest."

The robotic tones made it impossible to tell if the person was male or female. Desi guessed male from the cast list of suspects on her mental playbill. "Who are you, and what do you want?"

"I'm the Chief to all who work for me. You may call me

that. As for what we want? Well, our organization wants only what belongs to us."

"I don't understand."

"We want what your father hid from us, Miss Jacobs. We understand that you found the items. Attempting to keep them from us would be unwise."

Desi sat on the pavement and leaned her back against the Dumpster. Fury heated her chilled skin. "You killed my father! I want—"

"We killed no one."

The denial had the ring of authenticity—but then, so had Paul Dujardin's. She couldn't afford to believe either of them. Of course, the person on the phone could *be* Dujardin...

No. That doesn't feel right.

The formal speech pattern was similar, but why would the Frenchman pull off this elaborate stunt when he'd had her in his power and scared goofy yesterday afternoon? Besides, the man on the phone spoke as though he wasn't alone in this venture. What had he said? *Our organization? We want?* Dujardin seemed to be acting on his own behalf.

Desi rubbed a hand across her forehead. This little drama got stranger by the minute. Right now she had to play along, but she needed some assurances first. "What have you done with Max?"

"Mrs. Webb? I imagine she is asleep in your room."

"You don't have her?"

"Certainly not. But you understand from what has happened to you that we could take her anytime we chose."

"How did you know I found the items? I didn't tell anybody except—" Little crawly things scurried over Desi's skin. She swatted at herself. Nothing there…except a terrible knowing.

Max! What have you done? A vein throbbed in Desi's temple. She swallowed, then swallowed again.

Think about it. Only one person knew what she'd found. Plus the voice talking to her was electronically altered. Electronics equaled Max. Could Desi be talking to the woman who'd played the part of her best friend all these years? Could Max be the Chief?

Don't be stupid.

Desi shook her head. Wrong conclusion. If the redhead hadn't lost her Texas speech pattern in a decade on the East Coast, she wouldn't be able to disguise it now. Still…Max *could* have set this conversation up.

And the logic all came down to one undeniable fact. Max and only Max knew about the paintings.

Desi barely heard the Chief's next words over the soundless scream that rang through her heart.

"No more questions. You will turn our property over to us at once."

Desi lowered her head into her hand. "Yes." The word was a dull thud in her soul. Final. Reeking of defeat.

"Good. When we are finished talking, you will throw the phone into the Dumpster. Tell no one of our chat, and no one else need be…involved."

"I understand."

"I'm glad to hear that. You will be contacted with instructions when you return to Boston. Follow them to the letter, please. We would like to avoid more unpleasantness." The voice hardened. "But I believe you know we will do what we must to regain what is ours."

The line went dead. With a cry, Desi flung the phone against the wall.

A rap sounded at the hotel room door. Tony froze, his hand on the latch of Max's overnight case. Crane's head came up, nostrils flared like a hound catching a scent, and he rose from an undignified crouch on the floor where he'd been looking under the beds. Tony headed to answer before his partner could. As he passed the bathroom, he heard water running. Max must not have caught the knock.

Tony put his hand on his gun but didn't pull it out from beneath his jacket. He peered through the peephole. Desiree! Ignoring the rush of relief that greased his knees, he released his weapon and yanked open the door. He smiled down into the startled face of Desiree Jacobs. "Welcome home, Ms. Jacobs. Glad to see you in such good shape."

Desi stalked past him, trailing an air of disdain and a rank odor. She glanced at a scowling Steve Crane, cast her eyes around the disarray of a searched room, and then turned to glare at him. "Cheap sarcasm doesn't match your suit and tie, even if you do seem a tad rumpled." She scanned him up and down.

Tony grinned. He couldn't help himself. Her hair was matted to her skull on one side and stuck out straight on the other, as if she'd dried it standing sideways in a gale force wind. Her face was streaked with dirt, and her stained Bugs Bunny pajamas belonged in the Goodwill rejects bin.

She looked totally huggable. Especially with those wide, haunted eyes.

Tony curbed the impulse to step toward her. He was going to keep his head on straight if it killed him. "Are you all right?"

Her lower lip quivered. She bit it and turned toward the wall, swiping at her cheeks.

"Better question," Crane said. "Where have you been?"

The bathroom door opened, and Max stepped out. "What is that smell?"

"Eau de Dumpster." Desi gave a ragged sniff.

Max let out a squeal and raced toward her.

Desi backed away, arm extended. "You don't want to get that close."

Max halted, and her face went stiff. Tony frowned, watching the interplay. Was something going on between these two…?

"All of you, just give me some space here." Desi took another step backward. "I had a horrible night, in case you want to know. Went to sleep all comfy-cozy in my bed. Woke up in a nest of hotel garbage in the back alley…with no memory of how I got there."

Crane's laugh dripped scorn.

Tony cut him off with a wave of the hand. "Do you sleep-walk often?"

Desi's gaze dropped. "Not since I was five years old and ate too much deli pickle loaf." Her voice was as small as a miserable child's. "But I've been under an unusual amount of stress these days." Her head came up and her fists opened and closed.

Tony studied her, eyes narrowed. He sensed truth masking greater truth. She did that a lot. Despair ground through him. He'd failed to earn her confidence, and the cost might be more than either of them could afford.

"We want to see your briefcase." Crane's words charged the sullen air.

Fire and ice crackled in the gaze Desi leveled on him. "It's in the rental van, but you'll need a warrant to get at it."

Crane waved the paper in the air. She held out her hand, but he started to stuff it back into his jacket pocket. Tony snatched the folded sheet and gave it to Desiree. She scanned the document.

"This is an illegal search." She thrust the page back toward Tony. "Your so-called warrant is just a copy of the expired warrant you jokers used to search my house and office building weeks ago. You can both get on your knees and thank God if I don't press charges. Now get out!"

Tony gaped at the document. Desi was right. The warrant was no good. An honest mistake? Stevo must have the real warrant in his pocket... Tony looked at his partner.

The older agent stood with his arms folded across his chest, face ablaze like a schoolboy caught in the girls' locker room. He wouldn't meet Tony's eyes.

This nightmare wasn't about to end anytime soon.

"You said you obtained a warrant." Clenched teeth held back a steaming geyser of accusations.

"Yeah, well, I didn't have time to argue any longer with Balzac that she needed to get us one. And we didn't need it after Ms. Webb gave us permission to 'knock ourselves out' in the search."

Max huffed. "I assumed you had a warrant, or I would never have said that."

Tony jerked his head toward the door. "We're leaving." He didn't trust himself to say one more word until he had his partner alone.

Crane skirted past Tony like he expected a swift kick. Tempting thought.

Desi hadn't made another sound, but she must be laughing up a storm on the inside. Now she could take complete revenge on the agents who had hounded her father before his death and her afterward. Their careers were roadkill.

Desi wept in the shower. Sobs gusted through her as she scrubbed foulness from her hair. She swallowed a clump of shampoo suds, gagged, then slumped against the shower wall.

Her dearest and best friend had betrayed her.

Unless she'd been followed by the best tail on the planet, only one person could have told the Chief that she'd found the cache of paintings. And that traitor waited for her outside the bathroom door, feigning concern.

Max had demanded a full explanation of Desi's middle-of-the-night disappearance, but Desi gave her nothing more than she'd told the FBI agents. As if her false friend didn't know the truth. The woman must have let the abductors into the hotel room.

Desi shivered in the sauna heat of the enclosed space. She couldn't hold out anymore. Her resources were spent. This conspiracy was too big for her. The guidance she thought she'd received last night? Hollow idealism.

All right, she'd let the thieves have what they wanted on the condition that they leave her alone. It wasn't as if they were going to destroy the pictures. The pieces would disappear into private collections where they would be treasured and preserved, maybe even reemerge for public enjoyment generations down the road.

Yes, giving in was the smart thing to do. Even Tony and his partner would stay away after today's search fiasco. Too bad. She and the dark-eyed agent could have had something together, but it was too late now. She needed to keep her priorities straight.

The reputation of the firm and the jobs of the HJ Securities employees would be safe if she just gave up and walked away. A theft ring might continue to operate, but that wasn't her fault. What they did with the money wasn't her fault either. None of this could be laid at her door, and she shouldn't feel guilty for doing a duck and run.

Besides, as the new CEO of the premier security company in the world, she could entertain herself by making the thieves' lives a pure misery. What higher calling could there be for someone with her skills? Isn't this what her father would have wanted?

Desi finished her shower and dried off with deliberate strokes. Maybe she had lost this round to the bad guys, but the match wasn't over. She was clever enough to keep Max guessing. Then, in due season, the Texas traitor would find herself out of a job at HJ Securities—blackballed in the entire line of business.

Desi wrapped the towel around herself like a robe of righteousness and stepped from the bathroom with her game face on.

Sixteen

*T*ony handed his partner the car keys. Crane accepted them and climbed into the driver's seat. Tony buckled in, laid his head against the rest, and closed his eyes.

Sleep? Hah! He needed to deck someone.

The car stopped and went through traffic, but Tony didn't open his eyes or move a muscle. Not that he was fooling anyone. Clenched fists were a pretty good giveaway.

Why had Stevo laid both their careers on the chopping block for this wild play at Desi? Was this more than a manifestation of burnout? Was some personal vendetta involved? But why? Maybe Tony needed to dig deeper into his partner's background.

What if Crane was involved with the theft network and his obsession with the Jacobses—father and daughter—was a ruse to keep suspicion channeled in the wrong direction? As one of the two lead agents on the case, Crane made an ideal candidate for sabotaging the investigation. The man was within spitting distance of retirement, and his pension wasn't much to anticipate. Maybe he wanted the resources to live the high life when the agency cut him loose.

A pretty decent theory, except for a couple things. The

Jacobses were hardly candidates for innocent bystanders of the year. And six months ago, Crane had fought tooth and nail to stay in the Fraud program and not get transferred into the Organized Crime squad. Tony had considered the sudden switch at the eleventh hour of a man's career a little odd, but he hadn't questioned his superiors' decision. Maybe he should have.

"I'll take full responsibility."

Crane's rasp brought Tony's eyes open. His partner's gaze was fixed on the endless ribbon of interstate heading south. "Generous offer, but I'm afraid we're Siamese twins…*pard*. I should have checked your warrant, and didn't."

"You won't get dinged too bad for that little oversight. Partners are supposed to trust one another."

"You got that right. But be careful using big words like *trust* when you don't know what they mean. I've trusted you many days not to come onto the job hungover, and you've managed to disappoint a lot more times than I should have allowed."

A flush crept up the man's neck. "Yeah, you've been more than fair. Picked up the slack. Put up with me when I acted like a tiger with a twisted tail."

Tony sat up. "And you pay me back by filing a conflict of interest report about me and Ms. Jacobs."

Crane's lips thinned. "You saying you don't have feelings for her?"

"She's an attractive woman, but I'm no more sure of her than you are or I wouldn't be here right now."

"Good point." Crane jerked a nod. "Guess I was out of line then."

Tony waited for his partner to say more. He didn't. *Guess*

that's the best apology I'm going to get. "So why'd you fake the warrant?"

Crane rolled a shoulder. "Balzac got me steamed with her stonewalling about going to the judge."

"I told you we didn't have enough for a warrant. She's no dummy. Another reason I should have questioned your claim that you got one. Guess I'm the dummy." Tony punched the seat between them. "You know what I think?" He poked a finger at his partner. "Your problem isn't this case. It's personal. You've had it in for women since your divorce. That's why you stuck that gun to the back of Maxine Webb's head. You're dangerous, Crane, and I'm not going to let it slide anymore."

The man's Adam's apple jumped. "What would you know about lying, cheating females, Romeo? My ex was sleeping with my neighbor, but she gets this fancy lawyer and all of a sudden *I'm* the bad guy. You didn't lose your home, your savings, your kids. I've got two daughters who won't talk to me. Grandkids I've never seen! Women are trouble, and you should wise up."

Tony shook his head. "So you had a low blow. That was harsh. I'm not saying otherwise. But you'd be wrong if you think a woman's never stabbed me in the back. That didn't make me decide to put the whole sex in the same basket."

Or did it? He hadn't had a steady dating relationship since Meranda. What did that say about him? But this wasn't about him. It was about Steve Crane and the menace he posed.

Anger tasted rancid on his tongue. He clenched his teeth and subsided into his pseudo-rest position. *Lord, You've got to help me here. I've had it with this knothead sitting beside me.*

Help him heal.

The response rang in his spirit as clear as his mother scolding him for traipsing through the house with muddy feet. *So I'm just supposed to smile and pat him on the head? This is serious business.*

So is the condition of his heart.

Tony eased a long breath out through his nose. Stevo had bristled at Tony's every attempt to share his faith, even the most subtle mention. Why should this moment be any different?

Because he's humbled and hurting.

The answer came from his own heart, not the haunting voice of the Almighty in his spirit. To Crane, life must stink worse than Desi did this morning. As if all a person did was crawl from garbage pit to cesspool, from one trouble and disappointment to another, then up and die with not a soul to care.

He owned nothing, had no one. The bottle had him in a stranglehold. In a few months—or sooner if Desi made a fuss—he'd lose the sole interest he had in life: his career.

Tony looked at the man in the driver's seat. With a hand beneath his jacket, Crane caressed the butt of his gun, a look in his eyes like a man fascinated by the beauty of a serpent. Understanding dawned.

How long had Stevo been this close to taking the final way out? Tony should have recognized the signs, but he'd been too busy grousing to himself about his pain-in-the-neck partner. Crane was not going to make himself another statistic under his watch.

He slugged the man in the shoulder.

"Hey!" Steve jerked his hand from under his jacket.

"Eating your gun is not the answer." Tony glared at his partner.

"What do you know about answers?" He slammed a fist against his knee. "No, don't answer that."

"Too bad. You're a captive audience, and I'm a dead man talking, so you'd better listen up. No one knows the whole story about that shoot-out five years ago where a woman I loved was killed. Everyone thinks they do, but they don't because I never told. You'll be the first."

Cautious interest rose on Stevo's face.

Tony gripped the armrest on his door. "I'm going to say this once, so you'd better listen with both ears. You can draw your own conclusions, but all I know is that God's more real than you or me. And whether we like it or not, or even acknowledge Him or not, He loves us in all our dirt."

Even when we can't stand ourselves sometimes. Waves of helplessness, failure, and self-disgust flooded over Tony, ripping open the ill-healed scar.

Meranda stepped toward Tony across the tarmac outside the warehouse. The floodlight in the deserted parking lot haloed her figure.

All the angel I'll ever need.

He leaned against the side of a black Lexus—the perfect car for a hot young executive ready to deal in hot diamonds—and watched her approach. Waves of black hair bobbed around a face that could start a war. Tony's gaze fell to her full lips. After tonight, those lips...the whole package...would belong to him alone.

Meranda stopped in front of him, her eyes almost on a level with his.

They were blue like the sky just before dark. "You're late." She tossed her hair back over her shoulder.

Tony grinned. "I stayed under the speed limit. Wouldn't want to get a ticket. Or let your boss think I'm overeager. Might drive the price up."

Meranda pouted her lower lip. "Do we really need to do this? We could jump into that car and go—"

Tony laid a finger against her mouth. "Go where, baby? We don't want to look over our shoulders the rest of our lives. The team has a bead on the tracking device under the bumper. They'll swarm this place. Once Feng is out of circulation, we can have a future. Just remember that, and it'll get you through these next few minutes. "

She looked into his face. Her nostrils twitched. Then she sighed and looked down at her feet. "All right. I'll take you in."

Tony stepped beside her, nerves humming. This better go the way he told her. He was walking into the jaws of a man-eater without a weapon or a wire.

"Sorry to give you such a runaround." Meranda touched his arm. "It must have been maddening to follow instructions from one bogus location to the next, but Quent had to be sure you weren't followed. He's so paranoid, particularly since we've had trouble getting rid of this shipment. He can feel the feds breathing down his neck." She shot him a tiny smile. "Too bad he doesn't know how close they are."

Tony nodded, gut weighted with lead.

Mom, I hope you're praying tonight. Or maybe not.

His mother would never approve of his relationship with Meranda. Not that she wouldn't hug her and stuff her with gourmet linguine, but in Mom's narrow world a man and woman didn't share a bed until they were wed. Period. She also hated the way he charged into danger without "getting his heart right with his heavenly Father."

Tony gave a mental snort. He'd done all right without a father—heavenly or otherwise—so far.

He and Meranda arrived at the warehouse, and a door swung open from the inside. They stepped over the threshold into a well-lit shipping office. Two muscle-bound thugs waited for them, cradling AK-47s. One grabbed Tony, whirled him face-forward against the wall, and frisked him with rough hands. When the first one finished, the other ran an electronic wand over him.

"Clean," Number Two pronounced.

The first one nodded. "This way."

Tony followed the men through another door into a cavernous storage area. Meranda stayed at his heels.

They threaded through aisles of crates labeled soy sauce and other Far Eastern cooking ingredients. The spicy smells mixed with the acid in Tony's stomach as the men led him to the back of the building, where they faced a plain metal door.

Thug One opened the door and motioned Tony through. He stepped over the threshold, and his shoes sank into thick carpet. The room was furnished in a maritime theme. Captain's wheel on the wall, antique sea chest in the corner, a sampan in a bottle on the desk. But no one sat behind the desk. Tony scanned the room. In the corner, a pair of bamboo chairs flanked a round, ivory-inlaid table about the right size for a game of chess.

No board though. This game would be played out in the mind.

A man sat in one of the chairs, legs crossed, snifter of amber liquid in one hand. He wore a tailored suit and leather shoes. Thick gray hair hugged a bulbous head. A bull neck led up to an oval chin, and a patch covered one eye. But his other eye…easy to forget everything else about him, even the scars that crinkled one side of his face.

The eye studied Tony, indifferent as a shark with no appetite.

Meranda stepped past Tony and stood between the two men. "I've brought you the buyer I told you about." She looked from one to the other. "Mr. Lucano, please meet Quentin Feng. Quent, this is Anthony Lucano, late of the diamond exchange." She giggled.

The gangster set his snifter down and rose. Tony offered a bow. Feng returned the courtesy. The unscarred side of his mouth lifted.

"You honor me with your presence, Mr. Lucano. Please, have a seat. We will enjoy a little brandy and a chat before getting down to business."

"My pleasure." Tony took the chair opposite Feng. That British accent was downright eerie coming out of that Oriental mug.

The man lifted one finger from the arm of his chair. "Meranda, would you kindly serve our guest?"

"Certainly. Would you like another brandy, Quent?"

"No, just a refresher for me."

"And only a few swallows for me." He looked at Feng. "If I'm stopped for so much as forgetting a turn signal, I don't care to test over the limit."

The gangster nodded. "A cautious man. I like that."

Meranda returned from the wet bar with a snifter for Tony and the cut crystal decanter. She poured from the decanter into Feng's glass.

"Thank you, my dear. Now please wait in the other room until you are summoned."

She backed away, gaze on Tony. Her lips parted; then she pressed them shut. She set the decanter on the table, turned, and went out a side door, movements jerky and brittle.

Summoned? Who does this guy think she is? A slave? Tony hid his expression behind the snifter. Heat splashed across his tongue and boiled down his throat. He coughed.

"Easy does it, man." Feng chuckled. "Now tell me a bit about yourself."

Tony set his glass on the scrimshawed tabletop. "I assumed by now that your network had informed you about everything from my preference in toothpaste to the day of the week I visit my bookie."

The gangster smiled. "True enough. We've vetted you thoroughly. I, too, am a cautious man. But I always like to know a few bits of trivia straight from my buyer's mouth like...ah...aren't you the great-grandson of Dominic Lucano, one of Capone's right-hand men?"

Tony nodded. "You have done your homework. Not one of the stellar moments in our family history. Dominic was killed in a shoot-out with police. My grandfather took the family and moved to Iowa. My dad, Alonzo, was born there, and my grandmother still lives in the family home. We've all gone straight now." He grinned at Feng.

The man threw back his head and let out a full-throated laugh. "Oh, I do like you." He set down his snifter and shook his head. "A pity. Ah, well, certain matters must be finished. Come then." Feng stood and headed for his desk.

Tony followed. *Now we're getting down to business. The team should be closing in. Time to get those diamonds on the table.*

"I'd like to see the merchandise before I wire the money."

"Merchandise?" Feng stopped behind his desk, but didn't sit down. "There is no merchandise."

What the—? "Then why am I here?"

"How did your father die?"

Tony's mouth hung open.

"He left you and your mother when you were ten years old. Did she ever say why?"

Tony's heart rate kicked into overdrive. *Feng shouldn't know that. It wasn't part of Tony's cover. Had Meranda slipped up? Keep cool, Lucano. Damage control.*

"Look, I don't see what my personal business has to do with our business."

"Your mother never told you? Even after your father was dead?" The eye went bright. "Most interesting. She must have feared you would pursue me if you knew the truth. How ironic that her attempt to protect you has left you exposed."

"Explain yourself, and don't involve my mother in this. She's a good woman. It'd break her heart to see me here with you."

"Of that I have no doubt. Sit!" He pointed to a chair in front of the desk.

Tony lowered himself slowly. This guy was way too amused about something. What was going on here? And where was the cavalry?

The gangster opened the center drawer of his desk and reached inside.

Tony tensed. A gun?

The man pulled out two eight-by-ten photographs and studied them. "I knew your father. No, not the Midwestern drugstore owner invented as part of your cover. The real one. Al Lucano was an excellent agent. He did this to me when we both were young." Feng touched the ravaged side of his face. "A bit of a scuffle involving spilled acid."

Icicles formed in Tony's veins.

The gangster looked up from the pictures. "You're following in your father's footsteps as an FBI agent. Admirable. These past months pretending to be a disenfranchised member of the diamond exchange? A superb performance. Almost as good as Meranda's."

Tony leaped up, but Feng's only reaction was to lay the photographs on the desk.

Tony stared at the pictures—and his insides turned to ashes. "Dad?"

"They're both your father. Here he is, the day before his death, going into the mall to buy you a graduation present. And here is a close-up of him after the mysterious fire at a crime scene."

Tony stared at the blackened face that hardly resembled a man, much less one he knew and loved. But this was no stranger on the morgue slab. This was...

He retched and staggered away. The swallow of brandy and the pie and coffee he'd eaten at an all-night diner came up on the carpet.

"Oh, dear!" Feng tut-tutted. "I hadn't anticipated this. Meranda!"

The side door sprang open and Meranda stepped in, then recoiled, staring at the floor. Tony watched her face. Disgust was written all over it. She'd played him from start to finish.

The innocent meeting at a Red Sox game, where she spilled ketchup on him. The giddy plunge into a relationship so good he had to pinch himself every day. Her tearful confession that she was the unwilling mistress of Quentin Feng. That she needed his help.

All a lie.

"I thought we loved each other." Each syllable burst between clenched teeth.

She darted a glance at him, flushed, then gave him wide berth as she hustled over to Feng.

"Good girl." The gangster wrapped an arm around her. She winced. "My niece loves her pretty face more than anything. She doesn't care to look like me." He caressed her cheek. Meranda stood stiff as a pole, eyes wide.

Tony's heart wrenched. His niece? The sick pervert!

Feng smiled. "She does what I say."

"Well, I don't! Get your paws off her!" Tony charged the desk.

The business end of a Glock pistol pulled him up short.

Feng released Meranda, and she scurried into a corner. He smiled. "I did have more than photographs in my drawer." He shook his head. "A courageous young man and chivalrous. Just not terribly wise. Women are for one thing. A smart man would have tried for the door. Not that you would have gotten far." The gangster pushed a button on his desk.

The two armed thugs came back in through the warehouse entrance, followed by a slight, ferret-faced man.

Tony recognized the third man from FBI files. Ethan Coble, Feng's pet computer guru.

Feng nodded toward Coble. "You succeeded in your task?"

The little man bowed. "I removed the tracking device from his Lexus and placed it on a different vehicle while he dawdled over a piece of pie, awaiting your next call."

No cavalry? Tony's mouth dried up like the Sahara.

"Very good," Feng said. "Then we will have no unwelcome intrusions on our evening." He turned his eye on Tony.

The shark was hungry now. The hair on Tony's nape stood on end.

"Anthony Marco Lucano, this is a solemn moment for me. The fulfillment of what you Italians would call *vendetta*. A matter of honor. Not some hotheaded American notion of revenge. Much too sloppy." He waved a hand. "No, no, this sort of vow waits patiently, for years if necessary, until just the right moment. Your father understood this. He thought that by leaving you he would draw my whole focus onto himself. And he hunted me. Almost caught me a time or two. The game was quite exhilarating." The gangster chuckled. "But I caught him first." He tapped the morgue shot. "And now it is the time for Lucano's seed to end."

Tony felt dipped in Novocain. He shook his head as if he could make the last few minutes go away. Memories crowded in, stumbling over themselves—all the bitter words he'd flung at his father on the few occasions he'd seen him after he left. *Mom, why didn't you tell me?* But he knew. His parents both wanted him to stay far away from his father and the danger that surrounded him.

"Are the preparations made?" Feng looked at the thugs.

"Yeah, boss."

"Let's go then." Feng waved them ahead of him.

The meaning of the words slipped past Tony's comprehension. The gangster stepped around the desk, turned him with a grip on his shoulder, and shoved him out into the warehouse. Resistance was a low priority. He was a rotten son and a foolish man.

Mom, your prayers keep you safe. Stay that way. But I don't expect them to work for me.

They went through another door, stepped up a short passage and into a factory area. A greasy hot smell weighted the air. Tony didn't look at anyone, didn't see much of anything except the horror show of lost years with his father. So many games of catch never played. Karate tournaments missed. No father to cheer him on at basketball. A childhood cut short. Robbed. Because of this man behind him. Because of a rotten, twisted—

A roar tore from Tony's throat. He bent low and whirled, right leg extended.

Feng squawked and leaped back, but the kick connected with a beefy forearm and spun the Glock from his hand. Tony followed through with a jumping side kick to the solar plexus. Feng hit the wall, face contorted, then doubled over.

A blow to the head splintered Tony's consciousness, then another—then darkness.

Tony struggled to awareness. He lay on his side, a hard surface cramping his shoulder. Heat and an oily stink choked his airways. A strange bubbling noise brought his eyes open. He was in a clear space between manufacturing machinery. Several yards away stood a huge vat, the source of the sound, the heat, and the smell.

He started to lift his head, but laid it back down with a groan. A timpani section was using his cranium for practice. He reached up, but his feet followed. He gave a mental curse. His hands were tied in front of him and linked to his bound legs by a cord.

A large foot prodded him over onto his back. He looked up into Feng's eye.

"A hundred gallons of peanut oil. The method is quite humane. You will be dead before you feel much. A burn for a burn, and a debt is paid with interest."

Tony's stomach lurched, but he had nothing more to lose. His French-fried body might never be found or identified. He'd just disappear. His mother would be devastated.

Jesus, You can't do this to her! She trusts You!

"I don't want to stay," Meranda said from behind Feng. Her voice quivered.

"Me either." Coble's voice shook worse than Meranda's.

Feng turned his eye on them. "You'll both see this through."

The two nameless thugs hefted Tony by his shoulders and legs and carried him toward stairs attached to the vat. Tony bucked. They swore and dropped him. One kicked him in the temple.

Tony faded. He felt himself lifted and carried. Heat from the vat walls sucked at him, like he stood at the gates of hell.

Mom, I'm so sorry. My life...an empty waste. Out of chances... to make it right.

His captors grunted up one step. Then another.

"But, my Anthony, God is the God of new chances."

Mom? No, not his mother. Her words spoken years ago. He hadn't listened then.

Tony's brain cleared like a curtain had been swept away. *Okay, God, I'm listening now. I'll take one of those chances, if You'll give me one. I'm Your boy from now on, whether I've got two seconds left or a hundred years.*

The thug who had his feet choked. He scrambled back down the stairs, pushing the other ahead of him.

Feng snarled in Chinese.

"I...can't...go...closer." The hired muscle gagged. "Too...hot. Stinks." The man dropped Tony's feet.

"Use the pay loader," Coble said. "You can dump him in from the bucket. If you stupid clowns just toss him by hand, you're going to get splashed with boiling oil."

"Yeah!" This from the man who had Tony's shoulders. "Thanks for the warning after we almost got burned." The man let go of him.

Tony's head bounced on the floor. The room spun.

Feng laughed. "If you're so foolish, you deserve what you get. You won't be needing first aid anyway." He leveled the Glock on his hired help. "Can't have too many witnesses to the murder of an FBI agent, and you two are brainless enough to get caught and talk."

The hirelings cursed and backed away. One's gaze darted toward a barrel. Their AKs lay on top.

"Not another step toward your weapons." The gun cocked. "Ethan, drive the loader over here."

"M-me?"

"Be thankful I have use for you after tonight."

Feet shuffled out of Tony's line of vision. An engine ground, caught, then sputtered and died. The engine turned over again and rasped.

Feng spewed more Chinese. "Stop! You oaf. You've flooded it."

Coble stepped into Tony's view, stammering apologies. He passed between Feng and one of the hired thugs. The man lunged for his automatic. Feng turned and fired. Coble screamed. The thug jerked and went down, his automatic spitting in a ragged burst. Coble's head bloomed into a red flower. Blood spattered Tony.

The dead thug's weapon skittered across the floor. Meranda snatched it up, teeth bared, eyes wild. She sprayed bullets, and the second thug jittered like a rag doll and collapsed.

Silence rang. Bodies lay still.

Feng lowered his gun. "Good work, my dear."

Meranda looked at him, face carved in ice. She squeezed the trigger.

Feng duck-walked backward and slammed against a piece of machinery. Disbelief etched his marred face before his single eye went blank, and he crumpled to the floor. His gun slid within feet of Tony.

Chills rushed through Tony's body. These people had gone nuts and turned on one another, evil destroying itself, just like in one of those Old Testament Bible stories he'd been taught in Sunday school. The scenario was crazy. But it had happened…and he was still alive.

He looked toward Meranda. Her white face glowed. She clutched the gun and stared at her handiwork. A queen surveying conquered territory.

Tony raised himself on one elbow. "Everything's all right now, baby. I don't blame you for anything you did. Lay down the weapon and untie me. I can get you a good deal with the DA for saving my life."

She trained her gun on him. Her eyes flayed him. "Men are slime. My uncle taught me that when I was thirteen years old. Today, I go free."

"No, Meranda!"

Tony rolled. Pain stitched his left leg and side. His bound hands found the Glock. He fired from the hip.

Seventeen

Silence filled the car.

Steve Crane swore long and low and hard. Oddly enough, the words didn't seem like blasphemy, but like another man expressing the gaping wound of Tony's soul.

"So you shot her," Crane said.

"That's right." Slumped against his seat, Tony stared out the window. The scenery passed in a blur.

Crane whistled. "Office scuttlebutt has that shoot-out a big free-for-all where one of our own came out the sole survivor. You're a legend, you know."

Tony sat up. "I'm a what?"

His partner returned his gaze. No mockery. "I figured you knew. Guess not. Probably because you bite the head off anyone who mentions the old case to you. 'The job's done. Come get me.' You recognize that statement?"

Tony shook his head.

Crane wheezed a chuckle. "That's all you said when you called in. They've turned into Bureau buzzwords, like people spout Schwarzenegger's 'I'll be back.' Agents still talk about the team bursting in to find you covered in blood and sitting in Feng's leather office chair like the CEO of the world."

"You're making this up."

"Nope. When they transferred me, I was afraid I'd end up working alongside a schmuck with a big head."

"So that's why you try so hard to bring me down?"

The shadow of a grin lightened Crane's face. "You're not too dumb."

"I figure I'm a prize schmuck, like you said. The grace of God kept me alive."

"Maybe." Crane shrugged. "More like the girl cared about you."

Tony glared at his partner. "How do you figure that? She hated men, and last I checked, I was a card-carrying male."

"Then explain why her aim was so good when taking out that goon and her uncle, but she just winged you."

"God."

"Have it your way." Crane's face closed up. He stared at the road.

Tony sagged against the seat. *Had* Meranda loved him a little? A wonderful, terrible thought. If she cared, then their relationship hadn't been a complete sham. But that meant he'd sent a woman to hell who'd still had a chance of recovering from her uncle's abuse. Now he'd never know. His chin fell to his chest.

Let it go! The words crackled.

But—

Let it go now!

Yes, sir! His heart expanded.

Tony exhaled a long breath and with it went five years of hurt he'd tried to wipe away on his own. He chuckled out loud. *Thank You, Lord!*

His partner sent him a narrow-eyed look.

Tony grinned. "So I bare my guts about an experience with God that changed my life, and then my hard-shelled partner zaps me with a truth that sets me free. How does it feel to be an instrument of the Lord?"

Crane's mouth fell open. A shiver passed through his body, as if Tony had thrown a bucket of cold water on him. Which, in a way, he had.

Nothing like the finger of God to wake a guy up. Still grinning, Tony settled in to get some sleep.

Tony jogged through the deserted park in the predawn hush. Only the birds were up. His sunrise hill lay ahead. Puffs of praise and short prayers came from his lips in time with his stride. The little woods closed around him, and he slowed to pick his way in the gloom.

"Tony." The soft voice hardly disturbed the air.

Lord?

No, a flesh and blood person. Desi!

He halted and looked around. She sat as still as a tree shadow on a small bench beside the path. He could barely make her out. He approached with measured step. She stood to greet him. Her light perfume attracted him, as so much of her did, if only—

"I've decided to trust you."

He stared at her. "Say that again?"

She heaved a breath. "I've figured out that I'm nobody's savior, including my own. I need help."

Hope leaped in Tony's breast. He put a leash on it. "All

right. What have you got for me? No holding back."

"I'm way past that. After yesterday…" A shudder ran through her slight body.

Hands to yourself, Lucano. He crossed his arms.

She paced as she talked about death threats and secret messages, hidden pictures and warnings from her father about the Chief. A slow burn snaked through Tony's veins. *Whoever this Chief joker is, he messed with the wrong woman. And I'm the guy who's going to make sure he knows it.*

He let his arms fall to his sides. "So you didn't report the location of the stolen paintings because you were afraid for your life."

"And the lives of my staff. But that wasn't the whole reason." She stared at the ground. "I couldn't bring myself to betray my father as a thief."

"Okay, I can buy that." High marks for honesty so far.

She lifted her head. "When I went back and read the whole story, there were mitigating circumstances." She dug in the fanny pack belted around her middle and pulled out a small journal. The end of an envelope stuck out the top. "Here. You can read for yourself. And you can have this, too." She took out a CD case. "It's a recording of my conversation with Paul Dujardin. You should get some good mileage out of it."

Tony reached for the items. A thrill seized him, like when he left his stomach behind at the top of a ski jump. This was it. The case was on the downhill run to the finish line. His fingers brushed Desiree's. The cool, powdered slopes melted before the rush of a tropical storm. He snatched his hand back. Desi wiped hers on her sweatpants.

He stared at her. Desiree Jacobs was innocent. He'd

known that deep inside all along. History hadn't let him believe it, but that history was gone now. *Anthony Marco Lucano reporting for duty. Assignment: Get close to this woman.* For himself, no one else. A man could spend a lifetime on the task and not begrudge a minute.

Tony squelched a goofy grin. *Stick to business, buster. The bad guys are still out there.*

He tapped the book and CD against his palm. "I'll get to these as soon as I can." He put his foot up on the bench and tucked them inside his crew sock. "I could arrest you for withholding information, but I don't want to." He ghosted a smile. "Besides, I doubt the DA would seek an indictment, provided you continue to cooperate."

The rigid line of her shoulders softened. "Can you tell me anything new the FBI has on the case?"

"The Italian polizia caught the hired killer who pulled the trigger on your father. I interviewed him in Rome this past weekend."

Desi let out a cry. "Thank God! I've had horrible dreams… nightmares that no one ever found out who killed Daddy."

He stepped away a few paces—out of reach of her tantalizing perfume—and gave her the short version of his interview with the suspect and the aftermath of finding the shooter's apartment. "We hope Interpol will be able to break into his encrypted files and find the money trail."

Desi smacked her hands together. "Awesome news! Here's something specific to pray about."

"You're a special lady." High marks for godly pluck, too.

The light was sufficient now for him to see her blush.

"Tell me that after I finish my confession." She paused

235

and took a breath, but didn't look away. If anything, she stood taller. "I returned a painting yesterday."

"To Victor Gambel, the multimillionaire in Washington DC."

Her jaw dropped. "How did you find out?"

Tony grinned. The lady didn't know everything after all. "We had more than one retired agent on your trail. You and Maxine Webb were never out of our sight until you went to bed, and then you still gave us the slip. You're good, woman. Real good. So what clue were you digging for in the hotel garbage?"

The color left Desi's face. Tony stepped toward her. She whirled and leaned against a tree.

One day she'll choose me for support—and not just when she's out of her mind with grief.

In fits and starts, she told him everything she remembered about her kidnapping, the phone conversation by the Dumpster, and her realization about her best friend.

What was she thinking holding out on killers and debating with criminal masterminds? Did she figure that catching crooks was as civilized as a game of Parcheesi?

"I almost gave in," she said. "I was going to let them have the paintings. But I woke up in the wee hours this morning, and I couldn't do it." She stepped close and searched his face. "Is there any way out of this mess without getting someone else hurt or killed?"

Tony grasped her shoulders. "First off. Never—" he shook her—"and I mean *never*—" he shook her once more—"make yourself a target again." He wrapped her so close he didn't know if either of them could breathe. But breathing wasn't important. Not at the moment. He lowered his head and his mouth trapped hers. She molded herself to him, hands fisted in his sweatshirt.

God Almighty, help me! He set her away, but not too far.

She looked as dazed as he felt. "Why did you do that?"

Tony brushed a finger across her cheekbone and around the curve of her jaw. "I've been battling the urge for months."

"To shake me or kiss me?"

"Both."

She laughed, a sound he wanted to hear a lot more often.

He took her hand and led her over to the bench. "You sit here." He pointed to one end. "And I'll sit here." He pointed at the other end. "We need to keep our heads on straight."

She grinned. "Because?"

He arched a brow. "Because you and I, dear lady, are going to plot a trap for a nest of cockroaches."

Bruised but cherished! Heart still tripping over itself, Desi watched Tony settle in at the opposite end of the bench. *Mostly cherished. Thank You, God. You've brought me from pariah to princess with one decision. Who would have thought I'd melt— and like it—for a man I couldn't stand a few weeks ago!*

Too bad she had to bring up the next subject.

"I see that nimble brain at work," Tony said.

Desi sighed. "You're going to argue with me up, down, and sideways, but I believe someone in the Bureau is in on the thefts. Dad thought so, too."

Tony's eyes hardened, but he nodded. "Something's been funky about the handling of this case from the start. I'm going to look into a few things when I get back to the office."

"Oh, Tony, be careful." She reached toward him.

He grasped her hand and tugged her close, eyebrows raised. "Says the Queen of Careful." He stopped her protest with his lips on hers.

Thoughts of thieves, murderers, and danger receded to a realm of make-believe. He drew away, and she opened her eyes. His face hovered inches from hers. "So much for keeping our distance for the sake of productive discussion." He sat back. "You realize that after we leave this grotto, our relationship has to stay professional until after the case is over."

Desi snuggled into his shoulder and inhaled the scent of sweaty male. "I'm happy to stay right here for as long as I can."

Tony stroked her hair. "You could glue us to this bench, and I wouldn't argue."

They laughed together. *Oh, I like this! I'm addicted already.*

Tony's arm tensed. Desi lifted her head.

Approaching feet—more than one person. Could be someone from the neighborhood that would recognize one or both of them. Not a good thing when nobody was supposed to know they had met this morning.

"What should we do?"

Tony shot her a wicked grin. "Not let them see our faces." He turned so his upper body covered hers.

Tense muscles, soft lips. Snickers from the passing joggers. The footfalls faded over the hill.

Tony sat back, one arm draped around her shoulders. "Did the audience make you nervous, or are you having second thoughts about us?"

"Us?" She looked into his face. "I like the sound of that, if you've got more in mind than a casual date or two. What about 'after this case is over,' as you said? I don't pass my kisses out to any Joe Schmo, even when I'm scared and desperate beyond belief. Not even to the guy whose brown eyes make my pulse leap over Mount Everest."

His eyes sparked. "Good. Keep it that way." One finger traced the vein in her throat. "Woman, you have no idea what I've got planned for you as soon as we get you out of danger. But I can tell you this—there's someone who'll want to have you over for dinner as soon as possible."

"You cook?"

"Not me, darlin'. I'm a takeout/microwave kind of guy, but my mom makes lasagna that they must envy in heaven."

Shazam! With men, the mom-thing meant serious. She grinned at Tony; he smiled back.

His face sobered. "Okay, for now we need to go our separate ways. As soon as you have your instructions for surrender of the paintings, get to a public phone and call me. Don't use your house phone or your cell phone, way too easy for someone to listen in on those. Give me the info, and I'll set up surveillance. We'll catch whoever picks up the goods."

Desi shook her head. "Don't forget about the traitor in your midst. Your calls could be monitored, too. And who can you trust to help you? Besides me, of course. You sure better not bring that nutcase partner of yours in on the operation."

A quick kiss answered her.

"To tide me over." He grinned. "Now, one, you are not a part of the surveillance except to alert me to where and when."

"But—"

He stopped her budding protest in the usual manner. When he finally pulled away and spoke, his voice was less than steady. "I can't let you be nearby when this goes down. I'll be so worried about you, I won't be able to do my job right, and that could get us both killed."

"Oh, I see." That made sense. Of course, right now he could tell her that gravity was a hoax and she'd believe him.

"Two, not even a dirty agent would dare put a bug on an FBI office phone. They're swept with *beyond* state-of-the-art equipment. Three, you'll have to let me line up my team. I've got some pretty good ideas already."

With that, he stood. "I'm going to finish my jog now, double-time, or I'll be late for work. You wait a while, and then head down the path the other way."

Fears and questions still bombarded Desi's mind, but in her heart a new river of peace flowed. How good it felt to have another person step up strong and tall and make a few decisions. Someone to lean on…maybe even more. Had she found someone to love? Excitement bubbled. She banked it. Best leave that for later exploration.

"All right." She nodded. "I agree to the plans you've outlined so far. But there must be a role I can play. I'm not good at twiddling my thumbs."

"Don't I know it." Tony chuckled. "You're an asset I don't want to waste, so we'll figure out something." He leaned down and pecked her on the lips. "I've got to stop doing that."

"You better not." *Oh, boy, sappy smiles all the way around. Good thing he's as besotted as I am.*

"There is one thing I should tell you…" He gazed toward the top of the hill and put his hands in his pockets.

"No secrets. Remember? That works both ways."

One side of Tony's mouth lifted. "Fair enough. Right before I left for Italy, one of our electronics specialists showed me entries in your father's Palm Pilot. The notations suggest that he was seeing a woman. Memos like "Send roses" or a reminder to make reservations at one of the more romantic restaurants in the city. The start of the liaison coincides with his involvement in the theft ring. Do you have any idea who this person might be?"

Desi sat back hard enough for the air to woof from her lungs. "No. Daddy seeing someone? He would have told me..." She bit her lip. Or would he?

Not unless the relationship got serious. She relaxed. Then her stomach muscles knotted. Or unless the femme fatale had a connection to the thieves—and Daddy knew it.

Tony adjusted his tie as he headed out the door of his condo. He'd have to drive smooth and slick to make the office on time. He didn't want to do anything out of the ordinary, like being late, that would arouse suspicion in someone watching his movements.

He'd have to play it close to the vest with Desi, too. Now that he had hope of winning her, he didn't want to mess up. She thought she ought to be told his next move, but that might not be a good idea. She was going to have to let him do his job as he saw fit. He'd already decided to take a chance on someone that she wouldn't approve. But there was something that mattered more than her approval.

Her survival.

❖ ❖ ❖

Daddy with a girlfriend?

Desi turned the notion over in her mind as she got ready for work. She would have been happy for him. How terrible if he'd had an opportunity at love snatched away from him. She sat on the end of her bed.

This secret romance scenario doesn't feel right. Odd that no grieving stranger showed up at Daddy's funeral. Desi left her apartment shaking her head. No doubt the FBI had given a faulty interpretation to a few vague entries in his electronic scheduler. They didn't know her dad like she did.

She'd believe in the girlfriend theory when the woman showed up with smoking roses in her hand.

Eighteen

Tony walked into the office a minute shy of late. Something was up. Voices hummed. Agents hustled through the bull pen. One raised her eyebrows as she passed him, then stopped and looked back. "An all squad meeting ASAP. The brass is on the warpath."

Tony went to his desk and found Crane grabbing a pen and pad of paper. He wore the usual scowl on his face.

"Any idea what the meeting's about?" Tony snagged a pad and a pen.

Crane shrugged. "Rumor has it there's some terror alert for the area. Squads are being gutted to act as gophers for the Joint Terrorism Task Force."

Tony uttered a crude word. Crane stared at him like he'd sprouted horns.

"You catching a little devilment from me?" He grinned.

Tony shook his head and stuffed his hands in his pockets. "I know better, but I haven't made it even halfway close to perfect yet." Looking around, he noticed that the workspace had cleared out. "The Jacobs case is about to go volcanic. We've got to stick with it. Desi handed me the moon and then some this morning at dawn."

Crane's breath hissed between his teeth.

"You guys coming?" a team member called from the doorway.

Tony waved him away. "We'll be right there."

Stevo looked ready to chew nails. "You and me are going to have one big powwow after this meeting."

"You got it, but right now we're going to pray."

Crane gaped like a beached mackerel. "We're going to what?"

Tony suppressed a smile, took his hands out of his pockets, looked up, and closed his eyes. "Lord, it seems we might be heading into a conflict of interest here. Steve and I need to do one thing while the authorities over us might expect another. But You knew this was going to happen before it did. Desiree Jacobs is Your child, too, and she needs our help. Please arrange everything so we can be there for her and take some bottom-feeders off the streets while we're at it. We ask in Jesus' holy name… Oh, and by the way, this pug ugly next to me is Steve Crane. I know You care about the guy, but he likes to pretend he doesn't believe in You. I know he's not that stupid, so if You could get his attention, that would be great with me. Amen."

He opened his eyes. Crane was staring at the floor, red-faced and blinking like a debutante. Tony tapped him on the shoulder. "C'mon. We'll be late." He walked off.

The meeting room was almost full. They took seats near the back.

Bernard Cooke sat on a dais in front and to the side. He gazed over the room like a brooding eagle. Rachel Balzac stood near a whiteboard, front and center. Stocky and with a bulldog face, she dressed like she meant for the crease in her pants to cut paper. She threaded a laser pointer around and around between the fingers of one hand. Pretty smooth trick.

Her dark eyes honed in on the pair of stragglers. Those eyes would be her best feature, except they were cop flat. She frowned. "If we're not waiting for anyone else, let's shut the door and get under way. Hit the lights."

The room went dark except for the projection on the whiteboard. A Middle Eastern face with eyes colder than Rachel's stared out on the gathered agents. But the man's most notable feature was a jutting, ill-shaven jaw.

"This is the best recent picture we have of Abu al Khayr. His name means 'one who does good.' His definition of good includes blowing up anything that has to do with the U.S. or Israel. He's a high-ranking al Qaeda planner who likes to personally oversee his work. The list of his suspected involvements and other pertinent data is being passed around the room."

Paper rustled.

"And this is al Khayr debarking from a ship in Boston harbor yesterday afternoon." A grainy picture flashed onto the screen that showed clear resemblance to the first shot only in the chin.

"Anywhere this man is seen, a major strike follows. We need al Khayr caught and his plans stopped. As of this moment, every one of you is at the disposal of the Joint Terrorism Task Force. All of you except Lucano and Crane. Since those two saw fit to stroll in late, if you've got anything on a current case that needs immediate attention, you can dump it on them while you concentrate on this new priority."

Crane groaned. Tony did the same, but only because it was expected. A chuckle rippled around the room. Tony did an inner tap dance. *Thank You, God!* They had a clear field to take care of business with the Chief and company.

Rachel slapped the pointer against her palm. "Next up is a list of specific tasks for each squad to perform." The photograph left the board and was replaced by a bullet list. "I'm the liaison from this office to the other law enforcement agencies on the JTTF, so everything gets run through me."

Tony glanced at his partner. Stevo looked like he'd sat on a burr.

"Don't say it!"

No words were necessary. A little answered prayer spoke well enough.

Desi walked toward the HJ Securities building. The morning sun warmed her shoulders, but her heart went colder with every step.

Oh, Max, how did you get involved in a theft ring? What tempted you?

Desi's steps slowed. What would Max's arrest do to her children, her husband? The woman would pay for her crimes, but her innocent family would pay, too. How could Desi get through the day without tearing every red hair out of the woman's head? She put a smile on her face and walked in the front door.

"Hiya." The receptionist waved. "Your voice mail has backed up from here to next week since you've been out of town. Maybe some new clients. Let's hope!" The woman lifted folded hands.

"We're due for a break." Desi went up the hall toward her office at the rear of the building.

Now act like you don't suspect a thing, or justice might never be done.

But I want to spit in her face!

One traitor's office coming up on the right. Smile. Hold it together…

Blast! I can't.

Desi kept walking, but she looked down and pretended to fiddle with the latch on her briefcase. Out of the corner of her eye, she saw the electronics expert look up as she walked by. The furrowed brow spelled concern—or worry that Desiree was on to something.

Damage control, girl. She'd been cold and distant to Max on the commercial flight home from Washington DC yesterday. Today she had to do a better acting job. She had to!

Okay, just think about that kooky adventure from last spring— a kite, a tree, a determined Texan, and an angry blue jay protecting its nest. Desi turned on her heel and poked her head into her former friend's office. She grinned at the redhead. *Good job. I think I made it genuine.*

"We still on for tonight?"

Max grinned back, tension slipping from her posture. "Oh, yeah—7:00 p.m. sharp. I'll make that crab dip you love. Dean wasn't sure you'd want to go ahead tonight. Maybe you'd be too bummed about everything that happened in Washington. But I told him he didn't know Desiree Jacobs if he thought that. I'm going to pick up a comedy on the way home from work. We can sure use a few laughs."

"No argument there." Desi waggled her fingers and left.

Her mouth tightened. Max was babbling in her relief that all seemed well. *Laugh while you can, lady. This might be your last chance for a good long while.*

Desi entered her office and shut the door. She let out a pent-up breath. Seated at her desk, she booted up her PC and then turned to the phone's glaring red message light. Several hours slipped past while she returned calls, dealt with her mail, delegated tasks, and even picked up one new client.

But her mind was focused on one thing: When, where, and how was the Chief going to contact her? He'd been pretty creative so far—she'd give him that. What would it be this time? A box of chocolates and an innocent invitation to meet with an admirer? Yeah, right! She wanted to stuff the creep into a rocket and shoot him to Pluto without a tank of oxygen. He'd be wise not to choose a face-to-face confrontation.

She pinched the bridge of her nose. *Yeah, girl, you fantasize great, but if it came to a contest, you probably wouldn't fare any better than you did in your pillow fight with Leone Bocca.* Thank God for the SWAT team that day. Thank God for Tony now.

Desi brought up her e-mail and scanned the incoming addresses. Routine, routine, junk, more routine. Not routine! Desi gasped and shoved away from her desk. The wheels slid off the plastic mat, hit carpet, and jerked to a stop. She gripped the arms of her chair.

All right. This is what you've been waiting for. What Tony's waiting for. You can do this.

She crept forward. There in her inbox, like a viper lurking among an innocuous stack of entries, sat one from the Chief, subject line "Unfinished Business."

Desi held her breath and clicked the message open.

Against a mauve background, black letters crawled like ants across the screen. She closed her eyes, then opened them as she filled her lungs. Her vision cleared, and the letters stopped jiggling and settled into words.

Good morning, Desi.

Her teeth ground together. *No one gave you permission to address me like a long lost friend, pal!* This guy talked elegant, but had no manners.

In order to begin our business relationship on the right foot, let's make matters as simple as possible. Please crate the items and deliver them promptly by 7:00 p.m. to an address that will be communicated one hour in advance using a method you are sure to appreciate. At the drop point, you will receive instructions regarding your role in our next operation. I believe the plan will appeal to your sense of adventure and provide an enjoyable challenge for your capabilities.
Cordially,
The Chief

Desi leaped to her feet. What gave this jerk the tiniest inkling that she was now part of the team? She hadn't agreed to anything of the sort. Did he think that by giving over the pictures, she was part of the package?

Let's just give Chiefie-boy a major earful! She whipped the mouse pointer onto the reply icon, then stilled. She bit her lip. There was an attachment to his message. She didn't want to open it, but she had to. She clicked on the attachment button. The computer's internal security checked the message and gave its verdict. *No virus threat detected? Wrongo! You are the virus, buddy.* She clicked to download the attachment.

Her computer exploded.

Desi screamed, then slammed her hands over her mouth. No, the machine hadn't blown up. Just the picture on the screen. Her heart performed acrobatics.

A video appeared. Footage of smoking rubble. Dark smudges streaked the stone. Blood? The camera stopped on a mangled leg poking from the wreckage.

Desi choked and lunged to her feet. She raced for the bathroom. Barely made it to a stall. A long time later, she rinsed out her mouth and washed her face at the sink. A white Kabuki mask stared back at her in the mirror.

So this is what a war zone felt like. Since 9/11, Americans thought they were more aware of their vulnerability. They weren't—not nearly enough.

Could Tony guarantee to protect her building full of employees? No, he couldn't. Not when someone in his own organization was sabotaging his efforts. She'd allowed a pair of strong arms to lend her the illusion of safety.

What about My arms?

In the mirror, Desi saw color return to her face.

Of course! The real enemy wasn't flesh and blood, not even this puffed up painting racketeer, but the fear that choked faith. The Almighty knew her situation, and He wanted these people stopped more than she did. She needed His guidance and protection. So did Tony, and he knew it. If they relied on the Lord together, they would be more than twice as strong. The Bible said they could put ten thousand to flight.

Well, all righty then.

Desi got down on her knees on the chill tile floor, just as she had been in front of the toilet a few minutes ago. But this time she humbled herself before the throne of grace.

"I haven't responded to the e-mail yet." Desi stood by a pay phone in a mall several miles from the HJ Securities offices. "I wanted to talk to you first."

She shifted her weight from one foot to another and scanned the busy area for watchers. For all the attention paid to the nondescript middle-aged woman on the telephone, she might as well be invisible.

"Good girl," Tony said. "Can't hurt to keep the guy guessing for a while. So are you Myra today?"

"Who?"

"You know. Miss Frump in the tacky loafers."

Desi laughed a little longer than necessary. "You think of her as Myra? Sounds right. I'm getting rather fond of the woman. No one gives her a second look."

"Not like the real deal under the disguise."

Desi's skin flushed. *I think I like your brand of compliments.*

"Back to business," he said. "So this Chief wants you to deliver the merchandise in person? That's a no-go. We agreed to keep you out of the handoff, and I'm holding you to that. You tell him you'll hire the delivery to the location, but you have no intention of accompanying it or working for him."

"But what about that attachment? Max could have set a bomb in place already, just waiting for the signal to push the button. If I don't cooperate—"

"Take is easy, sweetheart. The FBI looks at these things seriously, but remember, it didn't cost this guy much to put that little kaboom video in there, and the threat may be just as worthless—nothing more than a scare tactic. It's pretty certain he won't do anything until after seven o'clock, even if Max did plant an explosive device. I promise you I'll have a bomb squad comb your building the moment we have suspects in custody tonight."

Desi scratched an itchy spot around the edge of her wig. "You sound pretty confident, Mr. Agent Man."

"I've been praying."

"Me, too."

A mutual grin stretched across the telephone line.

"Seven o'clock!" Her spine straightened. "I'm supposed to be at Max and Dean's for movie night."

"Go. There's the useful role you were looking for. You can keep an eye on Max. She can't be detonating bombs or skipping the country while you're looking at her."

"Good point. It's a deal. How do you think Mr. Chief will react when I turn down his little invitation?"

"I hope he gnashes his teeth and tears his hair out, but there's not much else he can do. He doesn't have anything on you like he did your dad. He can't very well expose you for turning the paintings over without exposing himself and—"

Desi interrupted. "He could still make Dad's theft public and further damage HJ Securities' reputation."

A beat of stillness. "Is that possibility enough to force your cooperation with this man?"

"If a bomb threat doesn't do the job? Not hardly. In fact—" Desi took a deep breath—"the thought of losing the business doesn't even raise a goose bump on my arm anymore. Life would go on. *I* would go on."

A gentle quiet fell, underscored by the conversation and laughter of passing shoppers. Scents from the food court got a rumble from Desi's stomach. Miss Myra was going to have herself a nice lunch before sending Desiree Jacobs back to work.

"I love you."

"Huh?" Desi jerked to attention. "I only half heard. I thought you said—"

"Is that any way to respond to a declaration of undying devotion?"

"Holy cow! You did say it?" *How do I respond to that? I think I feel the same, but how do I know what I feel about anything with everything such a mess?* When she told this guy she loved him, she wanted to know she wasn't talking out of emotional overload.

"I did say it, and I'll keep on saying it as often as you need to hear it."

Oh, heavens! Desi's legs went weak. "You're going to make me cry, and I can't do that right now." She wrapped the phone cord around her finger. "If you'll wait until this is over and my emotions aren't such a jumble, I think you'll hear me say the same thing back."

"I'll count on it. For now, all you need to do is return to the office and reply to that e-mail, arrange for the crating and delivery of the goods, and then let me know the instant you have a firm destination. I'll take care of the rest while you kick back with a bowl of popcorn."

"Crab dip." Desi wrinkled her nose. "Max is making my favorite tonight. She's a great friend, you know."

"I'm sorry, hon."

"I know. Me, too." She shook herself. *No pity parties now.* "One last thing. Explain the terrorist connection to this group of art thieves."

A short tone sounded in Desi's ear. "One minute remaining," the phone company's electronic voice warned. "Don't you dare hang up, Tony Lucano, before I feed Ma Bell some more change."

A few ka-chings later. "Well?"

"Who mentioned a terrorist connection?"

"One of those retired agents your partner put on our trail."

Tony muttered something about somebody with a big mouth. "The Bureau has a conniption about letting this kind of thing out to the general public, but you're in this so deep that I'm going to tell you anyway. The group your dad was involved in is something of an unusual animal. They operate much like a wholesaler might in a legitimate business, stockpiling goods and offering them in bulk to a bigger organization—the retailer, if you will—who sells the individual items at a substantial markup."

Desi's heart squeezed. "And the bigger organization is al Qaeda?"

"Woman, there are times when you're too smart for your own good. You connect the dots way too fast." Tony gave a dry chuckle. "The Bureau came to that conclusion when we discovered that the theft ring's fence is a key operative for the terrorists. If we could get our hands on this guy, we could do some major damage to the flow of terrorist funds. The Chief Thief may be able to point us right to him."

Desi collapsed against the wall to keep from landing on the floor. "Al Qaeda killed Daddy?" Her voice came out a squeak.

"No." Slight pause. "Well, some in the JTTF think maybe so. I don't agree."

"You don't?" A little air trickled into Desi's lungs.

"Whoever hired the hit on your father wanted to shut him up fast, and they didn't care whether the missing paintings were found or not. If terrorists had killed Hiram, his death wouldn't have been so quick. They would have made him talk first."

"Which brings us back to Paul Dujardin."

"Yes, he seems the most likely candidate, but I'm struggling to get a clear picture of his function. As far as I can tell, his main purpose seems to have been to recruit Hiram for specialty jobs. The al Qaeda fence could have received orders for particular pieces, and Dujardin was a tool to gain your father's expertise. The Frenchman's connection to the theft ring doesn't seem to be common knowledge among the members. It may be privy only to the Chief."

"Why do you say that?"

"I have reason to believe that Dr. Sanderson Plate is the forger for the group, and he went out of his way to implicate Dujardin. A dumb move if he knew the Frenchman was involved, since the finger would double right back on him."

The hairs under Desiree's wig prickled. Her mind blitzed through every experience she'd had at the Boston Public

Museum of Arts and Antiquities. She was overlooking something vital, but for the life of her, she didn't know what. And if she didn't figure it out in time, would someone else die? Maybe even Tony?

Her gut soured. She'd skip lunch today.

Tony hung up the phone.

Crane stood over him, shaking his head. "You let a whole herd of cats out of the bag, pard." He scanned the room, narrow-eyed. "Good thing I'm the only one within earshot to hear you blab."

"I don't regret a single word. Desi deserves to know the big picture. She's earned at least that much."

Crane plopped into his desk chair. "So you're going to do business with both her and me? You like to live dangerously, considering that she and I don't even agree to disagree."

"I'm not asking you to work with each other, just with me. What do you have against her anyway? Now that you've read her father's journal, you know she's not in the theft ring. Is it just the fact that she's female?"

Crane's lips thinned. Tony met his partner's glare.

The man looked away and flung a pen in the general direction of the holder on the desk. "Journal or not, she's got to be in cahoots with someone. How could a complete innocent hold up under that threat level so long all by her little lonesome, huh?"

Tony picked up the pen and put it where it belonged. "I'm not going to tell you what you already know about the way bitterness is eating you up on the inside. You heard my story about what a twisted woman did to me. But a good woman raised me. She's been living proof that in certain ways God made the female tougher than the male any day of the week."

"And Desiree Jacobs twice on Sunday." Crane's lips twisted.

"I'm going to ignore that cute remark, Stevo, and tell you something. For the sake of her father's reputation and the lives of others depending on her, Desi stood firm against pressure that would have buckled most grown men. You want to argue that?"

Crane frowned and held his peace.

Tony nodded. "That said, if she ever acts so crazy again, I'll personally hog-tie her and ship her to Timbuktu."

"Hah! I'd pay to see that. So where do we go from here, 007?"

"What's with the spook talk?"

The man grinned. "You, me, and Miss Nerves of Steel will be hung out to dry—flapping in the wind, no less—minus backup if we can't let another soul in the building know what we're up to. We have to grab the gang members who come for the paintings without alerting the rest of them." He held up one finger. "Then we get to persuade the pickup guys to tell us who they work with." Next finger. "After that, we round those dudes up, including El Jefe." Third finger. "And—presto!—they are so intimidated by our awesome prowess that they betray the whereabouts of a top al Qaeda operative." Fourth finger. "Then bingo! We go grab him and turn him over to who? MI6?"

Tony clucked his tongue and shook his head. "As much fun as all that sounds, it's better if we just figure out who's shafting the Bureau. Then we can have all the backup we want—including MI6. In the meantime, keep your retired buddies in the field. I want one on Maxine Webb's house tonight to watch over Desi."

"And make sure the Webb dame doesn't do anything funky like try to slip away," Crane said. "We've got enough trouble without another loose canon."

Nineteen

*H*ere ya go, girl."

Desi looked up toward the cheerful voice and the scent of fresh coffee.

Max stepped into her office, coffee in hand.

Desi laid her pen down on the ledger the bookkeeper had brought her a half hour ago. The numbers made no sense. No doubt they were accurate, but she couldn't string two thoughts together to say so. She pushed the printout aside and accepted the steaming mug.

"Thank you." She managed a grimace that masqueraded as a smile.

Max canted her head. "One of those days, eh? I'd tell you to take a vacation, but I know you won't. Dean and I will have to cheer you up tonight." She winked and walked out.

The unsolicited service was so Max. A smile started on Desi's face, but she squashed it and returned to the Sanskrit on the spreadsheet.

Her hand groped for and found the cup handle. She brought the mug to her lips, spluttered, and set it down. Coffee splashed onto the printout. *Oh, happy day!* She grabbed a few tissues from the box on the corner of her desk and dabbed at the mess.

What was I thinking? I can't drink this stuff! Ms. Traitor delivered it.

She tossed the wet tissues into the garbage, picked up the mug with two fingers, and set it behind her on a filing cabinet. Never mind that her mouth watered for a few swallows and her brain could use the pick-me-up.

Max. Oh, Max! Desi's vision blurred. *You can't be a dirty, rotten crook. You just can't be. I don't want you to be!*

She laid her forehead on the soggy papers and got them wetter.

Crane's eyes blazed at Tony. "The ASAC signed off on my transfer order? So what? How'd you wangle a look at my personnel file?"

Tony drove toward their next stop. The afternoon had already been a barrel of laughs cleaning up other agents' urgent business. He and Stevo needed to get on the same page pretty quick instead of barking at each other.

He shrugged. "One of the rotor clerks owed me a favor. And I didn't go through your file. Jen just took a peek and told me whose name was on the paperwork."

"A woman! Figures. You've got everything with long lashes and high heels wrapped around your finger."

Tony bit back a sharp reply. "I like Cooke as our mole. He's acting way too strange over this case."

"No way. Gotta be Balzac. Word has it she asked for me when your squad came up one short. She's the one who stuck us together as primaries on this case. Probably figured we'd get along like a couple of gangsters eyeing the same territory. The joke's on her that we bonded."

Stevo calls this rocky toleration "bonding"? Man, that's a sad statement.

This whole mess was going to turn out sad if they didn't figure out which agent was dirty. Prospects for tonight's trap succeeding were bleak to nil, with no form of authorized backup.

Who besides wild-man Crane would be willing to step outside the chain of command to expose one of their own? Not a soul, that's who. Plus they were all busy with the JTTF thing.

Maybe he and Stevo could tap another agency for help. Federal Marshals' office. City cops. The FBI worked with these people all the time.

Yeah, and they were all on the task force, too. Busting their rears to catch a terrorist while keeping the lid on the rest of their workload. They'd jump for joy to have a couple of rogue agents show up on their doorstep with an off-the-wall story about a theft ring and a mole in the Bureau.

Besides, every one of them would report right back to the people Tony and Steve suspected. Nope, no way around it.

They were on their own.

Desi locked the doors of HJ Securities and climbed into her car. She sat with it running and stared at the building that had been at the hub of her working world for so long. *Will this place still be here tomorrow?* Life didn't offer guarantees that things wouldn't change—sometimes drastically and in the blink of an eye. Whatever was in motion would lead to some kind of new territory. She'd either like it, or she wouldn't. But she'd adjust. She didn't have a choice. Her plans were set.

After she hung up with Tony, "Myra" had headed over to the pier, where she supervised the packing of the storage container's contents into a wooden crate. Then she arranged for a delivery company to respond to last-minute instructions for delivering the package.

She'd done what she could. Then why did she feel like she hadn't accomplished anything today?

Because the hardest part is yet to come. Tonight at Max's, pretending to relax and enjoy herself, while Tony risked his life to end the madness.

Desiree started her car and drove toward home. She looked at her watch. Dead weight compressed her lungs. Within the hour, she would receive delivery instructions. Some nasty surprise that would blindside her, no doubt.

Her stomach hurt. She needed to eat something. Just a bite. On impulse, she darted into a fast-food drive-through. Someone honked behind her, and Desi checked her rearview mirror.

They weren't honking at her. A Ford was cutting between a Chevy and a Cadillac to gain a place in the right turn lane.

Busted! You won't blindside me now.

Not FBI. Or terrorists. Those guys would be better trained.

A shiver coursed through her middle. She never wanted to find out how well terrorists were trained. Thieves were one thing—she pitted herself against them all the time. Greed she could understand. Old-fashioned selfishness. But fanatical hatred that demanded murder and suicide without mercy or compunction? Who even wanted to understand that?

Desi rolled down her window and pulled up in front of the microphone. The speaker crackled as an attendant greeted her. Desi didn't respond. She watched in her rearview mirror. The midsize Ford pull into a parking spot near the front door of the restaurant, and the driver got out. The car shielded all but his head, covered by a trendy fedora and sunglasses. A short, wiry man in a suit.

Not much of a description, but parts of it matched what the taxi driver had said about the guy who gave him that bus token.

An electric jolt shot through her. Had she just seen the Chief?

Or was she reading sinister intentions into innocent actions?

A little logic flushed her Chief theory down the tubes. Why would her contact for drop-off instructions go inside the restaurant when he could see that she planned to pick up an order and drive on? She shook her head. *Let it go, girl. You're driving yourself bonkers.*

The attendant greeted her again.

Desi leaned toward the speaker box. "Grilled chicken sandwich, regular fries, and a large orange soda, please." Good old comfort food.

Ten minutes later, she picked up her bag and pulled away. The scent of hot fries drew her fingers. She kept her eyes on the road and groped in the sack. Plastic crackled. What now? She glanced at the item. An action figure in plastic wrap? Whoever had filled her order must've thrown in a kid's meal toy by mistake. No problem. She'd give it to Max's children.

Some compensation for arresting their mom!

Munching her supper, Desi watched her rearview mirror, but the Ford never showed. False alarm for sure. *Should I be glad or sad? Let's get this over with.*

Desi turned into her driveway, licking the last bit of grease from her fingers. Extra gym time for a week, but hey, a girl needed to indulge once in a while. Today she had plenty of good excuses. She carried the fast-food bag, her purse, and her briefcase into her apartment. In the kitchen, she discarded the greasy garbage and kept the toy.

Strange. The toy wrapper was open. And that cardboard backing didn't belong in there.

Desi pulled out a glossy Boston postcard.

She flopped onto a chair, staring at it. The creepazoid in the fedora must have bribed the attendant to put this in her bag. Terrible as a tail, but off the charts inventive as a messenger. She'd written him off too soon.

The picture on the front of the postcard featured the white tower of the Dorchester Heights Monument, a Revolutionary War memorial. She turned the card over. Someone had drawn a map of the park, where the tower was located. Thomas Park. A big *X* marked a spot on the east side near G Street. A single word was scrawled: *Dumpster.*

Very funny. Har-de-har-har! Oh, and aren't we the budding artist? The jerk had drawn a winking smiley face in the upper corner where the stamp should be. *Well, Mr. Friendly, let's see how jolly you are by the end of the evening.*

If only she could be on the stakeout with Tony. She'd annihilate the cocky grin in a single slap.

Walk in the fruit of the Spirit, girl. Remember? Love, joy, peace, patience, longsuffering... Oh, just shoot the louse!

She grabbed her purse and took out the high-tech cell phone Tony had sent her this afternoon by special messenger. The phone contained an encryption device that would keep their conversation private. It was marked as FBI property, so it wasn't intended for an undercover operation, just privacy. She'd keep this baby tucked out of sight when she went to Max the Traitor's house. Clutching the phone, she went downstairs and stepped out into her fenced backyard. No good having a household bug pick up her conversation.

Tony answered on the second ring. "Lucano."

"Hi, it's me."

"Hey, hon. What's up? You doing all right?"

"Better now that I hear your voice. I got the instructions, and you'll never in a gazillion years guess how."

"Shoot me with it."

Desi relayed her near brush with the stranger in the fedora and the terse postcard message. She paced back and forth across the lawn. "If this guy hadn't already gotten on my last nerve, he'd be on it now."

"I'm with you there. Now let me do my job. Hang tight at the Webbs' house until you hear from me."

"I hate waiting!"

Tony laughed. "Is that a whine I hear?"

"Not with you out there confronting a killer. I can't do anything but support you. I'll be praying."

"That's the best thing right there. And I'll have the peace of knowing where you're at while I'm doing it. "

They said good-bye, and Desi closed the phone. She hugged herself. If only it were Tony's arms around her. Just his voice warmed the chills from her heart. Why had they wasted so much time battling each another? The enemy was so tricky—not the flesh and blood enemy, but the spiritual power behind all evil. One of *that* enemy's favorite game plans was to pit Christian against Christian. Kept them too busy to even remember he existed.

Almost worked, but not quite. And it's about time to shut you down!

One more phone call, and the paintings hit the road.

Desi smiled and went inside. She settled on her father's couch and picked up the living room phone. *If anyone's listening, enjoy yourself.* "Hello, this is Desiree Jacobs. I made arrangements this afternoon for a crate to be picked up at the Dock B warehouse. I'm calling with delivery instructions that must be carried out immediately."

Desi finished the brief conversation and hung up. If that dispatcher was as efficient as he was bored, everything should go off like clockwork.

She went into her bedroom and put on jeans and a sweatshirt. *And now…the shoes!* She got the box from the closet and flipped the cover open. Just ordinary brown lace-ups with chunky heels and thick soles. Hah!

Oh, Daddy, how could we have guessed I would use these to help in your murder investigation? We ordered them just weeks ago. Tears wet Desi's face. *Remember how we joked and laughed the day they came in the mail?*

"The game is *afoot*, my dear Watson," Dad had posed with slitted eyes while puffing an invisible pipe.

Desi groaned, but played along. "I say, Holmes, this is a nasty state of affairs we've *stepped* into."

Dad chuckled. "Nigel Bruce, move over. A twenty-first-century woman has upstaged your forties Dr. Watson."

"And I like you better than Basil Rathbone as Holmes." She kissed his cheek.

A good memory. One of many.

Desi went into the bathroom to wipe her eyes and repair her makeup.

Yes, the game was afoot, and Tony had neatly sidelined her. He acted downright casual about sending her to babysit a criminal. Did he know something she didn't? She wouldn't put it past him. The lovable hunk was bound and determined to protect her from herself. Well, if she found out he had a hidden agenda, she'd get even with him later.

Right after she thanked him.

"We're out of time." Tony strode up the sidewalk toward his partner.

The older agent lounged against their car, arms folded. "Took you long enough on that interview. I've got my end buttoned up. This running in different directions on everybody else's cases is for the birds."

"Yeah, well, it's keeping us under the radar. Forget everything else now. Desi called."

Crane straightened up. "Where's the drop?"

"Thomas Park."

"All right!" He smacked his gum. "I gotta go with my gut on Balzac. She knows something's about to go down with the Jacobs deal, so her little catchall assignment has kept us jumping through hoops all afternoon like trained mutts."

Tony climbed into the driver's seat.

Crane settled in beside him. "Your little answer to prayer looks more like female scheming to me."

Tony shook his head. Some people just had to fight for their right to deny the divine. "Keeping us busy isn't out of character for Rachel. You've just never gotten used to taking orders from a woman."

"Get off it, Lucano." Crane's glare could have melted stone. "I've never made secret my attitude about women in dangerous jobs. They should leave that work to the men. But I don't let my feelings interfere with my job." He jabbed Tony's shoulder. "Besides which, I had a mother, too, and learned 'yes, ma'am, no, ma'am' straight from the cradle."

"All right, all right, so there's some chivalry to your chauvinism." Tony rubbed his arm. "So it's down to you and me. Are we going to do this thing or let it go? Even if we succeed, we could be in hot water up to our eyeballs—this is so far outside standard operating procedure."

"In the immortal words of Clint Eastwood: 'Make my day.' I want to go out on a high note. Be remembered even when I'm out to pasture."

Getting rough and rowdy with a few bad guys wasn't the best motive for going ahead with the plan, but Tony would take it. "Quoting from *Dirty Harry*? You like old movies?"

"Nah, just action flicks where the bad guys—or gals—get what they got coming."

Tony started the car and pulled out onto the street. "You had me scared there, Stevo. For a minute, I thought you might have something in common with Desiree Jacobs."

Crane moaned.

Tony grinned. He'd better enjoy a little joke while he

could. Their real-world plans came with no guarantee that the bad guys wouldn't blow them away.

Desi stepped into the foyer of the Webbs' split-level home.

"Watch out for Dean." Max laughed. "His new jet came in today, and he's as giddy as a kid. He danced me through the house when I got home tonight, screaming 'the investors came through, the investors came through.'"

Investors? Or a suddenly rich wife?

Eyes narrowed on the redhead's back, Desi followed her up the stairs into the living room. Somehow Max coaxed Southwestern print sofa and chairs to look comfortable with Art Deco end tables. Dean made his mark with aviation prints on the walls. The kids got into the act with handmade pottery and popsicle stick creations from last year's Vacation Bible School. A wide-screen plasma TV took up most of one end of the room.

"Something else new?" Desi nodded toward the television.

"What can I say?" Max shrugged. "The charter flight business has really taken off. Pun intended. He's talking a fleet of planes, more pilots. Me, I'm talking new house. We could really use a guest bedroom."

"This plane—" Desi tossed her purse down beside one of the chairs—"is it the one he was crowing about that can zip to from New York to London in under six hours?"

"That's the one! He says he can fly the continent and back in less time than it takes for us nine-to-fivers to call it a day."

"What does Dean really know about the investors

who subsidized the plane?" *I shouldn't be baiting her, but I can't help it.*

Max lowered herself onto the sofa. She wasn't smiling now. "Yeah, that bugs me, too. He won't tell me much. Makes me wonder how careful he's been at looking into their backgrounds. But I can't rain on his parade, especially since…" Her gaze darted away.

"Hey, girl, I didn't mean to bring you down." *Yeah, right!*

"No, don't worry about it." Max shook her head. "You care, and that's a good thing." She smiled, lips compressed.

"So where is the man of the hour?"

"He went to the store." She stood. "I should finish stirring up that crab dip. Sit. Kick your shoes off. Get comfortable."

I'll leave my shoes on, thank you very much. "The kids aren't here either? This place looks way too neat for your pair of live wires to be around."

Max's eyes brightened. "Too true. Too true. We lucked out. They went with another family to a puppet thing at church. But they'll probably charge back in here about halfway through the movie and talk our ears off." She headed for the kitchen. "Just relax. I'll be back in a minute."

Relax? That's rich!

So Dean had a new plane, did he? Well, that settled it. No way he didn't know what his wife was up to. Desi should have seen the full picture sooner. That made not one, but two conspirators in this house. And she was plopped right in the middle of them with the case about to bust wide open.

She could only hope that Max's kids didn't come home too early. Or else they just might walk in on the FBI arresting their mommy and daddy.

❖ ❖ ❖

Tony sat in the parked car and sipped a hot coffee. Dusk softened the edges of the convenience store where he'd bought it a few minutes ago. In the passenger seat, his partner downed the last bites of a microwaved sandwich.

"I hate this part the worst." Crane wadded the wrapper and spoke with a full mouth. "Those last minutes of waiting until the whole thing goes ballistic."

"I'm grateful your guys were gung ho to help out. We've asked a lot from them lately."

"Nothing they didn't get a kick out of doing. They've got that park covered like fleas on a dog. They know good and well that we couldn't sit in a Bucar within eyeshot of the drop site. Not when someone's out there who knows how to see one. This is as close as I like." Crane dug out a fresh stick of gum and popped it in his mouth.

Tony glanced at his watch. 7:00 p.m. Drop-off time. He looked down at the two-way radio in the dash. Not a peep. *C'mon, people. Desi paid you good money. Don't mess this up because you can't tell time.*

"Heads up!" A quiet voice hissed over the radio. "I'm walking my dog past the Dumpster, and there's a delivery van here unloading a crate."

Tony opened communications. "Got it. That's good news. Just keep on strolling."

"You bet! My forty-pound pooch needs the exercise, you know." The voice chuckled. "Got nothing to do with *my* spare tire."

Crane grabbed the mic. "Don't want to lose that. Then

we couldn't roll you out of Sporty's so easy."

Tony winced. "Save it for happy hour, boys."

"Yeah, we're working stiffs right now." Crane put the mic up and rubbed his hands together. "The bait has arrived!"

"We haven't reeled the fish in yet, Stevo."

"Relax, pard. We will. This is one time I'm glad the ladies have a thing for you. No other way we would have scored all those lapel transmitters and mobile radios from central supply so quick and easy."

"Catherine does not have a thing for me. She's a friend from Quantico days."

"Whatever." Crane snapped his gum.

The radio crackled, and Crane's jaw stilled. Tony stiffened, waiting.

"Crane and Lucano, come in." A different voice than the man with the dog.

"Talk to us," Crane said.

"Me and the wife are situated on a bench about forty feet from the Dumpster. A gray commercial van with no markings just pulled up to the curb. It's getting too dark out to read the license plate, but I think it's smudged with dirt anyway. Surprise, surprise." A snort. "Okaaay. Two men just got out, and they're walking toward the box. One is short and overweight and bald and real nervous. He keeps looking around like the bogeyman is about to pounce."

"Plate," Stevo mouthed. Tony nodded.

"The other is big and bulky and doesn't seem to care who's watching. He moves like a man who knows how to take care of business. Can't see his face—he's keeping his head down—but he's not Caucasian. Now he's reaching for the box. Yep. As I suspected. The bulge of a shoulder arm."

Professional thug? Or law enforcement?

Tony raised his brows at Crane. "Cooke?" Stevo scowled and Tony smiled. Better save the razzing for later.

"We've got a third party." The voice came through clipped and urgent. "Someone opened the rear van doors from the inside. No glimpse of who it is though."

Crane grumbled under this breath.

The radio hissed. "Okay. Ghost Van is on the move, heading south on G Street. Copy that?"

Tony started the car while his partner keyed the mic.

"Loud and clear. We'll pick them up at the intersection of G and Eighth. Great work, Phillips. Go take your wife out to eat."

"Roger that. Let us know how it all turns out. Doing this made me feel like the clock turned back at least a decade."

"Yeah. I'm with you."

The wistful tone made Tony's heart sink. He turned out onto the road. Most of the time his partner was like sand under his collar. Plus he was a menace on the street. So why did he feel sorry that Steve was about to be benched? He shook himself mentally. Neither of them had time for sentiment right now.

"Enough old home week, Stevo. Let's kick it into gear!"

"I'm on it." Crane gave a flurry of instructions to the retired agents stationed in vehicles around the perimeter.

"Unsubs still en route toward Eighth," another voice said.

Tony pulled over within sight of the target intersection.

"Gotcha!" Crane flat-handed a drum flourish on the dash.

A gray van cruised up, signaling a right turn. Tony inserted their vehicle a few cars behind the unknown subjects. The van drove ahead a few blocks and then took a right onto Mercer Street. Tony kept going on Eighth. Crane notified their man on Telegraph Street. The new tail picked up the van and soon reported it turning right onto Dorchester, heading for West Broadway, a possible turnoff spot if the unsubs' objective was the I-93 Expressway. The whole route was a bit circuitous— probably trying to flush a tail.

Tony glanced at his partner. Crane's craggy face was locked into a feral sneer. Too reminiscent of the look on his face when he pulled that gun stunt with Maxine Webb. But they were in this together now. No going back. Tony knew the score when he kept Stevo in the loop.

He may have made a mistake. A big one.

Tony drove on a parallel route as fast as he dared. He turned onto West Broadway bare seconds after the ghost van passed by. They had to stay with the van from now on. Darkness had crept in, forcing both the hunted and the hunter to turn on their lights. For a fresh tail car, identifying the ghost van by sight would grow difficult to impossible as full darkness overtook them.

The unsubs' vehicle took the entrance to the Expressway north. Tony followed but stayed in the right lane while the ghost van moved over into the next one.

"I think they're heading for downtown."

Tony frowned. What was significant about that destination? Something…but what?

Keeping the unsubs' taillights in view, Tony stayed in his lane and allowed another vehicle to separate them as they went through the Central Artery Tunnel. Just past the Atlantic Avenue exit sign, the van signaled and moved into the lane in front of them.

Crane got on the radio. "Anybody in the downtown area in case we need to make another switch on tail cars?"

Two voices answered—one from the intersection of Broad Street and Wendell, another from North Street and Blackstone. Tony shook his head. The coverage was too loose. Who knew which street the unsubs would take after exiting onto Atlantic. Options were boundless.

"Sit tight," Crane said into the mic, "and we'll let you know if you're in position to take over the tail." Replies came in the affirmative.

Tony maintained the gap between their vehicle and the van, exiting behind it. After they got off the Expressway, he risked stepping on the gas to make up some distance. The ghost van glided into the heart of historic Boston and took a left at State Street. Tony followed but didn't crowd their quarry. Ahead, a stoplight went yellow. The van charged on through. Tony screeched to a halt as pedestrians stepped from the curb in front of him. Stevo thickened the air with curses. Tony steamed in silence.

They watched the van's taillights fade.

I should know where they're going. Something so obvious that I'm missing it. What is it, Lord?

The light flared green. Tony squealed tires away from the intersection, but the unsubs' vehicle was long gone in the flow of traffic.

Crane's gum snapped like the empty jaws of a steel trap. "I can't believe we lost them when we're this close!"

Tony's insight gelled. *Of course!* "It doesn't matter. I know where they're going. And we're a pair of prize chowder brains for not figuring it out sooner."

Twenty

I *shouldn't be here.*

Desi started, then looked around. *What?* Max was in her place; Desi was in hers. Jerry Lewis was yucking it up in *Cinderfella.* So where did that thought come from?

She shrugged and stuffed another cracker in her mouth. Better to keep on eating rather than try to talk. Not that either of them had seen two seconds of the movie. She was watching Max, and Max was staring at the kitchen as if her gaze might draw her husband through the garage entrance.

Where *was* Dean anyhow?

After waiting a half hour, Max insisted that they start the movie without him. The woman had practically force-fed Desi ever since, jumping up every few minutes to grab more dip or crackers or fluff the couch pillows. Enough already! Desi's nerves were about ready to dance the cha-cha right out of the house. Maybe that's where the chicken-out thought came from. Sheer pins and needles.

Had Dean already been arrested? Tony could be on his way for Max. Desi bit the side of her cheek—and tasted blood. Not good with crab dip. She set the partially eaten cracker on a little paper plate in her lap.

I really don't want to see Max arrested. But how do I leave without arousing suspicion?

Or maybe the time for subtlety was past. She was entitled to some answers, and she should probably get them before the Texan was hauled off to the hoosegow.

Desi set the paper plate on the coffee table, picked up the remote control, and shut the movie off. Max blinked at her as if awakening from a long sleep. "You might as well come clean. I already know something's rotten around here."

Max closed her eyes. A tear slipped down one cheek. "I've been tryin' so hard to keep my troubles from you. You've been through so much. I thought I was doin' a pretty good job of pretending...until now."

Desi's spine stiffened. *Max is confessing already? Way too easy.*

Max sniffled. "I think Dean's havin' an affair." The last word was a wail that morphed into a cloudburst. Max would have called it bawling like a branded calf.

Desi couldn't move. An affair? That's what Max thought? Was this tragic act for real? Of course, it was! Her Max didn't cry unless her heart was shattered. Desi sprang from the chair to the sofa and wrapped her friend in her arms. Max sobbed into her shoulder.

"Shh. Shh, Maxie-girl." She patted her friend's back. "There's got to be a better explanation."

Yeah, like he's out shuttling thieves around with their loot. Oh, rats! That's not *a better explanation.*

Max sat back and pressed the heels of her hands to her eyes. "He's hardly"—*hic*—"ever home anymore. And when he's around"—*hic*—"he's not really here." She took her hands away from her face and glared at Desi like she were the culprit. "A woman can tell when she doesn't have her man's attention."

"Why do you think it's an affair?" So where did this new wrinkle leave her theory that Max was one of the crooks? In the dust, that was where. Desi gritted her teeth. *What was I thinking?*

Max sucked in a long, deep breath as if gathering the scattered pieces of herself. "Phone calls that he doesn't think I know about at odd hours of the night. Sudden, unscheduled trips into the wild blue yonder. A la-la land smile on his face when he thinks I'm not looking. I know those cow eyes. He's in love, but not with me anymore." Her face reddened. "And things like tonight—we've got something scheduled, but he goes off on a flimsy excuse and doesn't come back." Something between a moan and a growl escaped her throat.

"Max, I don't think Dean is seeing another woman."

"Why not?"

Desi looked at the monster plasma television. What should she tell her? *"Hey, I thought you were a dirty thief and a liar, but now I think it's just your husband."* Sure, that would give Max her confidence back. No, she couldn't just blurt out an accusation.

I should leave now. Her stomach pinched. *Just take Max and go...*

Go? Where did that thought come from? She wasn't anywhere near done here. She had some fences to mend with her best pal in all the world. Fences that Max didn't even know had been broken. How could Desi have suspected straight arrow Maxine Webb of being involved in anything crooked? She ought to have her brain removed and forensically examined for discombobulated synapses.

"Max…did you tell Dean about the paintings I found at the storage company?"

"No way! You asked me not— Oh, dear." Her shoulders scrunched in toward one another.

"Oh, dear *what*?" Desi's chest tightened.

"Before I caught you at the docks, I was mad at you for keepin' secrets. I told Dean I was sure you'd found something and were keepin' it to yourself. He got pretty excited. Asked me if I knew what or where, but I never told—even after I knew." Max lifted her hands. "Honestly, that man's been fascinated with the inner workings of HJ Securities for months now. It's been murder tryin' to maintain confidentiality… Oh, no!"

Every freckle stood out on the redhead's face. She leaped from the sofa and paced up the room. "Oh, no, no, no, no! I'm nuts, aren't I, to be thinkin' what I'm thinkin'?" Her glance pleaded with Desi.

Desi stood. "International art thieves could use a private jet pilot."

Max plopped onto a chair. She stared, mouth quivering, eyes twin pits of shock. "Why didn't I see this before? My Texas horse sense must have galloped off into the sunset."

"Sorry, pal, but the Doctor of Densicology degree is mine. I had the wrong person tried and convicted."

Max frowned. "Who?"

Desi shook her head. Not a good time to explain. Later on, after the bad guys—including Dean—were corralled and put away, she could devote her life to making amends for wrongheaded suspicions. Right now, they needed to—

Get out!

Desi stopped breathing. Make that summa cum laude in Densicology. When would she ever learn to tell the difference between her own thoughts and the ones straight from the throne of grace?

"Max."

Her friend sat slack-jawed, staring into space. Desi could almost see the wheels turning as Max rearranged her thinking about her husband's behavior.

Desi grabbed her friend's sleeve. "We need to leave. Now. I've got a bad feeling."

"*You've* got a bad feeling!" Fire ignited Max's eyes. "I've been played for a fool by my own husband. How do you think I feel?"

Frustration clawed at Desi. High emotion didn't bode well for getting the stubborn Texan's cooperation, and Desi wasn't leaving without her.

"I'm going to stake the dirty polecat out over an anthill." Max squeezed the chair arms. "Better yet, turn him loose in the middle of Death Valley without a canteen. And no sunscreen either!"

Desi swallowed a sad laugh. "You talk like I think sometimes. We can flay bad guys alive later. Right now, we're leaving." She grabbed Max's arm and tugged her to her feet.

Snick! The garage entrance door opened. Footfalls sounded. Not one person. Several.

"Let's *go!*" Desi pulled, but Max put on the brakes, gaze riveted on the kitchen doorway.

Dean walked into the living room, white-faced. Beside him came the short, spare man in the fedora that Desi had glimpsed at the fast-food place. *Fedora Fella looks familiar. And not just from today. Where?*

Desi swallowed, attention arrested by the small pistol clutched in the man's slender hand. A third person barged between the first two—an ice-eyed bull of a man with an olive complexion, a big chin, and a much bigger gun.

Cloaked in shadows, Tony skirted the brick outer wall of the Boston Public Museum of Arts and Antiquities. Gun drawn, he edged toward the ghost van backed up to the building at the rear service entrance.

The wind had died with the setting of the sun, and the area was deserted and quiet except for the activity in the dim circle of light spilling from the open door of the building. Boston Public was located on the edge of the downtown district with no nightspots nearby. Traffic on surrounding streets was sporadic, pedestrians nil. Great for privacy.

Tony halted his approach for another examination of the surroundings. No lookout posted that he could spot. The thieves must've been confident that they could operate without interruption. Either that or haste overrode caution. Maybe both.

He'd been right about their destination. Wrong about their purpose. This was no unloading operation. These people were packing up the store for a getaway.

Still a good fifty feet away from the vehicle, Tony eased another foot forward. Grit crunched. He froze, gun raised.

Two unsubs hustled out the door of the museum, one chasing the other, voices raised. They stopped near the van's gaping cargo doors and faced off. Dr. Plate poked his finger at an unknown with his back to Tony, a man of medium build who resembled no one on the suspect list. Still, something about him tugged at Tony's memory. Was he the third accomplice who'd been in the back of the van at the park?

"…can't wait…" This from the unknown accomplice.

Where have I heard that voice before?

"Not leaving without…" Plate's firm response.

The mystery man shook his head. "Meet…plane…go *now!*"

The desperate inflection said as much as the words. Frightened crooks did one of two things when the law pounced—turned reckless or helpless.

Which kind are you, buddy boys?

Tony stepped closer.

He stopped again as the husky accomplice emerged from the museum lugging a box. Tony still couldn't see his face. His head was turned toward the arguing pair. Plate said something to the unsub with the crate and got a nod in return. The curator grabbed the other man's arm, and the two of them went back into the museum. No doubt who was in charge here.

Who would have thought Sanderson Plate was the Chief? I underestimated the little weasel.

The barrel-chested man deposited his burden in the vehicle, then turned and followed the first two. The van body seesawed. Someone was moving around in there. Unsub number 3 from the Dumpster pickup! A wild card. No way to tell if he was carrying. That left four bad guys—one, maybe two armed—against a pair of agents.

Tony smiled. They might just pull this off without backup after all.

The big man stepped outside burdened with another load.

Stevo, you'd better be in place on the other side of the doors. It's party time!

Tony shifted to the balls of his feet and rushed forward. "FBI! Hold it right there, Cooke! You're under arrest!"

The man dropped his crate and went for his gun. Tony fired. The man staggered backward as if kicked in the chest, and then sprawled, loose-limbed, to the pavement.

Tony's heart lurched. *God help me! I've just killed my ASAC!*

Shouts rang from the museum. Steve's blocky figure leaped over the downed man.

Tony waved him on. "Get Plate and the other guy inside. I'll take the one in the van."

Crane jerked a nod and darted away. *Pretty speedy for a man built like a gorilla.* Yelps came from inside the museum.

From the van, not a sound.

Tony stood to the right of the open cargo doors and trained his gun at the rear compartment. "Throw out your weapon, and come out with your hands in the air."

No response.

Running feet and more shouts from inside the building.

Tony watched for signs of movement in the vehicle. Nothing. The absolute stillness tied a knot in Tony's middle. Was the unsub waiting for him to show himself? Either the guy was cool, competent, and dangerous or a total jellyfish. He had to bet on the former.

A distraction. Something to draw initial fire. Tony glanced around.

Wood from the dropped crate scattered the area. A chunk lay at his feet. He hooked it with his shoe and flipped it past the opening, then leaped after it, weapon extended, elbows flexed.

A box slammed his chest. He jerked the trigger, but the bullet spanged against the pavement and went off into the night along with his gun. Tony fought for balance, tripped over the legs of the downed ASAC, and fell backward. His head hit the pavement hard. Sparks exploded in his brain.

He lay still, struggling to drag breath into his lungs. His mind's eye processed what his senses had been trying to tell him when he shot the man he thought was Bernard Cooke. The big guy was neither Hispanic nor a light-skinned African-American. He was Middle Eastern. Not the Boston ASAC!

Then who had he shot, and who was still in the van?

"Don't move, Lucano."

Tony's vision cleared. He stared up the barrel of a gun the same make and model as his, standard FBI issue.

Rachel Balzac in the flesh.

Stevo would never let him live this down. If he survived to hear the razzing. Rachel looked ready to do some serious damage. To him.

She wagged the gun barrel. "Put your hands behind your head, and get up nice and easy."

Tony obeyed, keeping his movements slow and careful.

The man on the ground groaned. He wrestled himself into a sitting position, unbuttoned his shirt with shaky fingers, and stared down at a dented flak jacket.

No wonder the guy seemed so barrel-chested. Is nothing in this case as it appears?

"Get up, Malik," Balzac said. "We're leaving."

Malik growled and dragged himself upright. "I will kill this one first."

His fist lashed out and caught Tony on the cheek. Tony slammed back against the museum wall.

"Stop it, you idiot!" Balzac danced from one side to the other. "You're in my line of fire!"

Malik drove in, swinging low. Tony deflected the punch with an arm sweep and answered with a strike to the face. The guy's nose crunched, and he staggered backward, blood streaming down his face. A jump side-kick to the chest sent Malik scissoring into Rachel. They both went down in a heap.

Bowling for bad guys!

"Steve, honey, glad you showed up." Balzac's voice came from the tangle of arms and legs on the ground. "It'll be worth your while if you subdue Lucano here."

Tony turned toward the museum, heart in his shoes. Steve Crane stood backlit in the doorway, gun barrel swiveling Tony's direction.

"Put your hands above your heads," said the big-jawed man.

Desi lifted her arms. Max did the same, but Desi didn't trust the mutinous look on her friend's face. Max's glare at her husband could have blistered paint. He looked away.

"Search this one's bag." The large intruder gestured with his automatic.

The guy in the fedora didn't move, and Dean didn't seem to hear. He stood with his mouth open, face screwed up like he'd bitten a skunk and needed a strong mouthwash.

"Do it now!"

Dean jerked, then lurched forward, not meeting his wife's gaze. He picked up Desi's purse and dumped the contents onto the tabletop. The cell phone from Tony skated across the glass surface and lay by itself, stamp of ownership uppermost.

Big Chin's lips flattened. "As I tell you. She is cooperating with the federal agents. Her person must be searched for a weapon or a wire."

Dean backed away, lifting his hands. "Uh-uh. Not me. I'm in enough trouble." He darted a glance at Max.

"You got that right," his wife said through gritted teeth.

Big Jaw muttered something in a foreign tongue—something distinctly nasty. He looked over his shoulder at the slender gentleman with the smaller gun and hooked his own onto his belt. "Keep them undercover."

The man grabbed Desi's arm and jerked her around so she faced away from him. Her heart did a backflip. His hands were powerful, rough, and intrusive to body parts she held private. Desi reacted as she'd been trained.

Her elbow rammed his stomach. A loud *hunh* sounded in her ear. She whirled and let fly with her foot where it would incapacitate the most. The deep grunt turned into a squeak. He doubled over, clutching himself.

Max let out a rebel yell and launched over the coffee table. A small caliber gun spat. Max cried out. Dean screamed. Desi whirled toward her friend. Max lay on the floor, groaning.

Cold metal jabbed into Desi's temple. She gasped and went still. The man in the fedora held his gun to her head. His features had a frightening calm composure, as well as a strange delicacy.

I know this person.

"Mr. Chin was…" She licked dry lips. "He got too frisky with his frisking."

Now why did I say something so stupid when Max could be bleeding to death?

Fedora Fella laughed—a feminine sound. The dapper gentleman pulled off his hat and smiled.

"You remind me so much of your father. We were dating, you know."

Desi stared, mouth agape. Of course.

Jacqueline Taylor, administrator of Boston Public Museum, smiled at her. "As you can see, you aren't the only one who can dress up to fool people."

"You murdered my father!" For the first time in her life, Desi knew she was capable of killing another human being. This one.

Taylor's attractive face went tight. "I *loved* Hiram. I never would have hurt him. You, however, are a different story if you continue to make trouble."

The man Desi had kicked started to get up. A steady stream of venom left his lips. Good thing she didn't understand a single word. Someone moaned.

"Max!"

Desi turned. Her friend was sitting up, cradled in her husband's arms. The redhead clutched her shoulder where a red stain blotched her shirt. Her eyes were closed, and she was white as wax.

Dean glared up at the museum director. "You promised my wife wouldn't be touched. We came for Desi. A necessary hostage, you said. Now look what happened! We've got kids, you know. And I'm not leaving them orphans."

Max's eyes flew open. "Like you care?"

"Care! I did all this for you. To get the extra money for the plane and all the stuff you and the kids deserve. Nothing was supposed to happen this way. I—"

"Spare me, jerk!" She shoved Dean away and began to struggle to her feet, still clutching her shoulder. "Annie Oakley here just winged me. I'll live."

Desi stretched a hand toward Max. "Here, let me—"

Something hard crashed into the back of her skull. Lights exploded in her brain—then melted into darkness.

Twenty-One

W hat are you trying to pull, Rachel? We haven't had anything going on for years." Steve Crane's weapon stopped in a dead aim at the pair on the ground. "I'd as soon shoot you as look at you."

Tony shook his head. Steve Crane and Rachel Balzac, an item? Boggled the mind, but at least he could breathe again. "Did you catch the two inside?"

Crane snapped his gum and grinned. "Cuffed to each other and a sturdy pipe. All ready for a ride to the lockup."

"Let's get these two packaged then, and I'll call Cooke with the news."

Stevo's grin widened. "You just do that, seein' as how he's clean, and—"

"I'm not going to prison!" Balzac pushed the bloody-nosed terrorist between her and Crane's gun.

Crane fired. The male suspect screamed and grabbed his leg, crimson spurting between his fingers. Balzac rolled, came up armed, and aimed for her former lover. Their guns spoke in echoes.

Tony dove low at Balzac. He slammed her stocky body to the pavement and wrenched her arms behind her back, stripping the gun from her. She struggled like a pro wrestler and spewed dockside words. *Guess Crane's bullet didn't hit her.* Tony slapped a cuff on one wrist, fed the metal through the bumper of the van, and then connected to her other wrist. She knelt, panting and glaring. A she-bear with its teeth pulled.

Tony got up, touching the tender spot on his cheek. He checked his fingers. No blood. But man there was a lot under the wounded suspect. Why hadn't Steve applied a tourniquet yet?

He looked toward the museum entrance. His partner sat against the door frame, eyes closed. The front of his suit jacket gleamed slick like silk. No, not silk. It was wet!

Tony stepped across the whimpering crook on the ground and hurried to his partner. Two fingers on Crane's neck found a weak pulse. Tony pulled his partner's coat aside and ripped open the man's shirt. The bullet had gone in close to the heart. He didn't dare move Crane from his awkward position. Tony pulled out his handkerchief and pressed it against the wound.

Crane groaned and opened his eyes. "Guess…a woman…finally got me."

"Don't talk. And don't you dare check out on me. You're not ready, and I'm not letting you go."

Crane's eyes widened, then the lids drooped. He moaned.

Tony held the cloth in place. *Lord, please make my words good.*

"I'm calling for help." He punched digits into his cell phone.

Sirens already sounded in the distance, moving closer. Someone must have heard the shots and called them in. Tony gave the dispatcher orders for an ambulance and asked that she relay status to the inbound city police. Then he pocketed his phone. His white handkerchief was soaked crimson. The scent of wet blood saturated Tony's nostrils.

"Be tough when it counts, pard." He continued steady pressure against the wound. Stevo didn't respond, but at least he kept breathing. Doubtful the suspect on the ground was doing that much anymore.

"Crane was a rotten human being and a misfit in the Bureau," Rachel said. "I thought he'd slow you down."

"Shut up, Balzac. He'll get a commendation for tonight's work. What are *you* going to get?" The fate of a dirty agent in a federal prison was beyond gruesome. And if Steve died, she'd face the death penalty. Tony couldn't work up any sympathy.

Sirens and flashing lights threw the alley into a bizarre nightclub atmosphere. A pair of squad cars squealed to a halt. A car door opened, but no one stepped out.

"We've got you covered," someone yelled. "Show your badge if you're Special Agent Anthony Lucano."

Tony held his ID in the air where the gleam of their headlights could pick out the FBI insignia. "I've got an agent down here!"

"Dispatcher told us. Ambulance is on the way." The speaker climbed out of his car.

Four officers left their vehicles, one of them bearing yellow crime scene tape, another with his unit first aid kit.

The rhythm of processing the scene took over. Tony sent two of the cops into the building to retrieve Plate and the other accomplice, while the officer with the tape marked the perimeter. The fourth uniform checked the prostrate male suspect.

"This one's had it," he said. "Can I help with your wounded agent?"

"Just hand me some clean gauze from the kit. This handkerchief is used up."

Another siren wailed in the distance. The ambulance. *Get a move on!*

"Hang in there, Stevo. Help is almost here. God, please… give him another chance…"

Balzac hadn't moved or spoken since the backup arrived. Tony glanced at her. She was hunched into a pitiful posture, eyes cast down, head drooping. The young officer with the tape gazed at her with questions in his eyes.

"She hurt, too?" He glanced at Tony.

"Scared spitless, probably. And she should be. She's the dirty agent who shot my partner."

The rookie's nostrils flared. He didn't look at the handcuffed woman again.

The ambulance screeched into the alley, and paramedics piled out. Tony surrendered his spot.

All right, Stevo. You're in their good hands…and God's.

He stepped into the building. Where were the officers he'd sent in after the other prisoners? He looked around. This area smelled warehouse musty. A few crates sat near the entrance, awaiting their turn to be loaded on the van. Sanderson Plate's voice rose from somewhere among the aisles of items stored on shelves. Tony walked that direction. An officer came toward him with the mystery suspect.

Under full light, Tony recognized the man who shuffled beside the uniform. Edgar Graham, the security manager. Made sense. With the curator and the head of security in cahoots, stolen goods could move in and out of this museum like roller skates through a revolving door, no one the wiser.

"Ah, there you are, Agent Lucano."

Tony looked around.

The second officer approached, a handcuffed Sanderson Plate by his side. The curator bolted toward Tony, but the officer jerked him back.

Plate let out a cry. "Please tell this cretin that I must speak with you."

"Bring him over." Tony waved them on.

The curator's pudgy face was red, and he breathed like he'd been doing push-ups instead of standing chained to a pipe. "Miss Jacobs is in dire danger. You must believe that none of us knew the sort of person who brokered our goods. Now they've gone to collect her."

Tony's heart skipped a beat. "Who are you talking about? We've got you and the rest of your gang, Mr. Chief. Who's left to round up?"

"Chief? Me? Oh my, no. Jacqueline Taylor, the museum director, she thought this all up. We did splendidly, too, until she got the bright idea to recruit her boyfriend, Hiram Jacobs. Then everything started to fall apart, and—"

"Get back to the point."

Plate took a deep breath. "As we prepared to go pick up the paintings this evening, a man of Middle Eastern descent showed up. He demanded the use of our courier plane and pilot to leave the country. Things were too hot for him here to complete his pet project. Jackie decided the time had come for us all to leave, but first they needed to get the pilot and grab Desiree for a hostage. This man—I believe his name is

Abu—left one of his henchmen with us, and we were to meet them at—"

"—the airport," Tony finished for him. The structure of the theft ring snapped into sharp, full-color focus. "Dean Webb is your pilot."

"Exactly."

Plate started to babble more, but Tony left him behind at a run. Stark terror snarled at his heels, but he dared not let it catch him. He had to keep a clear head.

Outside, the paramedics were loading Steve Crane into the ambulance. The older agent wore an oxygen mask, not a sheet, over his face. Still alive.

Tony sprinted for his car, punching in the number of Bernard Cooke's direct line. He needed more backup than a couple of squad cars.

Cooke answered on the first ring. "Lucano! Thank God! Where are you?"

"Driving away from Boston Public Museum." Tony left rubber in the alley. "We need a team here to take over a crime scene and another to meet me at Dean and Maxine Webb's home in Charlestown—pronto! Have SWAT ready to head for the airport if we miss our suspects at the Webbs'."

"Done. Anything else?"

"The city uniforms have several suspects in custody, including one of our own."

"Who?" The question razored the airwaves.

"Rachel Balzac."

The ASAC swore. "We'd hoped it wasn't someone higher than a street agent."

"You knew we had a mole?"

"We knew, but it could have been anybody...including you. Not that we took that idea too seriously, but we did have our eye on—"

"Steve Crane. Is that why you threw him in with me?" *That explained Half-Pint Henderson skulking around their desks, too.*

"You've had experience with double-cross before. We figured you'd spot shenanigans faster than anyone. Balzac seconded the motion. Looks like she had her own reasons for pairing the two of you. Kept our eyes off her."

"Well, I had my eye on you." Tony ignored the indrawn breath at the other end. "But Crane said Balzac all along. Those instincts the Bureau hired him for served him well. When he recovers, you might want to award him with a fat commendation check along with his pension."

"Recovers?"

"Your prime candidate for dirty agent caught a bullet from the real one. It's bad, but he was still breathing when they took him away."

No comment for several heartbeats. "We'll take your suggestion under advisement. Now update me on your situation."

Tony filled his superior in on everything he knew about the case and then dropped his atomic news.

Cooke gasped like a gaffed fish. "Abu al Khayr is going after Desiree Jacobs! How does that woman attract these people—? Never mind. This is our big chance. You get him, whatever it takes."

"My primary concern must be the safety of any hostages."

The ASAC made an exasperated noise. "Of course, you protect individuals as best you can, but nabbing al Khayr could save thousands of lives. I'm appointing you acting squad supervisor. You have a limited window of time to resolve the crisis. If the situation escalates into a standoff with terrorists at an international airport, we'll have to get CIRG involved, and it'll become a media playground. Let's not let that happen. There's only one set of words I want to hear from you: 'The job's done.'"

Cooke cut the connection.

Tony slapped his phone shut. If steam could escape out his pores, he'd be a toxic cloud.

The ASAC wanted al Khayr's collar credited to his watch. Bureau politics again.

But Cooke was right about the bottom line. Tony couldn't let the situation go sour enough to bring in the Critical Incident Response Group—though his reason wasn't the same as Cooke's. Every moment Desiree spent in terrorist hands decreased her chances of survival, and it would take precious hours to bring in the big guns. CIRG contained the best of the best in national crisis management, but once that behemoth was mobilized, there would be no ending the situation with speed or quiet.

Tony's teeth ground together. He steered with one hand, pulled out his gun, and checked the load with the other. The weapon didn't seem damaged from skittering across the pavement at the museum. He resettled the gun loosely in its holster.

A block from the Webb home, he slowed, killed his lights, and crept up behind the car where the retired agent was supposed to be on surveillance duty. No reaction from the vehicle. Across the street, lights showed in the living room area of the house where he'd sent Desi to keep her out of harm's way.

He should have known better. Desi and harm's way were a matched set.

Tony slid out his weapon and stepped from his car. He eased the door shut. A few steps took him to the driver's side of the surveillance vehicle. He looked inside and groaned.

The car window was shattered, and the former agent lay sideways across the seat. Something dark and ominous coated his head. Tony leaned in and felt for a pulse. None.

Thoughts blanked of emotion, he scanned the quiet neighborhood. No backup yet. Seconds counted. He wasn't waiting.

Tony crossed the street at a speed walk, watching the curtains. They didn't stir. The garage door was up, and the Webbs' big SUV was gone. Not a good sign, but he could assume nothing.

At the front door, Tony stood with his back to the house and tried the knob. It turned. Forget procedure. No way was he going to announce his presence with potential hostages' lives at stake. He entered fast and low, up the half flight of stairs on cat feet, and then a full stop.

The empty room narrowed to a single point—the splotch of crimson on the carpet.

Colors pulsed behind Desi's closed eyelids, keeping rhythm with the pounding in her head. She lay curled on her side on a hard surface that hummed with motion. Her temple and cheek rubbed against something fibrous, like carpet, but scented with an interesting mixture of old tennis shoes and orange peel—potent as smelling salts.

She pried her eyelids open and faced said tennis shoe, lying on its side a couple inches from her nose. Next to it was a chunk of something that, in the fitful illumination of passing streetlights, could be the shriveled peeling. Even her scrambled brain had little difficulty adding up the clues to mean that she was riding in the cargo area of the Webbs' mammoth Yukon Denali.

What? Why?

The last she remembered, she was eating crab dip and pretending to watch a movie with Max.

Max! Events rushed back—bringing along fear so rank she could taste it. What had they done with her friend?

Desi lifted her head to look beyond the shoe, and her stomach did a whirling skydive. She sank back down before crab dip and crackers could join the other odds and ends on the carpet. Another body lay close to her, but in what condition? The last she saw before getting clobbered, Max was bleeding from a gunshot wound.

"Desi? Thank God!" The redhead's voice feathered across the space between them.

Hope…adrenaline…maybe some of both pushed back the pain in Desi's head. "Max? Are you all right?" A heavy feeling of dread abraded her senses like a blanket of thorns.

"Relieved now that I hear your voice, but still spittin' mad."

"That's my Max. You got a plan?"

"Get untied and strangle a few people."

Untied? Desi checked. Yes, her hands were bound behind her, and her feet were lashed together. Okay, restraints limited their options a bit, but she had a few tricks up her sleeve—er, her shoe.

"Lynda Carter's got nothin' on you, girlfriend." Max chuckled.

The actress who played Wonder Woman? "Where did that come from?"

"The way you handled that terrorist fulfilled every red-blooded American woman's secret fantasy."

"How do we know he's a terrorist? Besides, I acted on reflex."

"You will be silent back there." The cold, accented voice came from the seat ahead of them.

Yeah, Max might be right on the terrorist peg. This guy scared her enough to deserve the title, whatever criminal organization he hailed from.

She angled her head to get a look at who might be riding where, but the seat back blocked her view—except for the shadow of a face turned in her direction. Mr. Terrorist. Jacqueline Taylor and Dean must occupy the front positions out of her line of sight. Dean was likely behind the wheel.

No need to guess where they were headed, not with a jet pilot in on the theft ring. The Webbs lived twenty minutes from the airport. How long had they been driving already? Desi had no idea. Not much time to act. She eased her knees toward her chest, lifting her feet toward her bound hands. No real weapons, but if she and Max could get loose, they could make a run—

Something slammed her already aching head, and Desi couldn't hold back a yelp. "Ow!" The creep had just hit her with his gun again! *Nasty habit you have there, bud!*

The terrorist leaned across the seat toward her. "Not moving. Not talking."

His hot breath brushed Desi's face. Her heart jerked.

"Abu, stop behaving like a Neanderthal!" Jacqueline Taylor's tone was as in command as always. "No wonder the rest of the world sees your fanaticism as little more than an excuse to indulge a savage nature."

Abu jerked around. "Woman, you have become corrupt. The West has filled you with greed. Do you forget we share a grandfather? While your mother married an infidel and moved to this country, my father's lifeblood watered the soil of our homeland. While your mother indulged herself and threw off the burka, my mother starved to death because the United States sanctioned our country."

"So you lump my side of the family in with your enemies?" Taylor sneered. "Never will I die poor. My mother made me swear an oath on it. She seared the horrors of her childhood on my heart. Yet you condemn her for escaping and assuring a better life for her children? If my mother hadn't made wise choices, I wouldn't have achieved a position to be of use to your precious cause."

Abu growled deep in his throat. "Do not mock. Our cause is just. Allah smiles. Our lives are a small price to pay for the destruction of our enemies—the Great Satan America and the terrorist nation of Israel."

Taylor trilled a laugh. "Well, while you beat your breast and utter war cries, why don't you thank me for funneling millions of the Great Satan's dollars into your coffers? You didn't much mind the euros and shekels either."

Abu subsided. Silence brooded like an unvoiced threat.

Desi kept a chuckle to herself. *Taylor, you're a disgusting Jezebel and a dirty, rotten thief, but I've got to give you credit for winning that debate.*

Desi had heard this type of rhetoric blasted over the news from terror leaders, and it always sounded utterly adolescent. IRA, Shining Path, al Qaeda—the terrorist mentality in any language never seemed to change. Maybe because it came from the same author—the real Satan. Unfortunately, these overgrown bullies liked to play with bombs and guns and treated human lives like disposable toys. Now she and Max were caught up in one of their games.

Desi lay still, pulling in shallow breaths. Thinking. Listening. Max had gone quiet with the air of a capped Mount Vesuvius. *Don't try anything stupid, girl.* The throb in Desi's head sharpened. Max's wounds went far deeper than her flesh, and the pain of betrayal must be making her crazy. No telling what she might try.

The SUV pulled over and stopped in a dimly lit area. The butt of the terrorist's automatic flashed upward, and the overhead light shattered with a crunch and spatter of flying plastic. Then the three in the seats got out.

A moment later, the rear doors opened. Night air rushed in, scented with cooling tarmac and jet fuel. They must be in the parking lot near the charter plane hangars. Desi lifted her head and tried to see out.

A pair of man's hands grabbed Max's ankles. She kicked. The man punched her in the leg. Max let out a sound between a squeak and a gasp.

"Stop it!" Dean stormed up to the rear of the vehicle.

Abu pointed his gun at him. "I lose patience."

"You'll lose a pilot if you touch my wife again. We leave her here."

"It's all right." Taylor said. "We can secure her arms to the metal bar on the headrest, then gag her and lock the vehicle. Someone will find her in the morning after we're gone. Rachel said we only need the Jacobs woman to keep Lucano in line."

Desi's jaw clenched. *Just let me scratch out a pair of coffee brown eyes.* What had Daddy seen in this woman?

Abu thrust his gun into his belt. He jerked Desi out of the vehicle and hauled her upright. Black buzzards swooped the death circle around Desi's consciousness. She swayed.

Smack!

Her head snapped back, cheek blazing fire.

"Do not pass out."

Abu clamped her under one arm. Her toes barely touched the ground. She struggled to inhale and hated it when she did. The man's nervous strain was evident in his body odor.

Dean produced a roll of duct tape from his glove compartment, then crawled into the cargo area beside his wife. Desi tensed for fireworks.

She heard a small sniffle. *What? You're not going to tear a chunk out of him?*

"You protected me from a terrorist." Another sniff.

"Sure did, sugarplum. Now, you know I have to tie you this way and then put this tape over your mouth so they'll agree to leave you here. When folks come to work in the morning, you just get someone's attention, and you'll be right as rain. Are you still bleeding?"

"I don't think so."

"In pain?"

"Not much."

"You're my strong Texas woman, honey."

The sound of a quick kiss, followed by the scritch of unrolling duct tape.

"Take care of Des—" Max's sentence was cut off.

"I'll send for you and the children when I get settled." Dean backed out of the Yukon's cargo area. He slammed the doors, turned, and led the way without a glance toward Desi.

Abu half dragged, half carried her like an overgrown sack of flour. They reached the hangar without seeing another soul. Dean unlocked the side door. They all stepped over the threshold and stopped in the darkness. A switch clicked and bright lights whitewashed the building.

Head throbbing, Desi squinted at a massive streak of silver. As her eyes adjusted, a plane took form.

No wonder Dean coveted this bird. It can't wait to fly! Lord, please clip its wings.

She pinched back a whimper. Once they were off the ground and out of United States airspace, she would have no value as a hostage. And when that happened, this magnificent jet would cease to be a miracle of aerodynamic engineering and become something entirely different.

A coffin.

Twenty-Two

"M rs. Webb!" Tony knocked on the window of the SUV. "Mrs. Webb, are you all right?"

The bound and gagged woman in the rear compartment lifted her head. She shuddered, eyes huge and wet.

A SWAT team van rumbled into the parking lot. Men in body armor piled out. Tony waved them over.

The team leader approached. "You Lucano?"

Tony stuck out his hand. "That's me."

"McCluskey." The man's grip was firm. "What's going on?"

"I'll brief you as soon as we get Mrs. Webb out of the vehicle."

"You want it slow and quiet or quick and noisy?"

"The people we need to surprise are no longer in the area. Just get it done."

"No problem." The man gestured to one of his team. "Janecek, front passenger window."

A rifle butt swung. Glass shattered. Doors opened.

Tony climbed into the rear of the SUV and sliced the tape from Maxine's wrists. He gripped an edge of the tape to ease it from her mouth, but she grabbed it and yanked.

"Thank heaven!" She fell against him, sobbing. "You've got

to help Desi. They've taken her. Some scary dude named Abu and this awful woman! And Dean, he's—"

"Sh-sh-sh. Yes, we know." Tony patted her back, and she stiffened and gave a cry. "You're hurt!"

"Bullet to the shoulder. I think it passed through."

"McCluskey!" Tony leaned out the hatch. "Get an ambulance here. But tell them no siren. And bring a blanket and a first aid kit from your truck." He turned and helped Maxine sit in a more comfortable position.

Had Desi been shot, too? What if she were in the clutches of a monster, bleeding and helpless?

Stop it!

"Was Desi wounded, too?"

"She wasn't shot, but she got a nasty crack over the head. She was awake and talking when they took her away. You're going to get her back, aren't you?"

"You can count on it!" A SWAT member handed him the blanket, which he draped around Maxine. "Where is your husband's jet hangar?"

Max gave him concise directions, and Tony nodded. "Thank heaven that bullet didn't take the edge off your mind. Now, you stay with these agents, and wait for the ambulance."

"Oh, no!" She gasped and swayed.

"Your wound?" Tony steadied her.

"My kids!"

"The paramedics will help you contact whoever you need to take care of them. Our people should be at your house right now, processing the crime scene. Someone will look after your children. I promise."

"Th-thank you." She clutched her blanket and wept.

Tony broke away and walked to the front of the SUV. His hands were clammy, and his mouth tasted like paste. Just seeing the feisty redhead shattered that way rocked him like a stampede had trampled through his gut. What must Desi be going through?

I can't let myself think about it.

Tony leaned a palm on top of a parking lot post. His other hand closed around the perimeter cable.

He could do this. He had to. Desi was counting on him. He couldn't fail. Not this time. Not when the Greater One lived within him. He didn't have to do this on his own.

And neither does Desiree.

You're right, Lord. Tony stared at the dark blobs of hangar buildings. She was out there, probably scared cross-eyed but, he'd wager, without an ounce of give-up-and-quit. God was with her, and somehow He would bring about justice. The time had come for evil men to be stopped. *Use me, Lord. Use me.*

Tony straightened. "Al Khayr, you've shattered and stolen lives all over this globe. But I declare in the name of Jesus that tonight you're finished. The blood of the Lamb stands between you and Desiree Jacobs."

Footsteps approached, and he turned to find McCluskey coming up beside him.

"You talking to yourself?"

"Nope. Laying a foundation. Let's get to work."

As Tony briefed the man, McCluskey put his foot up on the parking lot cable and leaned his elbow on his knee. "So what you're saying is we have to stop a terrorist from flying away with his hostage. Easy, just have the tower deny him clearance. We'll wind up with a standoff for a while. Could get tedious with him shut up in the plane and some hostage negotiator blathering at him from out here, but he won't be going anywhere."

Tony shook his head. "Push this man into a corner, and that plane will take off anyway. Al Khayr will be happy to cause an air traffic disaster. And to kill the hostage."

The SWAT leader looked at the ground. "Doesn't sound like the hostage stands much chance anyway. Best if we just storm the plane on the ground. At least it'll be over quickly."

"And some of your guys will wind up dead, too."

McCluskey straightened. "So we need to find a way to incapacitate the jet and al Khayr without him killing the hostage or risking any of our men. Just how do you propose to do that?"

"I don't know, but let's get in closer and take a look at the possibilities."

"All right." The man nodded. "I'll get my men deployed around Webb's hangar."

As he turned and strode away, a pair of Bucars and an airline open-topped Jeep swept into the parking lot, followed by the airport ambulance. Tony stepped toward the new arrivals, then stopped and turned.

Freshly set snubbing posts…new cable… What if…?

No, that was nuts. He'd gone past the border of lunacy if he thought anything like that could work.

His eyes narrowed. Maybe…

Lunacy was exactly what they needed.

❖ ❖ ❖

Abu shoved Desi into a plane seat and pulled a switchblade from his pocket. The knife snicked free from its housing.

Longer than a sword! Desi fought down a choking sensation. *Don't be silly. It's just a small knife.*

The terrorist yanked her around by one arm. Desi tensed, but the ropes on her wrists fell away. Abu let go of her.

Quivering in every nerve ending, Desi eased back in the seat and looked up at her captor. The knife had disappeared. Instead, he held the rope from her wrists, now sliced into two equal pieces.

"Put your hands on the arms of the seat."

Desi did as he said. *Dad, I hope I remember how to do this right. We didn't practice very often. Didn't seem like something I'd ever need. Wrongo!*

Abu bent over, focused on the ropes. Desi balled her fists tight and tilted her wrists twenty degrees. *Or was it supposed to be thirty? Probably not. Too noticeable. Too late anyway.*

The terrorist walked away toward the cockpit.

Desi's heart persisted in frog-jumping around her chest. *Get a grip, girl. You turn into a gibbering idiot, and you're done for.*

She took steady, even breaths and looked around. Dean wasn't kidding when he described his new baby as a luxury jet. This thing had everything a high-powered executive could want to finesse midair deals.

Six sets of passenger seats faced each other with oodles of legroom in between, and even a tall man like Abu could stand up straight without bumping his head. A gleaming ebony and chrome wet bar dominated the front of the cabin behind the copilot's chair. Crystal wine goblets hung upside down from a rack, and a large serving tray etched with gold was hooked to the back of the cabinet. A state-of-the-art sound system filled the wall behind the pilot's seat. The scents of new carpet and leather mocked Desi's nose.

Welcome to Crooked Air International, first-class getaway jet for the rich and nasty. All other passengers, please don't expect to land alive. Desi swallowed deep and hard. *Okay, Lord. I'll leave morbidsville behind. You must have this covered, because I sure don't.*

She wriggled her arms against the ropes. More give would have been nice. She was going to lose a little skin.

Better than losing her life.

"We're in position." The SWAT leader's voice came over Tony's headset. "The recon unit is almost to the hangar."

"Roger that. Sit tight. Our next move depends on their report."

McCluskey acknowledged the instructions, and then all was quiet from the team ringing the perimeter.

Just get me a look through those windows at what's happening in that jet hangar, boys. And don't get spotted while you're at it. Al Khayr doesn't need to know we're here.

Tony glanced at the man next to him in the driver's seat of the airline Jeep. The agent gave him a tense grin, teeth gleaming in the weak light of a half-moon. Their vehicle was positioned on the far side of the building next to the hangar containing Dean Webb's jet.

Out of sight and out of the action. For now.

Tony's skin itched. *Hang tough, Desi-girl. Don't worry about anything but staying alive.*

The driver twiddled his fingers against the steering wheel. "So if they're all shut up in the plane and we can't swoop in there and grab them in the open, we'll go with that idea of yours?"

"You got a better one?" Not that Tony blamed the man for being skeptical.

He shook his head. "Not me. You're in charge here. But if my opinion is worth two cents, I think the plan's got a strange sort of off-the-wall potential. Want to know what I'd dub the operation if I were you and had to write up a report on it and all?"

Tony shrugged. "Sure. Why not?"

"Operation Red Rover. Like the kid's game, ya know, where a bunch of them line up holding hands and dare people from the opposite team to break through."

Tony took a closer look at the agent. Big, blond Scandinavian type. "Erickson, isn't it?"

"Ben Erickson."

"Glad to have you along, Ben. Operation Red Rover. Works for me. If I end up writing that report, I'll—"

Tony's headset squawked. "The hangar door is opening. Recon took cover around the side of the building, but we have no way of knowing if they were seen."

Terrific! Ten minutes into the action, and we may already be blown.

"They have to tow the plane out of the hangar," Tony said. "Let's watch and see who's driving that vehicle. If it's al Khayr, we take him. Expect armed resistance, but if we get him out of the picture, we stand a good chance of talking Taylor and Webb into surrendering."

"Got it! My guys are in good posi… Hold on, I'm getting a report from the recon boys."

The air went dead. Tony counted the seconds. *C'mon, guys. You must have a look at who's driving by now.*

"You are not going to believe this!" McCluskey swore a blue streak in Tony's ear. "Some airport flunky just waltzed in the side door of the building right under our guys' noses. What do you want to bet he's going to tow the plane out of there?"

Better and better! Now we could end up with a second hostage.

The plane moved out into the night. Abu darted from window to window, cuddling his weapon like it was a treasured child.

Jacqueline Taylor sat down across from Desi and curled her lip at Abu. "Sit down, cousin. Do you think the FBI will show themselves if they're out there? They won't try to stop us when we have our little insurance policy along." She motioned toward Desi.

Thanks loads, lady! Like I needed more attention from a terrorist.

Abu leveled his dead gaze on her, and Desi scrunched down in the seat. *Attagirl, play small and helpless. Zero acting ability required.*

The man jabbed his gun at Taylor. "You are no longer of use to us. If you want to live to enjoy your wealth, be still."

The museum administrator pressed her lips together. Wise woman.

Abu went into the cockpit. He stood where Desi could see him, but Dean in the pilot's seat was hidden behind the dividing wall. "How long?"

"A good hour yet for preflight check and clearance," Dean said.

The automatic slashed the air. "Stupid son of a donkey! Did you not place us in the flight queue as soon we notified you from the museum? Is this not a less busy time for departure?"

"Yes and yes!" Dean's voice was about an octave too high. "But this is still an international airport, not some hick flight club. What do you want me to do? Call the tower and tell them that Abu al Khayr demands special attention? And what about those other friends of yours? Are we just going to leave them?"

The gun pointed at a spot about right for Dean's head. "If Malik were able, he would be here already. We must assume the worst." He glanced out the forward window. "We are free of the hangar. Get on the radio and invite the driver of the tow car to come inside. I believe that if our FBI friends are out there, they will try to stop him, and then we will know for sure."

Dean's hand appeared, then stalled over the transmitter. "Too late. That's him driving away."

Abu slapped the wall. "Start the engines, and get this plane into the air. Now!" He whirled and reached Desi's seat in three strides. His fingers closed around her throat, and he lifted her inches out of the chair. Black spots pulsed behind her eyes.

"Infidel woman, if you pray to the Christian God, beg Him that your boyfriend does not try to stop us."

Our options are getting slimmer by the second," Tony said into the headset. "We need to line up Operation Red Rover."

"Red what? Oh yeah!" McCluskey hooted. "Good name for it. Turns out airport maintenance had a bunch of stuff left, just like you thought. I already sent some street agents over to get the supplies while recon did their job. Just in case."

"Good work. Put everybody on setting it up. We don't know how much time we'll have."

"Got it!"

Out on the tarmac, Webb's jet taxied toward the runways. An airliner thundered over their heads, shooting for the stars.

The driver looked at Tony. "We following?"

"Absolutely. But no lights. They'll have to stop again and wait their turn. Just stay out of sight."

"No problem." The Jeep rolled forward.

Tony lifted his cell phone and punched in the number for the control tower. The chief controller answered on the first ring.

"Lucano here. All well at your end?"

"Ground control says Webb's pushing for early clearance. We're pretending trouble with the lights on his runway, as you asked. Uh, just a second…" The controller's voice went distant and indistinct. "Okay, I'm back on. Maintenance called to say your guys picked up the stuff you wanted."

"Great. Buy them as much time as you can."

"Will do."

Tony clenched his teeth. This wacko scheme of his better turn out to be more than just a product of his overworked imagination…

Or a blood-soaked warehouse would be the least of his nightmares.

The muffled scream of jet engines grew louder. The plane sat unmoving, but the cabin vibrated with leashed power. *Like I'm being held inside the belly of a winged monster.*

Desi swallowed. Her throat was swollen and sore. Why wasn't someone stopping them? There was only one good reason she could think of.

Tony wasn't out there.

He was busy nabbing the luckless crooks Jacqueline Taylor sent to pick up the paintings. Desi was on her own—except for God, of course. And He was going to have to come through majorly, unless He wanted to see her at the foot of His throne sooner rather than later.

Desi studied the woman across from her. The museum director's slim legs were crossed, her pants hiked above masculine loafers worn with no socks. The gap revealed a tattoo of a rose on one ankle. Evidence of an inner rebel? Interesting but not surprising. Desi's gaze traveled to Taylor's face. The woman stared out the window, jaw tense, nostrils flaring with every breath.

She turned and met Desi's look, and her mouth lifted in a sad smile. "I had hoped for a cordial relationship with you, but that hope died with Hiram."

"You killed him."

"I did not." The woman's chin came up. Her eyes burned.

"When you dragged an honest man into your dirty game, you as good as pulled the trigger. Did he know you were behind the theft ring? Was he trying to protect you?"

Taylor opened her mouth, then closed it. Her shoulders dropped. "Hiram thought I was being blackmailed. He tried to talk me into getting out, but..." She shrugged. "I'd never met a man like him. I didn't understand him like I should've... I thought he'd adapt, even enjoy the excitement, after he tasted the thrill of the heist and the good life of wealth." She drew a hesitant breath. "If it comforts you at all, my exile will be lonely."

Scalding words sprang to Desi's lips, but a sudden vision of her father's kind face froze them on the edge of her tongue. "Daddy would have forgiven you. And God still will if you'll ask."

The woman's cheeks went translucent.

"Me? I'm not there yet." Desi shook her head. "Not even close. And right now I'd just as soon not look at you."

Taylor's face smoothed into a composed mask. "As you wish." The woman rose with a regal inclination of the head and took a seat nearer the tail.

Desi closed her eyes. The museum director was a refined, intelligent woman. Daddy would have been attracted to her because of that. How long did it take for him to see her for who she really was?

Lord, give me Your perspective, or I'm liable to pluck Delilah Taylor as bald as dear old Sandy Plate.

Tony checked his watch. Only five minutes later than the last time he looked. *Get with it, guys.* Maybe he should go try to help them. He squeezed the change in his pocket. No. Sit tight. Wait. He'd just be a pair of hands getting in the way. If the SWAT boys couldn't handle this, then they should turn in their badges. Right now, he could happily chew on his.

"Take Me Out to the Ball Game" started to play. Tony pulled out his cell and checked the caller ID. He groaned. What did Cooke want now? He'd been downright generous with updates to the ASAC. Well, one anyway since arriving at the airport.

"Lucano."

"The lid just blew off this thing. Some reporter with a police scanner put two and two together from the raised terror alert, the shootout at the museum, and the buzz from the airport. You're about to have media company."

"Give me a break!" *Give me someone to kick!*

Tony got out of the Jeep and paced the grass beside the runway. "We need a few public relations honchos out here to keep them out of our hair."

"On their way, along with the head of the JTTF. He'll assess the situation and decide where to go from here. You'll put your squad at his disposal."

Tony stiffened. Some impersonal third party in charge with Desi's life on the line? Not a chance! "How long till he arrives?"

"Twenty minutes at the outside."

"A lot can happen in twenty minutes."

Blank air. Soft huff. "Officially I'm telling you to hold down the fort and do nothing. Unofficially? Well, I figure that nice carte blanche in your file fits this situation to a tee." The ASAC's voice hardened. "Just make sure the Bureau comes out smelling like a rose. Eyes will be watching."

"How about I just make sure the bad guys are stopped and the right people stay alive? That ought to make everybody happy."

Cooke chuckled. "Everybody but the bad guys."

Tony smacked the phone shut. His driver was staring at him, and Tony climbed back in beside him. "Bad news, Ben. We're about to get our ugly mugs splashed on the nightly news."

"They are out there." Abu's words lashed the air.

Desi gazed up into a face scoured clean of any human warmth. A bare-bones skull would have more appeal. Threads of revulsion tangled in her middle.

"I was checking the radio news, and there it was. A crisis at the airport. Federal agents on the scene. Sooooo—" he drew the slim FBI phone from his pocket—"we will talk to the boyfriend."

"Progress report," Tony said into his headset.

"We've got the line strung across the runway, but the boys are having trouble anchoring the cable."

"Tell them to step on it. Now or never is an understatement!"

His cell phone rang. Not again! *Cooke, if you don't know when to—*

He looked at the caller ID. His heart stopped, then jumped into overdrive.

Desi!

No. He shook his head. This would be someone nasty and dangerous. Tony opened the connection. The ill-muted whine of a jet engine filled his ear. "Lucano."

"You know me." The voice was harsh and male.

"Yes. What do you want?"

"Withdraw and get this plane cleared for takeoff. Now!"

"Fine, if you want to taxi down a pitch-dark runway."

"I think you will be able to fix that problem with a phone call. Do it! Or I will shoot off your woman's knee."

"Okay, relax. I hear you. Now let me hear *her*. We can't do any business without proof she's alive."

A woman cried out, and Tony's heart pounded. *Just give me one shot at this lantern-jawed lowlife—*

Al Khayr's voice had grown distant. "Tell the federal agent you live."

In Tony's ear, heavy breaths bordered on sobs. "Desi, honey?"

"Tony?"

"Buckle up, sweetheart. You're going for a ride. Don't worry, I'll be right behind you."

"O-okay."

Al Khayr's voice burst across the airwaves. "Are you satisfied?"

"Almost. How about I offer you a deal you can't refuse?" Tony stopped. *Let that thought tease a bit.*

"Such dealings are never what they seem."

Ah, but you're curious, aren't you? "Release Ms. Jacobs, and take me. FBI agent instead of a civilian? Hottest deal in town. Better grab it and run."

Seconds ticked past. That much more time for the SWAT guys to solve their problems.

A rusty chuckle. "You hear that, Ms. Jacobs?" The terrorist drew out each syllable of Desi's name, making it an intimate insult. "Your man wishes to trade himself for you. He is smart, but he thinks I am stupid. Release a harmless female who holds the heart of my enemy and take a trained warrior? No, Agent Lucano. No! I will not delay this flight. I will not open the door of this plane. But you will see that we are cleared, or you will hear much worse than this."

Shots spurted from an automatic. A woman screamed. A man yelled. The phone cover cracked in Tony's hand. *Desiree?*

"Stop it, you jerk!"

That was Desi—and she sounded too forceful to be shot.

Tony quit strangling the phone. "Okay. You've got your wishes. Your runway lights will be on shortly."

"Make it so, or the woman pays one limb at a time."

The connection broke off.

Tony ground his teeth. He punched the callback button. The phone rang. Then rang again. Then again. *You'll pick up. I know you will. You won't be able to resist.*

"Get back to your post." Abu waved his gun at Dean, who stood red-faced in the passageway. "We go!"

The cell phone started to ring. Abu and Dean glared at

one another; Jacqueline Taylor sobbed. Her scream echoed in Desi's ears. Evidently Ms. Chief kept her cool except when bullets whizzed past her head.

Dean lowered his head. "You shredded one of my passenger seats. You could have compromised the air pressure with a hole in the hull." He turned and stomped back to the cockpit.

The phone shrilled again, and Abu jerked it to his ear. "You are wasting my time and your girlfriend's chances at life!"

Tony could almost feel the steam rolling across the airwaves. "You forgot something, Abu."

"And what might that be, Tony?"

Tony chuckled. "So you've read the FBI playbook, have you?" *You just don't know how far I've chucked that thing out the window on this case.* "The part about negotiating on a first name basis?"

A sharp hiss. "We are *not* negotiating. I am telling; you are doing."

"No, we're not negotiating. The United States doesn't make deals with terrorists. So now I'm going to tell you something. Your flight plan says you're headed for Rio de Janeiro. I assume that's where Ms. Taylor and Mr. Webb plan to part company with you. When you get to Rio, you will leave Ms. Jacobs with Webb. Unharmed."

"This can be done."

Too easy. Too slick.

"Are we through then, Tony?"

You're laughing at me now. Be my guest. We'll see who gets the last one. "One more thing, Abu. If Desiree is not recovered safely, there won't be a hidey-hole on the planet where I won't find you."

"We stoop to personal threats now?"

"Just offering you a restful thought. Oh, and remember, we have Malik."

"My countryman will not t—"

Tony pressed the end button. He took a deep breath. *Did I buy the guys enough time?* He reopened the line with his men in the field.

Jubilation flowed over the headset. "Red Rover is a go!"

"Save the party, boys. He wouldn't take me for Desiree, so we don't have any spare seconds. Get to your places. They're coming at you. And God help us."

For some, that was an empty comment, a cliché tossed out in a moment of crisis. For Tony, it was one of the most fervent prayers he'd ever uttered.

Twenty-Four

*L*ights flashed on in the darkness. The plane taxied forward, and Abu swaggered to the copilot's spot, hugging his weapon.

Desi's scalp stung. The jerk had yanked her hair the whole time she spoke to Tony. To make matters worse, the back of her head still throbbed from the blow at the Webbs', but her mind was clear. No dizziness. Would she stay steady if she needed to move fast?

Tony offered to take my place. Way to cement a relationship! Now she just had to get out of this mess so they could actually have one.

She went to work on her right hand. The plane made a turn, then began to pick up speed. Her insides squeezed. What did it matter if she got loose? They were about to take off. What was she going to do? Overpower a terrorist with the gleam in her eye?

Can't worry about that now. Step at a time here.

Desi pulled. *Yowch, that hurt!* She shook her freed hand, ordering herself to take calm deep breaths. Calm deep breaths. She bent and worked the catch on the heel of her shoe. *Nippers,*

nippers. Here they are. The tiny wire cutters made quick work of the rope on her left wrist.

The banshee-keen of jet engines pierced her eardrums. Speed pressed her back against the cushioned seat, and she swallowed, then reached down to free her ankles. Too little, too late.

Once this jet lunged into the sky, she was trapped.

"Go, go, go!" Tony smacked the dash of the Jeep.

The driver jammed the accelerator, and they arrowed down the tarmac in the wake of the fleeing jet.

Hang in there, Desi darlin'. Here I come.

Heat from the jet's Rolls Royce engines washed over them. *Any moment. Any moment. Please! Before those wheels leave the ground.* What if Webb could get that bird up sooner than the specs allowed? The prospect of failure ate Tony like acid.

The aircraft heaved. The rear end bucked high, slammed down, and slewed sideways. As Tony watched, the nose plowed forward and the front wheel crumpled into the fuselage. Sparks flew as the engines screamed, spewing contrails of fiery exhaust. One wing plowed up a geyser of dirt, then folded. The plane somersaulted, hit the ground right side up, and skidded on its belly toward another runway. Wreckage of the destroyed wing left a flaming trail across the grass.

The Jeep screeched to a stop, barely missing chunks of debris. Tony stared after the mangled jet.

Oh, Lord, forgive me. What have I done?

❖   ❖   ❖

A jolt snapped Desi's head forward, then smashed it back against the seat. Her world bucked, whirled, and spun. Agonized metal shrieked. The seat belt sawed into her middle. A giant *whump* rattled her bones, snapping her teeth together.

Glass smashed and tinkled at the wet bar. Interior lights popped and sparked. Burnt wires spread a pungent reek even as the floor bucked and moaned.

Hang on! The Lord's the pilot here.

Though the aircraft shuddered and groaned, calm swept over Desi. Flames licked the window beside her head, then fell away. Desi rattled and bumped until she thought her teeth would fall out. Bit by bit, the craft slowed, then finally stopped with a shiver.

Silence boomed.

Desi sat in a dim, ruddy fantasy realm lit by a few surviving emergency lights. She strained to hear over the thunder of her heartbeat. *Plop…plop…plop.* Liquid plinking against metal. She drew a cautious breath and coughed. Jet fuel fumes.

Don't think about fiery explosions.

No sound came from the woman behind her. The cockpit was still—no sound or motion from Abu or Dean. A weak glow from the instrument panel illuminated the cabin enough that she could see the nose of the craft buckled up against a windshield that had been reduced to a mesh of shards held together by who knew what.

Time to "git while the gittin's good," as Max would put it. With shaking hands, Desi released her seat belt. She started to stand, then sank back down. *Silly putty's got more strength than I do.*

She struggled to her feet. Well, almost. The plane tilted forward at an awkward angle. She swayed and clutched the back of her seat. *Let go now. Take a step.* She shuffled into the aisle.

Shouts sounded outside. *Oh, goody, the cavalry…and Tony.* Strength flowed into her.

Okay, head for the exit.

But she didn't. *Daddy, you must be rubbing off on me.* She headed back toward the tail.

Jacqueline Taylor lay still, her head against the window. Something dark streaked the glass. Desi's breath hitched, and she touched the woman's neck. No life. Wait! There! Maybe a little. She didn't dare move her.

Desi touched the woman's arm. "I can't help you. I don't for the life of me know why, but I wish I coul—"

She tensed. *What was that?*

Sirens neared. No, that wasn't the sound she'd heard.

A voice mumbled in the cockpit. Dean? The mutter came again—not English.

Panic grabbed her throat. Desi stumbled to the exit and fell against the sound system. Knobs dug into her side. Breath rasping, she yanked the release catch on the door. Nothing. The door panel was rumpled like an ill-hung suit of clothes. She slammed her fist against it.

Outside, equipment rattled and clattered. Metal squealed as the rescuers went to work. They'd have the door open soon—but not soon enough.

Desi scanned for a weapon, some way to protect herself. Two-inch nippers wouldn't get her anything but a laugh. Shards of glass littered the floor, double-edged blades. She'd shred her hands on those. She looked higher. At the wet bar, the serving tray hung by a single tab. She half slid, half ran to the bar and yanked the tray from the wall. Diving back toward the exit, she pressed herself against the entertainment center. The oval of metal wouldn't stop a bullet, but Daddy had once told her something about guys with big chins.

"Lucano! I kill...your woman!"

Sounds of movement came from the cockpit. A stagger rocked the plane, followed by a foreign exclamation.

Fear tap-danced up Desi's spine. She drew in oxygen without feeling its benefits. Blackness edged her vision, and Abu's heavy breathing became a dull roar in her ears. Behind her the passenger door let in a small rush of outside air.

Should she duck and hope for rescue?

Too late!

The terrorist stepped into the cabin passage, gun brandished. Desi swung the tray. Bull's-eye on his most prominent feature! Aftershocks shuddered through her arms.

Abu reeled into the bar, slumped to the floor, and lay still. His gun tumbled from slack fingers. Score a big one for harmless females everywhere! Desi lowered the dented tray. *You were right, Daddy. Glass jaw.*

"Waytago, Ms. Jacobs!"

She turned. A SWAT member grinned at her from a wide open exit. If she wasn't mistaken, she'd seen this guy once before in her living room.

He offered his arm. "Let's get you out of here."

He didn't have to say it twice. Desi let him assist her down a short set of stairs onto solid ground. A wild cheer rose.

Activity boiled around her, as welcome as a holiday festival—FBI, airport security, fire and ambulance personnel, media. Flashing lights illuminated the debris-strewn area. Fire retardant chemicals hosed the plane. An EMT rushed toward her, but she waved him away.

There was only one person she wanted to see.

A tall figure strode toward her. Backlit by headlights, his face lay in shadow, but the rays picked out the strands of his hair. Messed up, just the way she liked it.

She ran. "Tony!"

He grabbed her close, and she buried her face in his chest. A few weeks ago when her world had crumbled at the death of her father, this man, her enemy, held her against her will. Now she never wanted him to let go.

"It's all right, honey." His arms tightened. "I've got you. You're safe. It's over." His fingers stroked through her hair, down her back, over her arms.

Desi had never quite believed people's stories of laughing and crying at the same time, but she was doing it. She turned her face up, and he claimed her offered lips.

"Hey, what's up with kissing the rescue subject?" someone said.

"Chill, Conroy," someone else answered. "Don't you know Lucano always gets the girl?"

I'll have to ask Tony about that sometime.

But not now. She was way too busy drinking deep of every good promise for a life and a future.

Epilogue

Tony halted in the doorway of Stevo's hospital room. Desi bumped up against him.

"Go fish!" Luke Webb laughed, bouncing on the edge of the bed.

Crane scowled, but his eyes smiled as he took a card from the pile on the tray perched over his bed.

Tony gaped. That *couldn't* be the Grinch of the Federal Bureau of Investigation enjoying a game with a child! Tony looked down at Desi, and she winked. This development was *not* news to her.

She tugged him away from the door.

"Max and the kids visit every day. She has a tender heart. And she feels guilty."

"She shouldn't."

"I know, but she can't help it. Things are working out better than expected anyway."

"How so?"

"The other day when she and the kids came to visit, Luke and Emily got right up next to the bed and prayed for him. Brought tears to his eyes. No kidding! He doesn't even mind when they sing him 'Jesus songs,' as the kids call them."

Tony shook his head. "If I knew what to say, I'd say it."

Desi tapped his arm. "Come on. Let's go join old home week."

He followed her inside. There sat Maxine Webb's three-year-old playing with her doll and Max herself lounging in the other guest chair.

Crane looked up. No fakery in his scowl this time. "Whatsa matter? Can't a guy relax over a card game without a bunch of cross-eyed looks?"

Tony chuckled. "Good to see you're on the mend, Stevo. A week in the hospital's got you back to your old self."

"Hi, Uncle Tony, Aunt Desi," Luke said.

Tony glanced at Desiree. "Uncle Tony?" he mouthed.

"Play along," she mouthed back.

Max offered a limp wave. Desiree gave her a hug, avoiding the sling on her arm.

"I gotta go to the baffwoom." Emily looked at her mother.

"I'll go with her," Desi said.

"That's all right." Max heaved to her feet. "I need a stroll down the hall. My muscles get stiff when I sit around."

Tony hated the pain in Desi's eyes as she watched her friend. She didn't smile enough anymore. So many wounds around here—both inside and outside. If only he could offer easy fixes.

He pulled a fistful of quarters out of his pocket and handed them to Luke. "Why don't you go along and get sodas and candy bars for you and your sister? Your mom, too. Uncle Tony's treat."

The boy smiled and hopped off the bed. "Cool! Thanks!"

He glanced at his mother and sobered. "I'll hold Em'ly's

hand, Mama. Don't want to hurt your arm."

Tony groaned inside. The kid didn't even know the first tenth of it yet, just that Mommy and Daddy had been hurt and that Daddy wouldn't be coming home anytime soon. Dean had two broken legs and a concussion, but he might as well be dead for as much use as he'd be to his wife and kids over the years he'd be in prison.

"I'll be right back to finish our game, Grampa Steve," Luke said.

"Be wight back, Gwampa," the little girl echoed. They scooted out of the room in their mother's wake.

Grampa? Tony stared after them.

Crane chuckled. He winced and touched his chest. "Guess I outrank you with the Webb kids, but I figure that'll be the only way. Cooke dropped by earlier. Told me you were a shoo-in to be confirmed as the new squad supervisor. I suppose I should say congratulations."

"Don't strain yourself." Tony sank into one of the guest chairs.

Desi took the other.

"Well, congratulations!" Stevo grinned at him.

Crane looked at Desi and lost his smile. "Better say something to you, too." He cleared his throat. "Any gal that can clock a terrorist like you did— Well, I just want you to know you've got my respect. And if you can settle this former pard of mine into domestic bliss, you've got my blessing."

Desi shifted, face pink. "Well, Tony and I haven't discussed anything quite that serious, Agent Crane. We're still getting to know one another. I just found out that this ambitious brainiac can do lots more than grab bad guys off the street. He's only a semester and a thesis away from a master's degree in criminal sociology, for heaven's sake."

Her look warmed Tony to his socks.

"Call me Steve." Crane pointed at Tony. "You're a sharp agent, but don't be dumb like me about family."

"Not to worry." Tony claimed Desi's hand. "My mother took one look at her and said she'd disown me if I didn't hang on to this one. I'm not about to get on Mom's bad side."

Desi laughed. "She said it right in front of me."

"Get used to it, hon. You're dealing with Italians." Tony looked from Desi to Steve and back again. "So what's this 'uncle/grampa' deal?"

"No way, Lucano." Steve zipped his thumb up the stack of cards. "First you spill whatever you didn't want to say in front of the kids."

Tony studied the floor. "Just got the word in this morning. Figured you should hear it from me, rather than the nightly news." He looked into Desi's eyes. "We've closed the file on your dad's murder."

Desi steeled herself to hear the worst—the FBI would never be able to prove that Paul Dujardin contracted the hit. A heartless killer would walk free.

Tony squeezed her hand. "Interpol traced the assassin's money trail to its source. We know who killed your father, and it isn't who we thought."

They got him! Then she realized what Tony had said. "Not Paul?"

"Close. Who else in that family would have been stripped

of power, prestige, and wealth if the scandal broke?"

Desi shook her head in slow motion. "No way. It can't be…Paul's son, the senator?"

Tony nodded, lips compressed. "Senator John Dujardin. His father must have confided in him about the trouble he was in. Senator Dujardin might well have lost his career in the scandal Hiram was about to set loose over his dad's head. He couldn't let that happen."

Desi gasped. "Paul knew. He *knew* that day I went to visit him. How awful for that old man."

Tony shook his head. "That's not the end of awful. When agents went to arrest the senator, they found him shot to death in the library. Suicide."

Daddy's murderer is dead! Triumph surged through Desi, then curdled into a sick feeling. She hung her head.

No one got the victory here. Everyone lost.

"That poor family. I saw the little girl. She looked so happy. Paul showed me…" She swallowed a lump. "He showed me a picture of them all together."

Crane muttered a curse. "The chump took the easy way out."

"There *is* no easy way out, Steve." Tony stroked Desi's hand. "We take our sins with us unless we grab God's offer of a pardon. I got that through my thick head while I lay in a hospital bed shot up like you."

Crane didn't answer, but he didn't scoff either.

Max walked back into the room. "Uncle Tony sure made brownie points with my kids."

Her face looks freshly scrubbed, but soap and water can't scour away the dark smudges under her eyes. Desi made herself smile. No need to share another tragedy with her friend until they were alone and could cry about it together.

At least they could feel happy about the future of HJ Securities. The spin the FBI had put on her father's involvement painted him as a crusader out to stop a theft ring. And the various parties who owned the art in the stolen cache were grateful to have their pieces discreetly returned. HJ Securities had more business than it could handle around the globe, and Hiram Jacobs's memory had turned to solid gold.

Thank You, Lord. You did that better than anything I could have asked or imagined.

Max stepped further into the room, and Tony got up and gave her his chair. She settled with a soft sigh and adjusted her sling.

"I told Luke that Grampa Steve wouldn't mind waitin' until tomorrow to finish the game. He and Emily went with one of the volunteers to the playroom over in pediatrics, happy as a couple of larks in a park." Max handed some quarters back to Tony. "I wasn't hungry, but thanks anyway."

Desi's blood scalded her veins. A misguided, greedy woman started this chain of events. If Jacqueline Taylor wasn't already in a coma, Desi would put her in one—

No. She wouldn't do that. She'd exercise some of that mercy Tony was talking about—and merely abandon her on a desert island with no phones, no lights, no motorcars, not a single luxury...

"So is anybody going to tell me what's going on?" Tony interrupted Desi's seriously bent *Gilligan's Island* fantasy.

Max frowned. "What are you talking about?"

Crane started to chuckle, then seemed to think better

about exercising his chest muscles. "Lucano wants to know how come he's now your kids' uncle and I'm their gramps."

A flush crept up Max's face. A smile teased the corners of her lips.

All right! There's life in Maxie-girl yet!

"Guess I let the cat out of the bag about you and my main girlfriend being an item." Max bumped Desi's shoulder. "They got so excited. I didn't see any harm. They need to know that there are some adults in their lives they can rely on. I figure you're good for it." She looked at Tony.

He flashed the Boy Scout sign. "I'm Uncle Tony till kingdom come. But this qualifies Crane as a grandfather how?"

Desi clamped a hand over her mouth. Max laughed outright.

"What can I say?" Crane spread his hands. "I'm a likable guy."

Max sent him a sidelong glance. "Chicken." She turned to Tony. "He told Luke that all he had were girls, and he'd always wanted a son and a grandson. Luke volunteered to be the grandson as long as Steve took Emily with the deal."

"Sounds good to me, but I don't get what's so funny."

Desi lost her battle with the giggles. She snorted. She hooted. She held her stomach. Max cackled with her. They looked at each other and went off again.

"Hey! It's not that funny!" Crane scowled. Then he grinned. "Well, yeah, maybe it is."

Desi wiped her cheeks. "Guess who gets to be the son in Luke's reckoning, *Uncle* Tony?"

"No!" The word dropped like a stone from his lips. He looked as if all the blood had siphoned out his toes.

Steve smirked and held out his good arm. "Sonny boy! Come to Papa."

"This can't be happening." Tony shook his head.

Still laughing, Desi stood and hugged him. "Get used to it, sweetheart. Italian mamas aren't half as scary as the trouble you'll get into hanging out with Max and me."

Tony held her close. "Maybe so—" there was a definite twinkle in those eyes—"but then you'll just have to make sure it's worth it."

Desi matched him grin for grin. "Oh, I think I can do that."

"I'm sure you can." Tony's laughter was deep and rich. "And I can't wait."

Neither can I, Desi thought as she reveled in the strength of his arms. *Neither can I.*

Dear Reader,

I hope you enjoyed reading about Desi and Tony as much as I enjoyed writing about them. After all, isn't it the characters who make us love a book or lay it down? I know that's true for me. Then, throw those characters into tense, heart-twisting situations, and I'm hooked. Maybe you can tell that I write what I love to read. I'm sure glad I'm not done writing about these two. Besides, they tell me their adventures are far from over. (An odd quirk about writers—our characters talk to us. How else would we know their stories?)

Did you know that art theft is listed right up there beside drug and arms smuggling and money laundering as a major criminal activity around the world? I sure didn't until I started researching this series. The FBI has a designated Art Crime Team, supported by special trial attorneys for prosecution. They also maintain a National Stolen Art File. Their website says, "Art and cultural property crime—which includes theft, fraud, looting, and trafficking across state and international lines—is a looming criminal enterprise with estimated losses running as high as $6 billion annually." http://www.fbi.gov/hq/cid/arttheft/arttheft.htm Whoa! No wonder why crooks are into this game. What gets me the most though is the fact that priceless cultural treasures are increasingly used as collateral in drug deals. I plan to incorporate that little nugget into book three of the To Catch a Thief series.

This book series was born because I literally dreamed Desi. One night I woke up with my muscles in knots from a dream where a woman sneaked into a home in the night to return a painting that had been stolen. I knew little about her except that she was an expert at what she was doing and that she mustn't get caught or the disaster would ruin many lives. My creative juices got busy after that. I truly believe that capturing the imagination with a gripping story makes an incredibly effective way for the Holy Spirit to deliver truth to the human spirit. It's a wonderful thing to reach one person with the love of Jesus, an awesome privilege to have the opportunity to reach thousands through a single avenue—the writing of a book.

It has been my honor and joy to provide you with what I hope were a few enjoyable hours in Desi and Tony's world. Please join me in their future adventures. And stop on by my website, browse around, and drop me a note. I'd love to hear from you.

Blessings in abundance,

Jill

www.jillelizabethnelson.com

Reader's Guide

1. At the beginning of the story, Desi can't stand Tony because he threatens someone she loves. She has her father on a pedestal and ignores signs that all is not right with him. She ends up being wrong about both Tony and her father. Think about a situation in your own life where you had blinders on and misjudged someone—either positively or negatively. How can we reconcile an honest assessment of human frailty (John 2:24–25) with the directive to "believe the best" (1 Corinthians 13:7, AMP) of others?

2. Steve is a "sandpaper person" in Tony's life. We all have them. Sandpaper people can rub us raw and create wounds in our lives, or they can shave off some of our own rough edges and refine us. Compare and contrast how Tony handles Steve with ways you handle sandpaper people. How can you adjust your attitude to allow the "sandpaper"

to have the greatest benefit for you and potentially to help that other person as well?

3. It could be argued that Hiram Jacobs did the wrong thing for righteous reasons. Can you relate to his motives for what he did? Why or why not? Is it ever appropriate to break the law to protect people? Can you think of examples from Scripture or life that might support either position?

4. An enormous weight of responsibility for the family business suddenly falls on Desi's shoulders after her father's murder. Max is a faithful friend (Proverbs 27:6) and points out to Desi her main stumbling block in dealing with that responsibility. What is that stumbling block, and how does Desi react initially to Max's advice? As God continues to deal with her on this issue, how does Desi's thinking change? Consider times in your life when a faithful friend spoke true words that were difficult to hear. How did you react? Did the truth ultimately change your life? Why or why not?

5. Desi is a strong-willed, independent person with a tendency to be more self-reliant than God-reliant. Her heart is to do the right thing, but she holds herself (and others) to an unrealistic standard of performance. Do you know people like this—so capable that they're scary? Are you one? Desi must come to terms with her own limitations so she can accept the help she needs from both God and

other people. Think about times in your own life when you attempted to "handle things" on your own. How did the situation turn out? What attitude did you have to learn before God could bail you out? Did Desi learn this attitude?

6. An unhealed emotional wound makes Tony deeply distrust his ability to judge the character of any woman he's attracted to. What does God require of him in order to be healed? Is this the same thing He requires of us in order to be healed of inner wounds?

7. Both Desi and Tony must take fateful steps of radical obedience during the conclusion of the book, and neither can see if their choices to obey will turn out well. Desi must trust Tony with all her secrets, risking everything she holds dear. Tony gets an inspired idea at the end of the story, but carrying it out could kill the love of his life. Have you ever been impressed to do something that made no sense to you? Something that was risky? Did you obey the leading or not? What happened? Look at Abraham in Genesis 22. What step of radical obedience did God require of him? How did that turn out? Consider other Bible heroes and heroines. Did God ask them to do the absurd to achieve the impossible? Would they have become heroes or heroines of faith without radical obedience?

8. The main villain stays hidden throughout most of the book, though the presence of this menacing figure permeates the plot. The mastermind thief is very clever and enjoys mind games, but when the Chief is unmasked, what proves to be the motive for every evil act? Read 1 Timothy 6:10. Now dig deeper. What is the seed that gave life to the root? Read Matthew 6:30–32. How often does this very seed infect our lives and bring forth sin? What is the solution? Read 1 John 4:18.

9. Terrorism is constantly in the news, yet it's a subject many of us shy away from in everyday discussion. Is the evil too black for us to comprehend? Like Desi says, "who even wants to understand" the terrorist mindset? Where does such impassioned devotion to a cause of hatred come from?

10. None of us cares to think that an act of terrorism could happen in our own backyard, yet the subtle fear lurks—the very real bogeyman behind the closet door we don't want to open. But is terrorism above the name of Jesus? What proactive steps should the body of Christ be taking to hold back this scourge? Confront yourself with this question, *Have I ever asked God to show me how to pray for someone like Osama bin Laden?*

11. At the end of the book, Max is dealt a devastating blow to her marriage and her self-esteem. She and

her young children have a long road of suffering ahead of them. Desi and Tony hurt with her and struggle to find ways to help. When we go through intense trial, what do we wish people would do to help us? What do we wish they wouldn't do? Are our expectations always reasonable? How can we apply these insights to helping others? (In Reluctant Runaway, the next book in the series, Desi, Tony, and Max continue to wrestle with this issue.)

DESI AND TONY'S ADVENTURES CONTINUE IN
RELUCTANT RUNAWAY

COMING MARCH 2007!

*D*esiree Jacobs swallowed and steadied herself on the six-inch-wide steel girder. The still September night pressed in on her like an urgent warning. She shrugged the unease away. Not the time or the place for second thoughts. Flexing rubber-soled feet, she held her gaze on the dim outline of the brick wall a half dozen yards ahead. Sweat trickled down her ribs under her Mylar jumpsuit.

E-e-easy. This little jaunt is no different than a trip across the balance beam at the gym.

Except no thick mat waited a few feet away to soften a fall. Only ten stories of empty air. A single misstep and she'd make a nice Impressionist splat on the pavement of the alley below.

Then Max can attend another funeral. Desi sighed. *All right, girlfriend. You win. Bungee cord it is.*

She took the single step backward onto the safety of the roof behind her. Amazing how easy it had been to get into this co-op apartment building next to the exclusive Tate Art Gallery of Washington, DC. A pizza delivery person got more perks than she realized. People opened doors at the scent of sausage and pepperoni, no questions asked.

Desi knelt beside her discarded delivery uniform and the

aromatic pizza box. She stripped off her backpack, then pulled out the bungee cord and clipped an end to the harness around her torso.

I hope you know, Max, that this is a serious cramp in my style. She wound the other end of the cord around a pipe sticking out of the roof. *And if I fall—which I won't—it'll still hurt like the dickens when I hit the end of the cord and swing up against that brick wall.* She hooked the cord and pulled it tight. *Then you can visit me in the hospital. Like you haven't seen enough of those lately!*

Lifting her arms, Desi stepped back onto the beam. *Okay, Max, ready or not, here I come. Go ahead! Try and keep me from that American artist collection.* She took a step, then one more, toes forward, heel to instep, every nerve ending abuzz.

And this one is for the Cassatt. She moved forward. *And this one for the Savage. And this one for that delightful Grandma Moses.* She hopped and switched foot positions. *Expect me soon Andy Warhol.*

At midbeam she stopped and looked up at the sky. One plump star winked at her. *If Tony could see me, he'd have a cow.* She winked back at the star. What an overprotective FBI agent boyfriend didn't know couldn't hurt him.

She quickstepped forward. The tenth-story ledge of the Tate Gallery building loomed close. Almost there. Almost…yesss!

Her breath came strong and even. She knelt on the two-foot ledge and glanced back at the wide open space she'd conquered. The girder was the only remaining connection between buildings that had once shared a roof support system.

So far, so good. She shrugged out of her pack and unhooked the bungee cord. *Good riddance!*

By feel, she located her narrow-beam flashlight and trained the glow on the window in front of her. The pane was an unimpressive standard thickness, and the wood frame showed wear from the elements. Desi kneaded her gloved fingers together but kept them away from the casement and glass.

Any tampering with the frame would set alarms shrieking to wake the dead. Enough to startle a poor, unsuspecting burglar straight off the ledge.

Desi gulped and peeked downward into the blank darkness. The ground was there, hard and unforgiving. Cold sparks skittered up her spine.

She stiffened her jaw, turned back toward the window, and pursed her lips. What about cutting the pane? Nope, that was out, too. A web of hair-fine wire covered the glass, not obstructing the view—such as it was—of the drab roof opposite. But any little slice would end in handcuffs for the would-be window surgeon. Nah-ah! She didn't need *those* bracelets.

Time to find another way in. And in a hurry. Tony really would snort and paw if she wasn't ready on time for the White House Midnight Masquerade. Rotten timing that the Tate Gallery wanted to open its collection the day after tomorrow, or she wouldn't be trying to pull a caper on this night of all nights.

Rising to her feet, she hefted the pack in her right hand and pressed the left side of her body against the building. She swept the flashlight beam ahead of her on the ledge. *All clear.* She lifted her foot and then halted midmotion.

Stupido! Dumkopf! Idiot! I cannot believe I almost made Max's day.

She planted her foot back where it had started and panned the light up the wall. Sure enough. Stubby plastic-coated censor rods stuck out from the brick at irregular intervals—no slipping around, between, or under those babies. Neither bird nor breeze could snap the sensors off, only a solid body of the Homo sapiens variety. A broken rod or an attempt to remove one from its socket released an ultra-sonic frequency that tripped an alarm, and voilà, one bagged burglar.

So where does that leave me? She frowned. *With a sack full of goodies and no place to go, except…* She looked down.

The opening scene from a movie about a female art thief played across her mind's eye. A masked figure, dressed much like Desi herself, leaps forward from a roof ledge. She hurtles gracefully downward, harness cord attached to an automated descender, which gentles her to a stop in front of a certain window. The woman flips upright, then uses telescoping bolts to pop an entire pane of glass from its frame, then enters a room, where she outwits other security devices and steals a priceless painting.

Desi wrinkled her nose and snorted. Hollywood hocus-pocus! Besides, she didn't have an automated descender.

However, Desi smiled, *I do have a grappling hook.*

Chuckling, she set the hook and clipped the end of the rope to her torso harness. Lying on her stomach, Desi turned and flipped her feet into open space. She balanced on the rim of the ledge, abdomen muscles and extended arms bearing her full weight as if she were about to start a routine on the uneven bars.

The bottoms of her feet sought and found the brick wall below. Blood pumping, she pushed away from the ledge. The tether flowed with steady friction through her gloved fists. *Piece of cake.* No dramatic leap from a tall building, just a few smooth hops and—*Cra-a-ack!*

Desi's line jerked. Bits of debris bounced off her head and shoulders. Her feet lost purchase. In free swing, her body rammed the wall. A grunt burst from her throat. Pain shot through her shoulders and hips. She dug her fingers and toes into the chinks between the bricks and went stone still—except for her heart, which threatened to backflip right out of her chest.

Well below, a series of muted smacks taunted her ears—cement chunks bursting against pavement. Her imagination went into overdrive, picturing the results on her body of a similar dive.

Stop it! Just stop it! Think. You can beat this.

A portion of the ledge above had given way. The stress of the hook and the weight of her body must have been too much for the aged cement. Thank goodness the ledge hadn't crumbled beneath her while she knelt by the window.

Now, any wrong movement… She sucked in a breath. She needed a better hold on the brick. Reluctant to disturb so much as an air molecule, she slid one finger over…another…another. *Oops!*

A toe slipped. Her weight shifted. She jammed her foot back in tight, gritting her teeth against a yelp. Her big toe had felt better after a collision with the bedpost in the dark.

Snap! Scra-a-a-ape… The tether line went limp.

She held her breath. *One… Two… Three…*

The grappling hook remained aloft, but the sounds from above indicated it must have pulled free and now rested without anchor on what was left of the crumbling ledge. If the hook plunged downward, the weight would pull Desi from her precarious hold on the brick. Now she was stuck like a human fly on the wall, not daring to move a pinky.

Great! Where's an angel when you need one?

Wasn't there a line in Psalm 91 about angels bearing up the servants of God in their hands lest they dash their feet against a stone?

Um, heavenly Father? This is as good a time as any to prove that one.

Neither she nor Max had considered that the cement on the ledges might be rotten. That was the double-edged sword when owners insisted upon locating art galleries in charming but antiquated facilities, which left them vulnerable to intruders and created unintended death traps for thieves.

Trust.

Okay, that thought hadn't come from *her* mind. Time to stop relying on her own resources. Hadn't the past months taught her a thing?

All right, I'm busted, Lord. Again. What's our next move?

No angelic chorus answered her plea with divine instructions.

Desi sighed. Her breath fanned the brick in shaky drafts. Her cheek stung, pressed against the rough surface. Her fingers started to cramp, and her leg muscles ached. She couldn't hang on much longer.

Should she try to climb up toward a ledge that she knew was brittle and crumbling, or should she risk moving down toward the lip at the next floor, its condition unknown? The latter option could pull the grappling hook off the ledge above before she reached the doubtful security of the next level, which would seal her fate as she joined the smashed cement chunks on the ground.

Let go.

Of all the kooky ideas… Wait… Maybe…

Desi licked her lips, mouth as dry as the cement flakes that powdered her shoulder.

All right, what might happen if she let go and performed a calculated fall onto the next ledge? She would need to hit leaning into the building. The impact might breach the cement if its condition was as unstable as the ledge above. Then again, the lip might hold her, and she'd be in a firm position when—not if—the grappling hook tumbled from above. Was the lower ledge strong enough to withstand the impact of her falling body? Only God knew.

Okay, Lord, I have to trust Your wisdom. Here goes!